TRAITOR

TRAITOR

DAVID HAGBERG

A TOM DOHERTY ASSOCIATES BOOK
NEW YORK

TRAITOR

Copyright © 2022 by Kevin Hagberg

A Forge Book
Published by Tom Doherty Associates
120 Broadway
New York, NY 10271

www.tor-forge.com

Forge® is a registered trademark of Macmillan Publishing Group, LLC.

The Library of Congress Cataloging-in-Publication Data is available upon request.

ISBN 978-0-7653-9426-2 (hardcover)
ISBN 978-1-250-30982-2 (ebook)

Our books may be purchased in bulk for promotional, educational, or business use.
Please contact your local bookseller or the Macmillan Corporate and Premium
Sales Department at 1-800-221-7945, extension 5442, or by email at
MacmillanSpecialMarkets@macmillan.com.

First Edition: 2022

Printed in the United States of America

0   9   8   7   6   5   4   3   2   1

FOR LORREL, AS ALWAYS

OPENING MOVES

The Arrest

ONE

☐

Otto Rencke, chief of electronic intelligence for the Central Intelligence Agency, parked his aging Mercedes sedan at his spot in the VIP garage beneath the Original Headquarters Building at the George Bush Center for Intelligence, and headed for the elevators to his third-floor suite of offices. It was just eight in the morning, a Friday, and he was worried about his wife, Mary, who'd been running a fever, but insisted that he get to work though he wanted to stay with her.

"I'm going to the Quick Care Clinic, honest injun," she'd promised, using one of her husband's phrases.

At five two and only a bit more than one hundred pounds, with a slight figure, she was almost the exact opposite of Otto, who, at nearly six feet, with a barrel chest, towered over her. Her hair was short and honey blond, while his was reddish brown and long, tied in a ponytail. She was a neatnik, but despite her friendly nagging, he was basically a slob, dressing mostly in sloppy jeans and ragged sweatshirts with either the old KGB sword and shield logo or the CCCP initials of the former Soviet Union.

"Call me soon as you see the doc," he'd said, and he reached down to give her a kiss, but she reared back.

"Do you want to catch whatever it is I've got? Just get out of here."

He'd thought about her on the way up from their house just a few miles away in McLean, and just now as he stepped off the elevator on the third floor he felt a sense of loneliness. Since they'd been married, last year, they had been side by side almost 24/7, and it felt unnatural to be without her.

She'd come over from her office in the New Headquarters Building, where she'd worked as a senior analyst, and joined her husband in his digs, known by just about everyone as the Wolf's Den. The unwritten sign above the door said: *Beware of the vicious beast within.*

Among senior officials in the Agency and elsewhere in Washington, and in most of the major intelligence agencies worldwide, Otto was known as an enfant terrible. His above-genius-level knowledge of computers and their advanced algorithms made him either a friend or a foe depending on which side of the fence you found yourself on. But everyone who knew anything about him both respected and feared him. Except for his friend Kirk McGarvey, who was the former director of the CIA, and Mac's new wife, the former Pete Boylan, who'd been the Company's chief of interrogations.

"Good morning, dear," an AI voice said from about eye level in midair as he got to his door.

"Good morning, Lou," he said. The lock buzzed, and he let himself in to

his lair, which consisted of three offices that had once been used by a team that developed legends—background stories—for agents going out into the cold.

Lou was the interface between him and the advanced computer systems he'd once called his darlings, that sampled the databases of just about every major computer anywhere on the planet, looking for what he called anomalies. They were the bits and pieces of intelligence information that were outside the normal day-to-day flow of data.

If there was a gunfight in Syria, routine intel would detail the strengths and weaknesses of the opposing forces, along with the orders of battle, casualties, and other obvious details. An anomaly could be the presence of a high-ranking officer, under very deep cover, from Russia, or perhaps North Korea, or China. Someone who should not have been there, and whose purpose was unknown.

Linking a series of anomalies together, his programs would come up with an assessment of risks for the U.S. and its allies. The greater the risk, the deeper the color lavender would appear on the many flat-panel monitors.

"How is Mary this morning?" Lou asked.

"She's going to see a doc and she promised to call."

"Nothing serious, I hope."

"A slight fever and cough, probably just a cold."

"Good," the program said.

Louise Horn had been Otto's first wife, but she had been killed in a shootout during an operation a couple of years ago. When he'd managed to bring himself back to reality, he reconfigured his darlings, upgrading them to a near-AI level and giving them his dead wife's personality and voice. Mary hadn't minded, and in fact she and Louise had known each other, and she and the program were friends. They shared the mission of keeping Otto on track and in touch with the day-to-day bits and pieces of real life beyond his work.

The first room contained three desks, and a number of file cabinets and map cases, filled with printed matter that had never been scanned into any database. The middle room was Mary's lair, with her computer interfaces. The inner sanctum was Otto's, with no keyboards, only a one-hundred-inch ultra-high-definition monitor on the wall, and a tabletop monitor about the size of a large pool table. Both surfaces were busy with streams of data, but the background color was only faintly lavender. For the moment all was well with the world.

Otto perched on the edge of the monitor table. "Anything I need to know about?" he asked.

"Beyond background noises, and the usual inquiries, in the past twenty-four hours mostly from State concerning North Korea's probable continuation of its nuclear program, and the attack on our embassy in Pyongyang, there is nothing of any real significance."

"Something will come up," Otto said.

He'd started smoking a couple of months ago, but when Mary had found out, she'd made him quit. He wished he had a cigarette right now.

"It usually does."

"Where're Mac and Pete?"

"They are currently on the island of Yakushima."

"Japan?"

"Yes. Fifty miles south of Kyushu."

"House shopping?"

"My confidence level is ninety-three percent."

"I thought they were on Nassau."

"They are on Yakushima."

"When did they leave the Bahamas?"

"Seventy-seven hours ago."

"It's only ten in the evening there, let me talk to him."

"Just a moment, dear," Lou said.

"What is it?"

"There is a message for you from Mr. Taft." Harold Taft was the director of the CIA.

"Is he on the phone?"

"No. Message is: 'Mr. Rencke please come to my office at your earliest convenience.'"

"Did he say why?"

"No. Shall I repeat the message for you, dear?"

"Thank you, Lou, but that won't be necessary," Otto said, pushing away from the table. "I'll go now."

He left his inner sanctum, but at the outer door he stopped. "Did you detect any stress in the director's voice?"

"It was a text message."

"My phone didn't ring."

"The message was sent directly to me."

Otto thought it was odd. Not Taft's style. He walked back to his office. "Show me the message on the monitor, please."

The text came up, letter perfect. Taft had always been a clumsy typist. "He didn't send it."

"No, but it originated in his office."

"Can you tell me who else is there?"

"Mr. Waksberg and Mr. Kallek."

Thomas Waksberg was the deputy director of operations, and Harold Kallek was the director of the FBI.

"Can you monitor their conversations?"

"No."

"You're being blocked?"

"No one is currently speaking."

Kirk McGarvey and Pete strolled down the tree-lined path from the Sankara Hotel and Spa to the cabanas overlooking the sea toward the nearby island of Tanegashima, from which the Tanegashima Space Center launched rockets into space. The late September evening was soft, in the midseventies, and only a slight breeze came from the Vincennes Strait separating the two islands.

McGarvey, Mac to his friends, was tall, athletically built, and extremely fit for a man of fifty. His brown hair was thick, his face honest, and his eyes, sometimes gray and at other times green depending on his circumstances, never seemed to miss a thing, which in his line of work as a fixer for the CIA was a definite plus. He was an expert with a wide range of weapons, including his old and trusted friend, the Walther PPK in the rare 9mm version, plus explosives and hand-to-hand combat.

"A penny," Pete said. Like Mac, she was dressed in resort wear, linen slacks and a light top.

"Serifos felt more like home, but this place could work," he said. He'd been moody for most of the afternoon, missing something that he couldn't really get a handle on, though it wasn't the converted lighthouse on the Greek island that he'd used as a refuge between operations, which most often ended in violence, and casualties at his hand.

After a recent incident that resulted in the deaths of six Spetsnaz operators who'd been sent to assassinate him and Pete, the Greek National Intelligence Service had politely asked them to leave and not return.

They'd compensated him for the cost of the lighthouse and the improvements he'd made—which amounted to nearly $1 million U.S.—and gave the two of them twenty-four hours to pack up and go, leaving the Greek military to clean up the mess.

"Are you asking or telling me?" Pete asked.

He had to smile, though he was getting the odd feeling that someone or something was gaining on them. And still he could not shake his fear for Pete. Every woman he'd ever been involved with, including his wife Katy and their daughter, Liz, had been killed because of who he was, what he did.

He'd started with the CIA just after getting out of the air force, more years ago than he wanted to remember, and after a long psychological workup by some of the best shrinks on the planet, he'd been offered the job as a black operator, an assassin, a program the Company steadfastly insisted did not exist.

And he'd been good, almost too good, and he'd quit the Company. But trouble seemed to follow him wherever he went, starting in Switzerland, where he'd run to hide after an incident in Chile that had gone bad for him. The CIA needed his help, the country needed his help. And he'd come back into the fold as a freelance operator.

"A little of both," he told her.

"Okay, so what's eating you? Another premo?"

McGarvey's premonitions—premos, Otto called them—had almost always come true. The Company shrinks had early on labeled him to be almost preternatural. He had a sixth sense of a sort that made him feel things that other people couldn't. It wasn't ESP, but rather an acute awareness of his surroundings, and especially everything in his past—good and bad—that warned him when trouble was brewing somewhere that might come his way.

"I can't put a finger on it."

Pete pulled up short. "Now you're starting to worry me."

This far from the hotel's main building, the only light came from low-power lanterns that lined the sand path. Away from the large cities, especially Tokyo, Japan had always been about serenity. Yakushima and the Sankara epitomized this philosophy.

Someone was behind them. Mac could feel it more than hear any specific thing.

He pushed Pete aside and as he turned around reached for the pistol usually holstered at the small of his back.

A slightly built Japanese man, dressed for the city, his tie loose and his suit coat draped over his arm, came out of the darkness and stopped short. "You cannot be armed, Mr. McGarvey, unless you somehow smuggled your Walther through customs at Narita. Of course, that isn't the case, nor did you meet with anyone who could have given you a pistol."

McGarvey let himself relax a little.

The man was a cop or an intelligence agency officer, he had the look, but he smiled as he took out an identification wallet and opened it.

"I am Enki Fumiko," he said. "Officially I'm badged with the prefectural police department's security bureau."

"In reality you work for the Cabinet Secretariat, I assume?"

"Actually, military intelligence. I'm Colonel Enki and I was sent down from Tokyo to have a chat with you and Mrs. McGarvey, but only after it became apparent that you were looking at properties to buy here on Yakushima."

"Which is uncomfortably close to Tanegashima," McGarvey said.

"That does not concern us. Serifos does. May we talk?"

"Here or back at the hotel?"

"Let's walk along the beach, no one is there at the moment, and I won't take up much of your time."

McGarvey exchanged a glance with Pete, whose expression was neutral,

and they headed the rest of the way down the path, which led to a spectacular beach with open cabanas under thatched roofs.

"This is a beautiful island, Mr. Enki, will we be allowed to buy property here?" Pete asked.

"At this point I can give you only a provisional yes, that will depend greatly on your cooperation this evening."

"What do you need?"

"What happened on Serifos to cause the government to ask you to leave?"

"Someone tried to assassinate us twice in Georgetown, and once at our home in Florida, so we tried to get out of the way on the island," Pete said.

"Who and why?"

"It was a personal vendetta," McGarvey said.

Enki pulled up short. "A Russian? North Korean? Pakistani?"

"Actually an American with a serious amount of money who was probably playing a game," McGarvey said.

"'The Most Dangerous Game,' I read the short story in English class when I was ten," Enki said. "And you hoped that island would eliminate any possible collateral damage."

"The Greek government didn't see it that way," Pete said.

"Neither would we have."

"Which is why you came here to interview us."

"We would like a reasonable assurance that such an incident wouldn't take place on this island. We value our serenity, especially in places such as this. Can you guarantee such a thing?"

"From the same man who attacked us?" McGarvey asked.

"For a start."

"Then yes, I can give you my word that he wouldn't be coming after us here or anywhere else for that matter."

"How can you be sure?"

"Because we know who he is, and he knows that we know."

"Then arrest him."

"We don't have the proof," Pete said. "Yet."

Enki was troubled, but he nodded. "I'll take your word that this particular man would be no further threat. But trouble does seem to follow in your footsteps, Mr. Director."

"That's something I can't help," McGarvey said, and he was about to say that they would be leaving Japan first thing in the morning, but Pete interrupted.

"It's something that we can't help, Mr. Enki. If you want assurances that trouble won't follow us here, we can't give it to you. But if another assignment comes up, it will almost certainly not involve Japan. Can you give us your assurance that no one in Japan will be gunning for us? Because we value serenity as much as you do. It's one of the reasons we're here."

"And the other reasons?"

Pete smiled. "It's beautiful, the people are friendly, and the food is terrific."

"Like Serifos?" Enki asked.

"Better."

"More isolated, fewer tourists, and therefore easier for us to keep a close eye on who comes here," Enki said. "I sincerely hope you find what you're looking for."

THREE

□

Otto did not go directly up to the director's office. Instead he went across the enclosed walkway, past the *Kryptos* sculpture in the courtyard, to Mary's old office in the New Headquarters Building.

Lately she'd been paying visits with her analytical group. "Working on something you might find interesting," she'd told him a couple of weeks ago.

His ex-wife had been very smart, one of the leading experts on satellite intelligence gathering and data interpretation, but Mary was even brighter. The way she approached a difficult problem, how she broke it into pieces manageable enough to be understood, was even better than most computers. And over the months they'd been married he'd come to rely on her.

Toni Mulholland, who'd been Mary's number two and had been promoted to chief analyst, came from the bullpen where the team of five foreign intelligence service eggheads met once or twice a day to hash out whatever issue was pressing at the moment. She was an attractive curvy woman in her midthirties.

She was startled. "Is it Mary?" she asked.

"She's got a bug, but it's nothing serious," Otto said. "I just stopped by to see what you guys were working on. She pestered me this morning to find out."

Toni's left eyebrow rose. "Bullshit, Otto. This is me you're talking to. What's up?"

Sometimes Otto was so wrapped up in his own world that he forgot a lot of people in the Company were seriously smart. In fact, there were more Ph.D.s per capita on this campus than at Harvard. He bobbed his head. "Taft asked me to come up to his office. Tom Waksberg and Kallek are with him."

"They've probably got a problem they want you to sort out. What'd Lou have to say?"

"Nothing."

"She didn't know?" Toni said. "That's hard to believe."

"It's why I came here to talk to you first."

"She hasn't developed a glitch, has she?"

"No, but I have a feeling that some of her inputs have been blocked."

"Have her run a diagnostic."

"If she's blocked, it wouldn't matter right now," Otto said. "Whatever's going on, and I have a feeling something is going on, will be humint, and out of the dataverse." "Humint" was CIAspeak for human intelligence—face-to-face intel methods—versus intel information in the data universe.

"What's going on that's made you come over here before you go up-stairs?"

"Do you have anything tickling your fancy on the threat board? Anything that catches your eye? Something odd?"

"Other than the usual crap with the DPRK, Iran, Pakistan, the Ukraine, and the shitstorm going down in Venezuela, nothing unexpected," Toni said. "What's your color?"

"Barely lavender."

"But something has you worried. Have you talked to Mac?"

"He and Pete are over in Japan looking for something to buy. I didn't want to bother them because you're probably right, Taft has a problem he needs help with."

"Tom is there, which could mean we have an internal problem. But if the FBI's involved it's more than us. Maybe something to do with Mac?"

"I have nothing from the Serifos aftermath, but a couple of Bureau people got caught up in the middle of it, and one of them was shot to death."

"I haven't picked up any complaints from the Greeks other than Mac and Pete's expulsion," Toni said. "But maybe Kallek wants to have a face-to-face and he's afraid that Mac would tell him to screw himself, or something to that effect. And they want your help to rein him in."

It was the Marty Bambridge effect. Bambridge had been the deputy director of operations, sometimes called clandestine services, and he and McGarvey had gone seriously head-to-head on more than one occasion. In the end, Bambridge had been involved in a plot to bring down the president, and had died in a shoot-out when the operation went bad. Because of McGarvey and Pete. And now many of the upper-echelon officers in the CIA and over at the FBI walked with care lest they cross McGarvey. No one wanted to end up in McGarvey's gunsights like Bambridge had.

Otto was troubled. "Probably."

"But you don't think so."

"I'll find out," Otto said.

Toni stopped him at the door before he went out. "Look, you're the one guy in this organization that no one is going to screw with. Everyone's afraid of the havoc that you and Lou could wreak."

"Your lips to God's ears," Otto said, but he wasn't sure.

On the way back across to the OHB, he thought about stopping at his office first to reinforce Lou's passwords, just in case, but they were already strong. He'd once worked out that even a Cray working full-time would take a half century to break in. And that was assuming Lou wouldn't fight back to protect herself.

Taft's secretary looked frightened when Otto walked in. But she nodded toward the door to the DCI's office. "They're waiting for you."

Taft's office was not terribly big, but the windows gave a nice view of

the woods behind the OHB. The director was seated on a couch in front of a coffee table on the other side of which Waksberg and Kallek sat on a matching couch—almost the twins of the ones in the Oval Office across the river.

A side chair was placed at the end of the coffee table facing the three men, who looked stern, even a little frightened, Otto thought.

Taft motioned for him to take a seat.

"Do we have a problem, Mr. Director?" Otto asked, sitting down.

"Are you armed, Mr. Rencke?" Kallek asked. He was a stern-looking man with salt-and-pepper hair, who looked and acted the part of a high-end New York banker.

"No. Are you?"

"Yes."

It wasn't the answer Otto had hoped for, but seeing the looks on their faces, especially Taft's, he wasn't surprised. "Lou?" he said.

There was no answer.

He took out his cell phone and tried to connect with his office, but the call wouldn't go through.

"This room has been shielded," Waksberg said. He was a portly man whose clothes never seemed to fit. "We had some good people figure out at least that much. And now that you're here, power to your offices has been cut. You're on your own, Mr. Rencke."

"We'll see how long that'll last. But in the meantime, are you guys going to tell me what this is all about, or do I have to guess?"

"Give me your phone, please," Waksberg said.

"Fuck you," Otto said, and he started to rise, but Taft motioned him back.

"Believe me, this isn't easy for any of us," the DCI said. "But I promise you that you'll have a full hearing."

"On what?" Otto asked, sitting down.

"We're in the early stages of the investigation, and we have a long way to go," Waksberg said. "How long will depend entirely on how willing you are to cooperate with us and with the Bureau that has taken the lead, but with our help."

"Am I being charged with a crime?"

"Actually, yes," Taft said.

"I'd like to have Carleton sit in on this."

"He will represent the Agency, not you."

"Then I want to hire a lawyer," Otto said. Mary would have to help him with that, because other than Carleton Patterson, the Company's longtime counsel and his and Mac's friend, he didn't know any legal beagles.

"In due time."

"Your phone, please," Waksberg said.

Otto took it out and tossed it at the man, who had to scramble to catch it.

"Are you going to tell me what I'm being charged with, or am I supposed to guess?"

"Treason," Kallek said.

"You have to be shitting me," Otto said, as though he'd been slammed in the gut.

FOUR

When she hadn't heard from Otto for more than a half hour, Toni Mulholland tried calling his office, but the line was dead. She went across to the OHB and tried the door, but the entry lock wouldn't work with her ID, and in fact it seemed to be dead.

"Lou, I'd like to speak with Otto."

There was no reply, and a worry started to nag at the back of her head. He'd been on his way to a meeting with the DCI, and now Lou was apparently off-line. She turned on her heel and headed for the elevator.

Toni had started out as a junior lawyer, clerking for Leonard Blakely, an assistant attorney general in the Department of Justice's Criminal Division, but she had tired of her job within the first year, because she was smarter than her boss. On a whim she'd applied for a position with the CIA and was hired after an extensive background check and several interviews.

Originally, she'd worked in Carleton Patterson's office, but in less than six months he'd suggested that she would be happier as an analyst. It was then that two things became evident: She was an extremely curious person for whom face value in any investigation meant absolutely nothing, and she was finally working with bright people, many of them smarter than her, and that was a refreshing thing.

She got off on the seventh floor and went down to the DCI's office, where Madge Lyons, his secretary, was just getting off the phone. The woman looked up. "Is the director expecting you, Ms. . . . ?"

"Toni Mulholland, I work in the DI, but no, Mr. Taft is not expecting me." The DI was the Directorate of Intelligence. "I'm looking for Mr. Rencke. I was told he was here."

"No, he's not."

"But he said he was coming up here to speak with the director."

Madge picked up the phone and buzzed Taft. "A Ms. Mulholland from the DI is here looking for Mr. Rencke." She nodded, said, "Yes, sir," and hung up. "Mr. Rencke isn't here."

"Crap," Toni said.

"I'm sorry, dear, but he left ten minutes ago."

"How about Mr. Kallek, did he leave at the same time?"

Madge glanced at the director's door, but then nodded. She was worried. "They left together."

. . .

Toni went back downstairs to the third floor, but this time a strip of yellow DO NOT CROSS tape had been placed across the door to Otto's office.

She used her cell phone to log into the CIA's internal directory site and tried to pull up Otto's address, but it came back ACCESS DENIED.

"Shit, shit, shit," she muttered. None of this seemed real.

A man in shirtsleeves came out of an office down the hall and looked at her.

She turned on her heel and hurried back to the walkway to the NHB and up to her office, where she grabbed her purse. Hank Rogers was at his desk in the cubicle nearest to her office, and he looked up. "Did you find Otto?"

"I guess he's still in conference with the director, I'll catch him later. Right now, I've got a couple of errands to run."

"We're going over RP's latest this afternoon."

GKRP was the designator for one of the Company's deep-cover agents inside North Korea's Nuclear Scientific Research Center at Yongbyon. "GK" meant top secret and "RP"—Rice Paddy—was the code name for their NOC agent. "NOC" meant their agent was working under no official cover. If he was outed, the U.S. would deny his existence.

"I'll be back by then," Toni said.

She went to the OHB and took the elevator down to her five-year-old Porsche Carrera, parked in the VIP ramp. She'd bought it as a gift to herself after her divorce. A friend had advised her that the way to get rid of a hundred and eighty pounds of ugly fat was to divorce the bastard. Her reward was the car.

She drove down to the main gate, but waited until she reached the GW Parkway and was heading south before she called Mary's phone. It was answered on the second ring.

"Hi, Toni," Mary said. She sounded stuffed up.

"How about a cup of coffee at our Mickey D's?"

"Now?"

"If you're up to it."

"Where are you?"

"On the parkway. I can be there in ten."

"Right," Mary said, and she hung up.

Mary was seated in a corner of the McDonald's on Old Dominion Drive in McLean with two cups of coffee, one black for her and the other with milk and sugar, when Toni came in and sat down across from her.

"You don't look so hot."

"I've felt better," Mary said. She was dressed in a patterned orange blouse, and white leggings. "But what's so important that it brought you away from your think tank in the middle of the morning?"

"Otto's missing."

Mary inclined her head slightly. "Hibernating? Locked himself in his Wolf's Den?"

"Missing. He stopped by my office to tell me he'd been called up to the seventh floor to meet with Taft, Waksberg, and Harold Kallek."

"Okay?"

"He said he was starting to get a little worried because Lou had been locked out from eavesdropping on the director's office."

"That had to happen sooner or later, but Otto said he would fix it if and when he had the time."

"Anyway, after an hour or so, I tried to call him but it didn't ring through, so I went up to Taft's office. Madge told me that Otto was there, but that he'd left with Kallek. And that was all she could tell me."

"Or would tell you."

"When I went back down to Otto's office, Do Not Cross tape had been put across his door, and when I tried to pull up Otto's internal website, it came up access denied. So I called you."

Mary looked away for a longish moment or two, biting her lower lip. Toni noticed a small artery throbbing at her left temple. Only a few people were in the restaurant at this time of day, and no one was paying them any attention. This was where they sometimes met to ostensibly talk over girl stuff, but in reality to discuss whatever current problem or problems they were facing.

"If he and Kallek left together it probably means only one of two things," Mary said. "Either the Bureau needed his help, or he's been arrested."

"Help, I can understand. But arrested, for what?"

"To get at Mac," Mary said. "My guess would be the incident at Serifos. Otto figured that the Russians were bound to put pressure on us to find out why six of their Spetsnaz people were gunned down. We'll have to check the diplomatic channels through our Moscow embassy and theirs right here."

"That's something I can do," Toni said. "But I didn't know that Otto was involved."

"He's always been involved with whatever Mac was doing. So was I over the past year since Lou was shot dead."

"That being the case, the questions are where'd they take him, and when and where will the arraignment be held?"

"If he's been arrested there won't be an arraignment anytime soon," Mary said. "But I'm the wife, and I'll find out where they're holding him. And why."

"What about Mac?"

"Let's find out what's actually going on before we bother him and Pete."

FIVE

Kallek had handed Otto over to a pair of stern-looking FBI agents, who cuffed him and placed him in the backseat of a black Cadillac Escalade, the agents sitting on either side of him. A third agent was behind the wheel. All of them were very large and looked fit.

"Are you sure you want to do this, Mr. Kallek?" Otto had asked, but the FBI director didn't answer, instead merely turned away and walked to where his limo and driver were waiting.

They had taken I-95 south, and after twenty miles took the exit at the Fairfax County Parkway, never exceeding the speed limit, the driver continuously glancing in the rearview mirror.

"I was wondering where you guys were going to stash me," Otto said, realizing where he was being taken.

No one responded.

"Fort Belvoir, home to the army's Military Intelligence Readiness Command," he said. "Lot better than Quantico if you wanted to cover your tracks. But this is also the HQ for the National Geospatial-Intelligence Agency, where my former wife used to work part-time. Just about like coming home, ya know."

The agent to his left glanced at him, but said nothing.

"Treason's a pretty big deal. I hope whoever is the lead investigator knows what the hell they're doing, because it's going to be pretty hard to prove, even if Lou cooperates with you, which she won't of course unless I tell her to do so."

Ever since Kallek had taken him from Taft's office, Otto had been racking his brains trying to figure out what game they were playing. He didn't think it was going to be so easy as investigating the Serifos thing. For that they would have brought Mac and Pete in for questioning, but that wouldn't have been so easy either.

It was possible that they were going to use him as bait, just as the Cuban intelligence service that had forced him to come to Havana had done a few years back, in order to lure McGarvey. Of course, that hadn't worked out so well, especially not for Fidel Castro's illegitimate daughter, who'd orchestrated what became a royal cock-up.

They were passed through the main base gate and wound their way past the administration area, and finally back to the sprawling NGA Campus East, the nine-story main building of which was bisected by an atrium so large it could easily accommodate the Statue of Liberty. More than sixteen thousand people worked in this building, which was almost as big as the Pentagon.

Where do you hide a needle? Otto had wondered. The answer was right here. You hide a needle not in a haystack, but in a pile of needles. Simple.

"Not such a smart idea, trying to stash a computer nerd in the middle of a techie's haven," Otto said half to himself. "Quantico would have been better."

By now Lou's power had been cut, but unless the technical services guys looked closely enough it might be hours, or even days, before they discovered her backup source. He'd never trusted the Company's campus-wide emergency generator system, which was way too vulnerable to attack from the outside.

So, after he'd switched from his old system to the AI algorithm to which he'd given Louise's persona, he'd hidden it in the guise of the Cray he'd modified to take up less than one-fourth of the space a normal Cray needed, leaving plenty of room for the series of lithium iron phosphate batteries a friend over at LG Chemical had supplied him with.

The modifications had taken nearly a month to make, but at least for the moment Lou was safe. When the power dropped, she would go to sleep. Unless someone tried to screw with her. Then she would automatically go into a search mode looking for him, or in the end if that failed, self-destruct.

They pulled up at a service and supply dock at the rear of the main building. One of the overhead doors opened, and the agent driving backed the Caddy into the receiving bay where everything from food for the cafeterias to parts for the vast number of computers and communications systems in use 24/7 was delivered.

When the door closed, two men came from the rear of the bay, one of them in his midthirties, tall and whip-thin, with dark black hair and a scowl, whom Otto didn't know, and the other much older, with long silver hair, a belly, and the complexion of a big drinker, whom Otto had known for years.

The agents with Otto got him out of the SUV.

"Take those stupid handcuffs off the man, will you for God's sake?" Bill Benkerk, the older man, said. His voice was booming, but his demeanor, normally jolly, was deadly serious. He was a chief investigator for the CIA's Directorate of Management and Services—which included security. He and Pete had worked together before she'd left the Agency, and he'd known Otto and Louise for several years.

"That's not such a good idea," the other man said, but Benkerk waved him off.

"You'll give us no trouble now, will you, boyo?" he asked Otto. His father was English, his mother had been Irish. Benkerk took after his mother.

"Honest injun," Otto said.

"Good enough," Benkerk boomed, and he motioned for the agents to do it.

"I hope you know what you're getting yourself into," one of the agents said while the other removed the handcuffs from Otto's wrists.

"He's an old friend. And we'll be fine. Thanks for dropping by."

The two agents got back into the Caddy, and when the overhead door was open again they backed out, and the door closed.

"Mr. Rencke, you've been charged with treason," the thin man said.

"I know what I'm being charged with. You have a name?"

"My name is of no importance. But I've been tasked with overseeing your interrogation."

"Why this place?"

"When we heard two weeks ago that they were bringing you here I was asked to help out," Benkerk said. "They figured having an old friend at your side might calm you down."

"This is a load of crap, and you know it," Otto said, though in actuality he wasn't all that worried. He and Mac had bent a lot of rules together over the past few years, but nothing that ever could be called treason. Mac's motto had always been "Truth, justice, and the American way." It was a little hokey, in Otto's estimation, but it had grown on him. And once Mary realized that he'd dropped out of sight, she would let Mac and Pete know.

"I surely do, but we've set up some reasonably comfortable accommodations for you."

"Thanks, but I don't think I'll be here that long."

"That will depend on you," the interrogator said.

From the moment her power had been cut and she'd switched over to batteries, Lou had gone into search mode looking for Otto, whose last destination known to her was the DCI's seventh-floor office.

The surveillance system that monitored sounds had been disabled, but the infrared sensors, which were actually sophisticated heat and smoke detectors, were still operating. No one was in place except for Taft's secretary, and she was currently not using her computer, though it was online, nor was her telephone in use.

Expanding her search to the archives of all surveillance cameras from the DCI's office in widening circles, she found Otto and FBI director Harold Kallek as they walked down the seventh-floor corridor and got aboard the VIP elevator. The time stamp on the recording was forty-seven minutes ago. They did not speak on the way down, until they reached the parking garage, where two men in FBI windbreakers were waiting.

"Are you sure you want to do this, Mr. Kallek?" Otto had asked, but the FBI director had just walked away.

Next, Lou called up a number of U.S. surveillance satellites, but nothing easily accessible was currently pointed at the CIA's campus, or the greater Washington, D.C., area, so she went searching farther afield to Russian satellites, starting with the Resurs-P, which was a commercial Earth observation platform in sun-synchronous orbit.

Simultaneously she searched other systems, including the Persona reconnaissance constellation starting with the Kosmos trio of 2441, launched in

2008; 2486, launched in 2013, which had some early technical issues; and 2506, put into orbit on June 23, 2015.

She got lucky with the Resurs, pointed at the U.S. eastern coast, looking as far north as New York City and as far south as Norfolk. It was tasked by Roskosmos, which at one time had operated as the Russian Federal Space Agency.

Bringing up the archival downlinks for the past sixty minutes and scrolling forward at the speed of one millisecond per actual minute of images, she picked up the Cadillac Escalade leaving the OHB, passing through the gate, and finally disappearing into a service garage at the National Geospatial-Intelligence Agency headquarters on Fort Belvoir.

She had discovered the where, and now she went looking for the why.

☐

Mary still maintained her Company credentials, which allowed her entry not only to the campus but to just about every section in every building, including the NHB. She followed Toni back to Langley, where they parked several spots away from each other, and caught up as if by chance on the way to the main entrance.

No one else was around, and the surveillance system for the various parking lots was not sophisticated enough to pick up conversations. It was believed that if you made it through the main gate, you had been initially vetted and posed no real or immediate danger.

"I want you to get your people together and see what you can dig up about Serifos, and as far back in Otto's history as you can," Mary said.

"We can do that, but what am I looking for? Specifically?"

"Whatever the Bureau wants with Otto could have something to do with what he and Mac have done or are still working on. I want you to see if there are any patterns. Some connections between each operation they've been involved with."

"You know more about stuff like that, especially over the past year, since you two were married and started working together."

"You're right, but Hank Rogers was my number two when I was sitting behind your desk, so he can point you in the right direction. And two or more heads are better than one."

"What about you?" Toni asked.

"I'm going up to Otto's office and see if Lou's come up with anything."

"How will you get in? The card reader doesn't respond and neither does Lou."

Mary took an ordinary key out of her pocket. "The old-fashioned way," she said.

Once through security in the OHB lobby, Toni headed the long way across to her office, and Mary took the elevator up to the third floor. All of the doors in the long corridor were shut, and no one was about when she went down to Otto's office.

"Lou?" she said, but there was no response.

Using the key, she got the door open, then ducked under the DO NOT CROSS tape and went inside, closing the door behind her.

For a moment she stood stock-still, waiting for some sort of an alarm to sound. But the suite was dark, and nothing happened.

She tried a light switch, but all electricity had apparently been cut.

"Lou, it's me, I'm alone," she said.

"Yes, Mary, I know," Otto's AI program responded.

Thank God the batteries hadn't been discovered. "I need your help finding out what's going on."

"Yes, and I need your help because my batteries are at ninety-three percent and falling."

"What's your threshold?"

"I need twenty percent to maintain my memory and logic circuits, below that Otto has designed me to shut down."

"What about if someone tampers with you in sleep mode?"

Lou uncharacteristically hesitated for a beat. "I will die."

"Christ," Mary said softly, and she hurried into the primary office, where both the wall monitor and horizontal display table were lit up bright lavender. "Otto's been arrested. Do you know the charges and his current location?"

"He has been charged with treason, and the FBI has taken him to the National Geospatial-Intelligence headquarters at Fort Belvoir."

"Do you know the specifics of the arrest warrant?"

"There is no record of the charges or of his arrest in any database I have accessed—that includes ours as well as the FBI's."

"How did you find out where he was taken?"

"I tapped into the Resurs bird overhead and got lucky."

Mary suppressed a laugh. "The Russians, very inventive."

"Otto designed me to think, to learn, and to invent."

"Can you tell me the specifics of his current location and situation?"

"He was delivered to a service dock. No mention of him shows up in any NGA database."

"For all practical purposes he's disappeared."

"Yes."

"But why take him there?" Mary asked. "I don't understand."

"No one would think to look there," Lou said. Again, the program hesitated for just a beat. "Will you call Mac and Pete?"

"As soon as I can find out the specifics of what my husband's been charged with."

"I can offer limited help."

"I'm working with Toni Mulholland on this."

"I know."

"Can you give us the details of the last few field operations that Mac has worked on and that Otto has helped with?"

"I'm sending that information directly to Toni now."

"Good. When that's finished, I want you to go to sleep."

"I'm finished," Lou said. "Good night and good luck. Please wake me from time to time to keep me advised."

"First. Do you know where Mac and Pete are at this moment?"

"They are at the Sankara Hotel and Spa on Yakushima Island."

"Japan?"

"Yes."

"Do you have a password for me to use?"

"No, Mary, just your presence in this space."

"Good night."

Both monitors went blank.

When Toni got to her office, Hank Rogers came in and shut the glass door. He was a man in his midfifties, with boyishly long hair and a scruffy beard that made him look like a professor of philosophy at some small junior college rather than a senior intelligence analyst.

"Okay, what's going on?" he asked. "I just got a big data dump from Rencke's AI, and it's all about four ops that he and Mac were involved with. Pakistan, North Korea, and two in Russia."

"Otto's been arrested and charged with treason."

Rogers was skeptical. "You've gotta be shitting me."

"I wish I was," Toni said. "But we're dropping everything else and working on this. RP can wait."

"What's the plan?"

"Since Otto was involved, it almost certainly means he hacked into the mainframes of all four intelligence agencies: Pakistan's Inter-Services Intelligence, DPRK's State Security Department, and Russia's SVR and GRU."

"If I know Rencke, he left a back door in each so that if need be he could get in again with no fuss and bother."

"That's the bad news," Toni said. "Looked at the wrong way, it could be construed that he left his calling card and since none of those intel agencies have raised hell—accusing us of spying on them—someone thinks that he has developed friendships in all the wrong places."

"Treason."

"Yup. What we need to do is find contact names at all four, during the times of those ops."

"Then what?" Rogers said.

"Let Mac know."

Mary showed up at the door and Rogers buzzed her in.

"We need to get a handle on a possible reason for Otto's arrest, and it's not going to be easy," Toni said. "We'd better call Mac."

"He and Pete are in southern Japan, Yakushima Island," Mary said. She glanced up at the clock; it was just coming up on eleven. "Unless my geography is bad, it's one in the morning over there."

"I think we should call him anyway."

"I'll take care of it, but from off campus."

SEVEN

Pete was already in bed when McGarvey got out of the shower, dried off, and with the towel wrapped around his waist came out of the bathroom. He was troubled and he suspected that Pete was as well.

Her head was turned away.

"Are you asleep?" he asked.

"No," she said, turning toward him. "I was waiting for you. We need to talk."

He sat down beside her on the edge of the bed, and she sat up.

"This place doesn't feel right to me," she started.

"If you mean Enki, I don't think we'll get any more pressure than we did from the Greeks at first, or even from the cops in Florida. We're the troublesome couple that everyone in the business knows about."

"That, too," Pete said. "We're carrying a lot of baggage, and the load doesn't seem as if it'll get lighter any time soon. But I mean this island, this entire country, it just doesn't feel right to me."

"The Japanese are a good people."

"Not bad, just alien. I can't get a handle on it, but from the moment we landed at Narita I felt like a bull in a china shop." She shook her head. "Kirk, I don't know if I could ever be as comfortable here as I was in Greece or even in France. If you want an island refuge why not somewhere in the Caribbean? The USVI?"

"Too isolated," Mac said, but that wasn't right.

Pete laughed. "And this place isn't?" she asked. "Look, I happen to be in love with you, if you needed reminding, and I'll gladly fly off to wherever you want us to go."

"But?"

"Georgetown has some bad memories for both of us, but it still feels like home. Just like Casey Key. And I almost lost you when the bastards put a bomb in your car in Sarasota, but it's still home to me."

Pete reached down and touched his left leg with her fingertips. Dr. Franklin and a team from Johns Hopkins had replaced McGarvey's prosthetic left leg from the knee down with a scaffolding of titanium and carbon nanofibers that were connected with the still-functioning nerve endings in his knee.

Over a series of operations, more mechanical than medical, they had covered the scaffolding with padding of gel that closely mimicked the overlying muscles and tissues of his real leg, then covered it with a plastic skin that looked and felt like the real thing.

Afterward it had taken months for McGarvey to learn how to use his new leg, working mostly at the CIA's training facility near Williamsburg, Virginia, until in the end he stopped thinking of it as artificial. And except for the fact that he had no real sense of touch in the skin, and the muscles never became fatigued, the new leg was just as much a part of his body as if he had been born with it.

"You can't feel my fingers, can you," Pete said.

"No, but I know how it's supposed to feel and I like it."

Pete laughed. "I'll buy that, but I've watched you on the confidence course at the Farm, and walking on the beach in front of our house in Florida, and making love. It's as real as Franklin and his team could make it, but at the back of your head, you're still having a hard time accepting it."

She reached up and brushed her fingertips across his lips. "You can feel that because they're real. And your problem, my lovely man, is that you think that it's me who is having an issue accepting you—the whole you. But I don't."

McGarvey took her into his arms and kissed her deeply. When they parted, he studied her face, her lips, her small nose, her eyes. He'd loved before but never so completely as he loved her at this moment, because she was more than a wife, she was a partner in every sense of the word. And more of a part of his body than even his real arms and leg.

"Something's catching up with us, you can feel it, and I know it," Pete said. "But make love to me now, Kirk, and we'll deal with your premo in the morning."

Mary left the campus from the back gate to Georgetown Pike that connected a few miles later with Dolley Madison Boulevard and she was home in McLean in under fifteen minutes.

She was driving Otto's old Mercedes 220 diesel sedan with 350,000 miles on it, and when she had it parked in the garage, she went into the kitchen, where she did a thorough diagnostic test of his sophisticated antisurveillance system, which could detect even a soft intrusion. But no one had tried to call the house, let alone ring the doorbell, test the locks, or make a drive-by in an unidentifiable vehicle.

Despite the hour, she poured herself a glass of pinot grigio and sat down at the kitchen counter, her tiny hand shaking as she raised the glass to her lips.

This business with Otto was coming as she'd known for a long time that it would. They'd even discussed it at one point a few months ago.

"You've crossed a lot of swords with a lot of people right here at home, let alone just about everywhere else," she'd said. "Sooner or later something's going to rise up and bite you."

Otto had grinned. "I'm surprised someone hasn't tried already."

"Everyone's afraid of what you're capable of doing."

"Just the bad guys."

"You're not listening to me," Mary had insisted. "You've made enemies on both sides of the pond. And a lot of people on campus don't think it's funny that you walk around in sweatshirts and windbreakers with the old KGB's logo, or your CCCP baseball caps."

"They're jokes."

"The statements you're making or the people?"

"Both."

"Well, I'm worried about you," she'd said. She'd been angry then because she loved him.

"Mac and I have never done anything to hurt this country, and everyone knows it."

"Mac's heading for a fall, too, and if that happens first you'll go down with him."

"We'll see," Otto had said, and that was the end of it. Until now.

Mary glanced at the clock on the kitchen stove. It was coming up on one thirty in the morning in Japan. She got her cell phone and called McGarvey's number.

Mac answered on the third ring. "Otto?"

"It's me," Mary said. "And I'm sorry to bother you guys at this hour, except we've got trouble."

"Okay, what's happened?"

"The FBI arrested Otto and took him away this morning."

"What was he charged with?" McGarvey asked, and it didn't sound to Mary as if he was surprised.

"Treason."

"Has there been an arraignment?"

"Not yet."

"Okay, this is important. Where was he arrested, at home?"

"In Taft's office. But before he went up he asked Toni Mulholland if she had anything urgent on her threat board. Maybe something Lou wasn't picking up."

"That's doesn't make any sense."

"No," Mary said. "Anyway, he told Toni that Taft had called him upstairs, and that Tom Waksberg and Harold Kallek were there, too. She thought that it was likely the Bureau needed some help with something. But when she couldn't get ahold of Otto, she went upstairs to find out what was going on. All Taft's secretary could tell her was that Otto had left with Kallek. And when she went down to Otto's office, Do Not Cross tape had been placed across the door, and all power to the suite, including the card reader on the door, had evidently been cut."

"Do you know where they took him?"

"NGA headquarters on Fort Belvoir."

"That doesn't make sense either," McGarvey said.

"Lou confirmed it."

"I thought they cut the power to the office."

"Otto installed an emergency battery power pack. She said to check the most recent operations you guys had with Pakistan, Russia, and the DPRK. Toni's on it now, but we need your help, Mac. Otto needs it. I'm afraid for him. And for you."

"Pete and I will be there as quickly as we can."

"Do you want me to arrange military transportation?" Mary asked. "It'd get you here faster."

"That's the last thing I want," McGarvey said. "Just hang in there, Mary, we're on the way."

□

EIGHT

NGA on-site security, including surveillance monitors, plus a rotating staff of one hundred officers, was located in the basement in one wing of the head-quarters building. Otto's quarters, which he guessed had been recently put together, were in an opposite wing and consisted of a small, windowless room furnished with a narrow bed, and an easy chair and side table, plus a bathroom with a shower.

Several magazines, including a couple of *National Geographics* and *Smithsonians* from a few months back, lay on the bed, along with white coveralls, paper slippers, white socks, T-shirts, and underwear. The bathroom was equipped with soap, shampoo, and towels but no razor.

"A waste of time and energy," Otto said, looking around. "Be it ever so humble."

"I don't like this any better than you do, boyo, but the evidence I've seen is compelling," Benkerk said. The interrogator had left.

"What evidence?"

"We'll get to that at your first interview. But what beats the hell out of me is why? You were always the wild man ever since you started working with McGarvey, and especially since the Company hired you and Mac was appointed as the interim DCI, but what you did defies any rational explanation."

"What I'm accused of, Bill, not what you say I did," Otto said. "Let's just get that part straight right off the bat. I shit you not, ask me whatever you want, and I'll tell you. Get me a link to my office and I'll even let your people have free rein with my AI."

Benkerk grinned. "That won't happen any time soon. In fact, your technical service people shut down all power, and cut all the phone lines to your office. So, Lou is dead and will stay that way."

"She's been dead for more than a year now," Otto said, his heart suddenly heavy.

Benkerk understood his gaffe. "Look, I'm sorry, I didn't mean Louise, I meant your computer. Your tech guys are scared shitless of going anywhere near her. So is everybody from the NSA to the Pentagon because we all know just what kind of a shitstorm you could rain down on us."

Otto shook his head. "So why don't you guys just shoot me and get it over with?"

"It was suggested."

"Mac will straighten it out when he gets here," Otto said after a beat.

"We think he's out of the country for the moment, and no one will be

calling him any time soon," Benkerk said. "Get changed, and when you're ready, knock on the door and someone will come for you."

"What about lunch?"

"Something will be provided," Benkerk said, and he left.

As soon as he was gone Otto tried the door, but it was locked.

Once Mary realized that something was wrong, she would start raising hell and her first stop would be Harold Taft. If she got nothing from him, her second call would be to Mac, and the shitstorm that Bill and everyone else were afraid of would begin to happen.

Benkerk walked next door to the room that had been set up for the interrogation. It was small, just ten feet on a side, and until last month it had been used by the computer maintenance people as one of the several spare-parts storage spaces. Now it contained only one small steel table, three chairs, and a video monitor in a corner on the ceiling.

"Will he cooperate?" the interrogator asked. His name was Lazlo Smits and he worked for Homeland Security's Office of Intelligence and Analysis. His background was Coast Guard intelligence, which he'd been assigned to after the academy in New London, Connecticut, and then four years at Columbia Law School. He held the rank of commander, but seldom wore the uniform.

"He says he's innocent, and I want to believe him."

"What about McGarvey?"

"He's expecting that his wife will call him."

"She's done so already, but it'll take him and his wife at least twenty-four hours to get here."

"And then what?"

"McGarvey will do everything within his power to prove his friend is innocent, which is exactly what we want, because everything he turns up will prove the opposite. In the meantime Mr. Rencke won't be able to help himself from giving us the keys to the kingdom."

"You're a son of a bitch," Benkerk said. "I just wanted you to know it."

"I do," Smits said. "Now go fetch your friend, please."

Otto, still wearing his CCCP sweatshirt and jeans, was sitting on the bed when Benkerk came in.

"You didn't change."

"And you didn't knock."

"I'll wait outside until you're ready."

"No."

Benkerk shrugged. "Suit yourself, but your attitude won't help."

"Are you hearing yourself when you talk? Your people, whoever they are, already have me guilty. All they want now are the details—how and why."

"Homeland Security."

"Intel and Analysis. Coasties," Otto said, getting up. "They're a pretty decent bunch of people. So let's get the show on the road."

Smits was seated at the table, and when they came in he motioned to the chair opposite. "Have a seat, Mr. Rencke."

Otto took a seat and Benkerk took the third chair in one corner.

"This is the initial interview with Rencke, Otto Calhoun, time and date stamped," Smits said. "Could you please state your full name for the record."

"Let's not waste time, okay. What do you want to know?"

"How long have you been working with the intelligence agencies of the Russian Federation, Pakistan, and the Democratic People's Republic of Korea?"

"I've hacked their mainframes from time to time, especially the Russians' SVR and GRU. But if that counts as working for them, then I suppose it's been years."

"Possibly."

Otto had to grin. "Honest injun, I don't think their guys think so. In fact, I always got the impression that they were pissed off."

"But you left calling cards in each of their systems. Can you tell us why?"

"Back doors?"

"By another name, yes."

"So I could get in anytime I wanted to."

"Did it occur to you that they were aware of your back doors, and were allowing you access only to feed you disinformation?"

"No."

"How can you be so sure, unless you were in fact in collusion with someone in each of those agencies?"

"I'm sure. But what I don't know is who are your informants in those intel agencies, or here, because that's the only way you could know or guess about my comings and goings."

"I ask the questions here, you provide the answers."

"Then I suggest that you get your head out of your ass and start asking me something worthwhile. If there's a traitor, and it looks as if there is one or more, and if it's not me, we'd better get to work finding out who the fuck it is."

McGarvey and Pete had taken the early-morning hydrofoil across the strait to Yakushima, where they cabbed it to Skymark Airlines facility and chartered a private jet up to Tokyo's Narita Airport to catch the overnight All Nippon Airways flight direct to Dulles.

They'd not been able to sleep after Mary's call, and situated in business class with seats that opened to flat beds, they were still too keyed up to get any decent rest. The food was terrific, and they'd been offered champagne, but Mac declined, his mind racing ahead to what sort of a buzz saw they were going to run into when they got home.

This morning before they'd taken off, McGarvey had phoned Mary, but she was not answering, possibly because she herself was under surveillance and couldn't talk, so he'd called Toni Mulholland at her apartment, but after the first ring it rolled over to her office on campus. It was nine thirty in the evening in D.C.

"It's McGarvey."

"I hope to God that you're on the way," she said. She sounded excited. "Mary said she was going to call you."

"We're at Narita waiting for our flight. Should be landing at Dulles at ten thirty tomorrow morning. Mary told us that you guys were working together. Have you come up with anything?"

"He's being held at Fort Belvoir of all places, and from what we've been able to piece together the Bureau seems to think that he's been working with intelligence officers inside the SVR and GRU, plus Pakistan's Inter Services-Intelligence, and DPRK's State Security Department."

"He's hacked those mainframes plus a hell of a lot of others over the past ten years or more. Any hint at why those four?"

"My guess those are just for starters," Toni said. "I have Hank and the team working on it."

"Under the radar," Pete broke in. They were on speaker mode but seated well out of earshot of anyone who might be listening. And they kept their voices low.

"Oh, hi, Pete. Of course."

"What's your thinking to this point?" McGarvey asked.

"It looks as if someone in Science and Technology, possibly with a grudge, went looking down your tracks to see if they could come up with something interesting, and found it."

"Otto's back doors."

"SOP, but the recipients should have discovered traces by now and closed

them. Either that or set up traps that could be recognized. Just like the Russians hacking our elections, especially in '16."

"That's been going on almost from when the KGB got smart in the seventies and eighties," McGarvey said. "It's nothing new. Just about everybody does it to everyone else." So far this business was making absolutely no sense to him, except that whoever had pointed a finger at Otto had to have an agenda beyond simply a grudge.

"Yes, but I think the Bureau came up with a specific name or names in each of those four agencies that they think Otto was working with. Directly working with them, as in an old boys' network. That would be treason."

"Only if it could be proved that Otto passed information to them," McGarvey said.

"Hank suggested Otto wouldn't need to actually pass data. By the simple fact he'd left the back doors open it could mean he was giving those officers roaming rights in our mainframe."

"He would have left safeguards against that possibility."

Toni hesitated. "Then I don't know where to look next."

Four hours out of Narita the aircraft's cabin lights were dimmed, simulating nighttime, and would remain so for several hours to begin acclimatizing the passengers to the time change that would put them on the ground in D.C. in midmorning, while it would still be late night in Tokyo.

When the lights came back up they would be served breakfast—American or Japanese, each passenger's choice. Several hours later the lights would be dimmed again, after which a light lunch would be offered, and again a few hours later, dinner.

The routine helped eliminate much of the jet lag, which in Mac's mind was a good thing, because once he and Pete hit the ground they would need all their wits about them.

They'd managed to get a couple of hours of sleep between cycles, and when McGarvey woke up, Pete was just returning from the head, her eyes a little puffy. It was still evening their time, but coming up on 7:00 A.M. in Washington.

"I don't know about you, but wherever we settle next will have to be either on our side of the pond, or not much more than a six-hour flight away," she said, buckling up.

"Either that or take a slow boat," McGarvey said.

"Except we always seem to be in a big hurry." Pete got serious. "So, who the hell is behind this and what are we going to do about it?"

McGarvey had done a lot of thinking about it, since the first call in Yakushima. "Start at the top and work our way down. See if we can get some answers without making too many waves."

Pete's left eyebrow rose. "That doesn't sound like you."

"We're going to have to take it easy at first. This whole deal could be like a house of cards. One wrong move and we'd be screwing the pooch."

"Crude."

"This is not going to be easy, sweetheart. Before they grabbed Otto and stashed him at the NGA someone must have started an investigation, and there had to be a reason for it. Just about every intel agency in the world either is scared silly of what Otto can do, or at least respects him."

"Okay, but the question stands, what next? Taft?"

"First Carleton," McGarvey said.

Carleton Patterson was the CIA's general counsel, and had held that position longer than just about anyone could remember. Each presidentially appointed director of the Agency had been advised by the DCI they were replacing that whatever personnel changes they wanted to make, leave Patterson alone.

Tall, slender, always impeccably dressed in a three-piece London-tailored suit, his ties knotted with the classic Windsor, his shoes handmade in London just down Savile Row from where his shirts were crafted, he was the consummate gentleman. East Coast bred, a product of Harvard Law School, he'd worked at a prestigious New York firm until he outgrew his position and was accepted at the CIA as assistant to Roger Engel, then the general counsel.

Engel died two years later, and Patterson took over. Now eighty-three, he had lost none of his acumen, nor had he shown any signs of slowing down.

He and McGarvey went back to the beginning of Mac's career, and the men had a deep, abiding respect for each other.

It was seven thirty in the morning when Patterson's houseman answered the call. "Good morning, Mr. McGarvey. Mr. Patterson has been expecting your call."

Patterson came on a moment later. "Good morning, my boy, are you and Pete well?"

"Yes. We're landing at Dulles in three hours. What can you tell me about Otto?"

"He's been charged with treason and arrested by the FBI, though no warrant was issued. Of course, I've been assigned to represent the Agency."

"He's not a traitor."

"Of course not, but the man has had the deplorable habit of thumbing his nose at whoever he didn't respect. He's made enemies."

"We all have."

"Indeed."

"Have you seen a copy of the specifics?"

"I'm scheduled to meet with Taft at nine."

"We can be there by eleven," McGarvey said. "Hold off till then."

"I'm sure that you're expected."

Otto had spent a troubled night alone in his cell, worrying about Mary, who had been sick with something, and seriously doubting the sanity of his chief interrogator, Lazlo Smits. But what he couldn't fathom was Bill Benkerk's involvement.

Dinner last night had been fairly decent, shrimp and rice, though he could have used a split of pinot grigio. But this morning's breakfast of oatmeal and an English muffin was crap, though the coffee was okay. Right now, he wanted a couple of packages of Twinkies and a pint of half-and-half. Comfort food.

Benkerk came for him after breakfast, bringing along an older man with long walrus mustaches and thinning white hair who was carrying a small leather bag and a white cotton cloth draped over an arm.

"Good morning, boyo. Before we get started we need to give you a haircut."

Otto remained seated. "No."

"It's for your own good, you can see that much. A sign of cooperation. Easy peasy."

"No."

"Goddamnit, Otto, we can do this the easy way or the hard way. Your choice."

"I'd be willing to fight whoever you want to send to force the issue. Who knows, maybe I'd get hurt and end up in the hospital. Or you could try drugs, but I don't think you guys really want to fuck with my head—at least the brains part."

Benkerk was at a loss.

Otto was enjoying himself, at least for a moment. Win the first battle no matter how small, Mac used to tell him. After that you'll have the high ground.

Benkerk dismissed the barber, who left the cell. "What to do?"

"I'm not a traitor and you know it, so get your head out and maybe we can figure out who's behind this happy horseshit."

"You have to know that we can't give you access to Lou."

"She's safe for now, but under what rock did Smits crawl out from? He looks and acts more like an undertaker than a Coastie."

"I was told that he knows his job."

"I stand corrected," Otto said. "He's not a mortician, he's Gestapo. And with everything going on in the media these last few years I hope to hell his name doesn't go public. If it did Homeland Security would take a serious hit."

"All that aside, it still comes back to right here. You have to prove your innocence."

"Wrong country, Bill. On this side of the pond a guy gets to be innocent until someone like Smits proves him guilty."

"Not this time. Too much is at stake."

"And you're a willing part of this bullshit?"

"The director asked if I would lend a hand. He figured that you would need a friend who could help blunt the ragged edges."

"Taft sent you?" Otto asked. He was surprised. "I never thought that the man liked me."

"He doesn't. Not many in the Company do. But he, along with everyone else, respects you."

Smits, his jacket draped over the back of his chair, was sitting at the small table, an open file folder in front of him. He looked up when Otto and Benkerk came in. His expression and language were bland, as was his voice.

"You can leave us now, Bill, if you would."

"I'll just stick around for a bit."

"As you wish," Smits said, and he motioned for Otto to sit down.

Otto sat opposite the man, and held his hands out, wrists together. "No shackles?"

"Will they be necessary?"

"You can never tell," Otto said.

Benkerk took up a spot leaning against the wall next to the door.

"Let's begin, then," Smits said.

"No waterboarding, or drugs?" Otto asked, keeping his tone light though the bastard frightened him.

"Perhaps later," Smits said. "Is the name Dalir Padishah familiar to you?"

"It's Pakistani, maybe Pashtun, but no never heard it."

Smits took an eight-by-ten black-and-white photo from the file folder and slid it across the table. It showed a man of moderate build, wearing Western jeans and a white shirt, halfway upstairs to the entrance of a large building. Something had caught his attention and he'd turned to look over his shoulder. The picture had been taken from long range and was grainy, but the man's face was clear.

"That's one of the ISI headquarters buildings in Islamabad."

"The man is Mr. Padishah. Have you ever met? Perhaps in a videoconference? Or perhaps in or around the UN General Assembly building, or Pakistan's UN mission's office on East Sixty-Fifth Street. Or seen a photograph or photos of him?"

"No," Otto said, and it was the truth.

"I see," Smits said. "But Mr. Padishah knows you, or at the very least knows of you. Can you explain that?"

"No. But I suspect that he might work in the Joint Intelligence Technical Department. By the looks of him maybe a lieutenant."

"An army captain when that photo was taken seven years ago—the first time you hacked the ISI's mainframe."

"What was his job at that time?"

"From what has been gathered by backtracking, he was assigned as a junior officer helping develop anti–electronic warfare methods and tactics."

"And now?" Otto asked, but he knew where Smits was going.

"Within the year after your first incursion into their computer system, Captain Padishah was promoted to major. Six months later he was a lieutenant colonel and eight months after that he was promoted to full bird."

"Phenomenal."

"Extraordinary, I was told."

"He must have been very good at his job," Otto said, almost enjoying where this was headed. It was like witnessing a slow-motion train wreck.

"It is suspected, though not yet proven, that his product was nothing short of stellar."

"Particularly his work just a few years ago."

"Almost from the beginning," Smits said, a slight smile on his narrow lips. "Because of the back door you'd left for him, which allowed the ISI practically a free rein within the CIA's mainframe."

"The potential, let's get that straight right off the bat."

"A near certainty."

Otto laughed, and turned to look at Benkerk. "Is this the best shit that you guys could come up with?"

"Treason, Mr. Rencke," Smits said.

Otto turned back to him. "Does the name David Harris ring a bell? Or didn't you take a look at his track record?"

"The case files are mostly sealed, but we do know that McGarvey was sent to assassinate him."

"David was a Company project manager whose expertise was Pakistan. Turns out he was a traitor—an Islamist double agent—who was trying to bring down the legitimate government in Islamabad. And except for Kirk he would have succeeded."

"Your word," Smits started, but Otto overrode him.

"Taft will open the case files, you dumb bastard. And I would suggest that before you try any more of this bullshit you might get your head out of your ass and pay more attention to your fucking homework."

Patterson's driver met McGarvey and Pete at departures. "Good morning, Mr. Director, Mrs. McGarvey," he said.

He took their bags, led them outside to the black Mercedes-Maybach at the curb, and opened the rear door. Carleton was waiting inside, and they got in as the driver put their bags in the trunk.

"You two look remarkably fresh this morning," Patterson said. He was sitting back, one leg crossed over the other, *The Washington Post* on his lap.

"We got a few hours' sleep," McGarvey said.

The driver got behind the wheel, and they took off for the fifteen-mile ride to the CIA. Patterson handed a slender file folder to McGarvey. "This is a brief summary of the charges, pending the outcome of what looks like an unusually brief investigation. Open and shut, I was told."

McGarvey opened the folder which contained only one page, and held it so that Pete could also see.

"Told by whom?" Pete asked.

"Mr. Kallek."

"Has the president been informed of the details?"

"Not until after Otto's initial interview."

McGarvey looked up. "They wouldn't find out anything from him, even if he was guilty. He'd play with them until they went crazy. But what about his computers?"

"Power to his offices was shut down, and the door sealed," Patterson said.

"When did you find out about all this?" Pete asked.

"Not until last night. Taft called me at home and asked for the meeting this morning."

"Does he know that we're coming?" Pete asked.

"He wasn't surprised," Patterson said. "But he agreed to see both of you."

"This is circumstantial," McGarvey said. "Otto left back doors in four mainframes, and that's it?"

"It is felt by some that the doors were left open intentionally."

"Felt by whom?"

"Charles Noyes," Patterson said.

Noyes headed the Directorate of Science and Technology. He'd come over from the National Security Agency, and was considered to be a steady hand and a professional who didn't tend to go off half-cocked. That he had signed off on the charges was bothersome to McGarvey.

"There has to be more than this to order his arrest," McGarvey said.

"Taft promised he'd have the entire file for me. He said that it was extensive, running to more than one thousand pages."

"Whose was the originating signature?" Pete asked.

"I was told that I would be given that information as well."

"Good, because I'll want to talk to them," McGarvey said. "They're screwing around with a good man, and this will come to an end immediately, if not sooner."

Pete reached over and touched the back of his hand, telling him with the gesture to take a deep breath and calm down.

Patterson's driver was cleared for entry to the campus, but only to drop off at the VIP garage beneath the OHB. He offered to take the McGarveys' bags to their apartment in Georgetown, and Mac gave him the key.

"It'll be a long day," Patterson said. "I'll call when I'm ready to leave."

"How about you, Mr. Director?"

"We'll take a cab," McGarvey said.

Patterson had thought to bring visitor's badges for them, and they took the elevator up to the DCI's seventh-floor office, which overlooked the woods and rolling hills sloping to the south.

"The director will see you now," Taft's secretary told them, and they went inside.

Taft was a short man, well under six feet, in his late fifties, with a slight build and the military bearing of the navy four-star he'd been until eight months ago, when President Weaver had named him to head the CIA. During his navy career he'd spent two years as special envoy to the Joint Chiefs, where he helped completely modernize the intelligence operations of all five services, including those of the Coast Guard plus the Department of Defense Central Security Service. He was well respected within the Agency.

He was behind his desk, three chairs across from him, which he gestured to. "Have a seat please," he said. His jacket was off, his tie loose, which was very uncharacteristic for him.

"Thanks for holding your meeting for us, Mr. Director," McGarvey said.

"I expected that you and Mrs. McGarvey would show up, though I can't say I'm pleased," Taft said. He passed a thick file folder across to Patterson, then picked up his phone. "Madge, have Mr. Noyes join us, please."

Patterson opened the folder, the first page of which was the specifications of the charges against Otto.

"Let me know when he arrives," Taft said, and he hung up. "Charlie is on his way from the Bureau. He'll be back shortly, and he should be better able to answer some of your questions. We can have lunch when he gets here."

"No thank you," McGarvey said. "Otto is innocent, and everyone on this campus knows it. All I need to know is who the hell came up with this crap."

"He's your friend, everyone knows and respects that. As we also knew that you and Mrs. McGarvey—"

"My name is Pete."

"I was saying that we know you've come to try to prove his innocence."

"Whatever it takes."

"You have been a great service to this organization and to this country, for which you have been gravely wounded more than once, and near death on more than one occasion. But in the end, you have always been a black operations officer whose methods have at times been unorthodox to say the least."

Pete started to say something, but Taft held her off.

"You've gone head-to-head with many of the officers in this building, and the NHB. You've even butted horns with a couple of presidents. And every time the body count was high, but when the dust settled you were always proven right. It's the only reason you're not spending your life in a super-max."

Patterson looked up, a slightly amused expression on his narrow face.

McGarvey said nothing, pretty much knowing where this was going, and understanding that Noyes would be the first link in whatever chain of evidence led to the four intelligence agencies.

"But this time the evidence against Mr. Rencke is overwhelming."

"We've read the preliminary specifications," McGarvey said.

"In each of the cases, the officer who was in charge of their agency's cyber security was given promotions completely out of line with ordinary SOP for any branch of service in just about every country on the planet."

"Amazing, don't you think?" Pete asked.

"Yes, unless you knew the reason."

"Which in each case was the officer's mining an absolute gold seam of intelligence out of the clear blue."

"On the contrary, each time it closely followed the back doors that Mr. Rencke set up and then abandoned."

"Maintained, not abandoned, Mr. Director, let's just get at least that much straight," McGarvey said. "But I have two questions before Charlie gets here, to which I'm sure that someone on campus has already given you the answers. Otto was hacking those mainframes as well as others, as part of his job here. Do you have a précis of the gold seams he mined for us? And I'm sure that you've been told exactly what damage the gold seams you say were opened for the ISI, SVR, GRU, and North Korea's apparatus caused?"

"If any?" Pete asked.

"The specifics are in the report Mr. Patterson—who is representing the Company, not Mr. Rencke—has in his hands now."

Patterson, who had been skimming the file, looked up. "Innuendo, Mr. Director. Clever speculations, I have to admit on first reading, but nothing that would hold up in any court of law."

"There's more," Taft said. "Much more."

TWELVE

Otto was given an early lunch of tomato soup, a grilled cheese sandwich, and pickles, plus a sixteen-ounce aluminum bottle of Michelob Ultra beer. He figured that sooner or later he would have to go on a hunger strike, because once it became clear he wasn't going to cooperate, they would move to drugs, but in the meantime, he ate reasonably well.

Benkerk came for him again and they walked together down the hall to the interrogation room.

"Are Mac and Pete back from Japan yet?" Otto asked before they went in.

"I'm not sure."

"Bullshit."

Smits, his tie loose and jacket off the same as this morning, was sitting again at the small table. Two gray file folders, both with diagonal orange stripes on the covers denoting classified information, lay on the table in front of him.

He looked up. "Leave us for now, if you would, please, William."

"Mr. Hughes called a few minutes ago, he wants to see me," Benkerk said. Kevin Hughes was the deputy director of the NGA.

Smits pursed his lips. "Did he say why?"

"Actually, it was his secretary who asked me to stop up as soon as I was free."

Smits nodded and Benkerk left.

"Perhaps you know the name Ivan Aladko?"

"Ivan Petrovich Aladko," Otto said. "He used to work in the KGB's First Chief Directorate, in what was called Department V for executive actions—assassinations—until '91 when the KGB folded. I heard that he went over to the SVR, but by now he has to be an old man, probably retired."

"You evidently knew him well."

"I was doing work for Kirk in the old days, just like now, so it was my job to know guys like Ivan."

"Knew him well, did you?"

"You could say intimately. I hacked into his bank accounts, he had three of them, only one in Moscow. I knew about his chubby wife, Svetlana, and his Bolshoi Ballet mistress Inna Savin. Pretty girl. Got run over by a bus, at the height of her career. I'm pretty sure it was Svetlana's doing."

"And did you work with him?"

"Absolutely."

"Can you explain how, exactly?"

Otto had to laugh. "I suggest that before we go any further you either get

a replacement who knows what the fuck he's talking about, or at least go back to whatever rock you crawled out from under and do your homework."

Smits didn't react.

"Every intel agency worth its salt knows who the opposition is. Departments like V—which by the way the Russians tried to hide by calling it the Thirteenth Department, or Line F—are tasked with identifying and either turning or killing field officers. Our field officers, the NOCs, who work out in the cold with no official cover. You might want to stop by the lobby of the OHB and take a look at the stars on the wall, just to the right, with no names. They were the guys, and some women, who were outed and assassinated. So you're damned right it was my job to know guys like Aladko."

"Did he get into your computers?"

"He tried."

"But?"

"I've always had pretty good firewalls."

Smits glanced at something in one of the file folders, and looked up. "Your darlings, you used to call them. But you renamed all of your programs after your wife . . ."

Otto sat forward all of a sudden. "Don't fucking go there," he said, his voice low and even. "Or I swear to Christ on a cross that I will destroy you."

Smits didn't react. "I still need an answer. Was there any possibility that Mr. Aladko or anyone else in V could have defeated your firewalls, and actually gotten inside the CIA's mainframe?"

"No."

"A guilty man would say something like that."

"Show me the proof."

Smits shrugged and smiled. "We'll get there."

Mary showed up at the NGA's main gate a few minutes after one, and handed her CIA credentials to the guard. "I'm here to see Dr. Marston." Nicholas Marston was the director of the NGA.

"Do you have an appointment, ma'am?"

"No. But if you tell him that I'm here, he will want to see me."

Mary had from the beginning of her career with the CIA been able to neatly compartmentalize her thoughts. She'd been taught that to do otherwise in the business would wreck her within a year or less.

Her first boss, Alex Alonso—his people called him the Amazing Alonso—who was a chief analyst in the DI, told her to leave her work at the office.

"When you go home to your hubby and kiddies, think about fixing dinner, or reading bedtime stories, not the office."

"What if a nuclear war is imminent and I'm the only one who knows it?" she'd countered.

"Especially then," he'd said. "It's the only way you'll stay sane. Look at the poor bastards in the Watch down the hall from the director's office. Twelve

on, twelve off. Within a few months, sometimes weeks, they become information addicts. No cure."

The Watch was manned by a small crew of a half dozen people, who were connected by computer and phones to just about every intelligence source available in real time. It was their job to produce the daily report, which used to be sent directly over to the White House, but since the National Intelligence Program was set up to oversee all fourteen U.S. intel agencies, the report was sent to the NIP's director.

"Those folks don't know how to step aside from the job, because they get high on believing that they know everything."

The guard came back out and handed back her ID. "Dr. Marston's secretary asks that you call to make an appointment, sometime next week."

"Call back and let them know I'm on my way," Mary said, and she floored the gas pedal.

She'd been here several times over the past few years, and knew her way, though it was impossible to miss the headquarters complex on Campus East. Her only concern for the moment was some fool opening fire on her.

Glancing in the rearview mirror, she was in time to see the guard duck back into the gatehouse to alert base security.

Marston's secretary, an older woman with her gray hair up in a bun, burst into his office. "She's on her way just as you said she would probably be."

The NGA director, who had his Ph.D. from Cornell in international relations, had run the Central Intelligence Agency's Directorate of Intelligence ten years ago until he'd taken the job as deputy director, rising to run the entire agency just two years ago. He had never met Mary, but he knew of her, and her genius husband.

He had a lot of respect for both of them, and he knew that she'd be showing up soon. But he figured that his biggest problem would be when Kirk McGarvey stormed the gates.

"What would you like me to tell security?"

Marston, a big man, six four, with a barrel chest, a large square face, but kind gray eyes, got up and put on his suit coat, which had been draped over the back of his chair.

"Have her escorted up, please," he said. "And we'll have coffee."

THIRTEEN

Charles Noyes arrived fifteen minutes after Taft's call, and the DCI's secretary showed him in. When he spotted McGarvey and the others, he hesitated for just an instant at the door, then came the rest of the way in. He was in his early fifties, of medium build, with bland, undistinguished looks that would never cause someone to take a second glance.

McGarvey had a good deal of respect for the man, and he offered his hand. "Glad you could come, because we need some answers."

Noyes shook hands and took a seat. "I don't know if my answers are going to be anything you want to hear."

"Otto is no traitor and you know it," Pete said.

Noyes's mouth turned down at the corners. "I would have bet my life on it at the beginning."

"But?" McGarvey asked.

"Look, when this started six months ago I was just as shocked as you are now. But stuff just kept piling up. And after a while it got really clear that this was no plot to bring Otto down, nor was what was showing up circumstantial."

"Six months?" Pete asked.

"I wanted to make absolutely sure."

"Was Otto aware that you were looking down his track?" McGarvey asked. He was confused, except that Noyes was a good man who knew his business—not quite as well as Otto, but close enough that his judgment had to be respected and trusted.

"If he was, I never got any indications."

"But you were looking, so Lou must have picked up on it."

"I was careful," Noyes said. "Believe me, Mac, I have done everything I could think of to prove him innocent, not prove him guilty."

"Whose idea was it to take him to the NGA, of all places?" Pete asked.

"Mine. He'll be out of sight out there, and two good men are conducting the initial interview."

"Who?"

"Bill Benkerk, who's known Otto almost as long as you have. I thought he would need a friend."

"And?"

"Lazlo Smits."

"Jesus," Pete said. She turned to Mac. "We have to get Otto out of there right now, Smits is a piranha."

"It's why I partnered Bill with him," Noyes said.

"But Smits?" Pete countered.

"I'm looking for the truth, and the only one who can provide it is Otto himself."

Pete started to say something else, but McGarvey held her off.

"We're going to involve ourselves with the investigation."

"No," Taft said.

"With or without the Company's help," McGarvey said.

A silence hung heavy for a moment or two.

A look passed between Taft and Noyes, and Taft finally nodded.

"To this point I've found four instances in which Otto hacked into the mainframes of Russia's SVR and GRU, Pakistan's ISI, and North Korea's State Security Department," Noyes said. "In each case he left back doors with, so far as I've been able to determine, no safety locks."

"So far as you have been able to determine," McGarvey said.

"In each case I've found the officer in charge of North American data. And in each case, within months after Otto left back doors those officers were placed on the fast track to promotion."

"We were told that. But you're saying it was because they were able to hack our mainframe."

"One may have been a coincidence, a fluke, a mistake, whatever, but not all four," Noyes said.

"Did you do follow-ups?"

"I just told you that I did. I followed the career tracks of the officers in charge."

"No. I mean, were any of our NOCs outed in those countries because of information taken from our mainframe?" McGarvey asked.

Noyes didn't answer.

"Were any of our sensitive operations compromised?"

Still Noyes held his silence, and he looked uncomfortable.

"Any of our people in badland rounded up and maybe shot while trying to escape?"

"Otto hacked into those four mainframes," Pete said. "Did you run diagnostics on the intel he was able to gather up? Maybe the names of some deep-cover people here in-country? I mean, Otto was a one-man gold miner who gave the Company a lot of good stuff. He sounded the initial alarm on the Russians hacking into our elections in '16. Any other good shit like that?"

"Most of that material has been deemed for-your-eyes-only," Taft said. "Need-to-know."

"Deemed by whom?"

Taft hesitated. "We're not going in that direction."

"Jesus Christ, Admiral, who put the lid on it?" McGarvey demanded. "And why?" But he suddenly had it. "The president?"

"Not directly, but it was Donna Blakely."

"His chief of staff," McGarvey said. "I want the names of the four intelligence officers who got the big promotions."

"Why?" Taft asked.

"I'm going to have a chat with each of them."

"Will you assassinate them?"

"If need be," McGarvey said. He turned to Patterson. "Are the names included in the file?"

"No."

"I want the names, Mr. Director," McGarvey pressed.

"Ivan Aladko, KGB," Noyes said.

Taft's lips compressed, but he held his silence.

"Captain, now one-star, Felix Svirin, GRU. Dalir Padishah, ISI. Ryang Se-jun, SD."

"Are they all still in service?"

"I believe so."

"Do you have their physical locations?"

"Where they work?" Noyes asked.

"Where they live," McGarvey said. "Their wives, children, relatives."

Noyes shook his head.

"We don't go after each other's families," Taft said. "What kind of a son of a bitch are you, after all?"

"Tell that to my wife Katy, and our daughter Liz and my son-in-law Todd," McGarvey replied bitterly. "And just about everyone else I've ever been close with."

Neither Taft nor Noyes said a thing.

McGarvey got to his feet and Pete followed.

"If need be I'll have the Bureau place both of you under arrest," Taft warned.

McGarvey took a step closer to the DCI and pointed a finger at him. "Don't try, Mr. Director. Otto is innocent and I'm going to prove it."

"We're going to prove it," Pete said.

They left Patterson with Taft and Noyes in the DCI's office and took the elevator down to the lobby, where they turned in their visitor's passes.

"Have a cab sent up from the gate, if you would," McGarvey told one of the security officers.

"Yes, sir," the man said.

McGarvey and Pete walked across the lobby, passing the stars set in the granite wall to their left, but didn't speak until they got outside and were at the curb to wait for the taxi.

"What's next?" Pete asked.

"We have to talk with Mary and Toni first, but not here on campus."

"Then Otto?"

"You can do that. I'm going to have a chat with my friend Dalir in Islam-abad. I'm sure he hasn't forgotten me."

FOURTEEN

Dr. Marston put his coffee cup on the low table separating him from Mary, and sat back and crossed his legs. They had been meeting for twenty minutes and he had no real idea what she wanted other than to press her belief that her husband was not guilty of treason. She was a pretty woman, and very bright, but he'd met her before and knew both things, along with the fact that she was determined.

"As I've told you, this agency is not involved with your husband's investigation," he said.

"Then why was he brought here?"

"I can't confirm that."

"But you can't deny it," Mary said.

"What do you want, Mrs. Rencke?"

"To talk to my husband."

"I can't help you."

"Goddamnit," Mary screeched. "I want to talk to my fucking husband. I want to hear from his own lips what I already know, that he's innocent. And I want him to tell me about the back doors he supposedly left in his search engines, so I can prove he's no traitor."

Marston had agreed to house Rencke here as a personal favor to Harold Taft, who was a close friend. Right now he was regretting the decision.

"We want him someplace where no one would think to look," Taft had explained several days ago.

"We're not equipped for something like that," Marston had said. They were sitting in the DCI's office at Langley.

"Two, maybe three days at the most, just until we get through the preliminary interrogation."

Marston was an academic who despised the very idea of interrogation. "You have your own facilities for things of that nature."

"He has too many friends here."

"I meant just about anywhere in the world, not just here in the Washington area."

"As I said, he has too many friends. And there must be absolutely no chance that he'll get to a computer terminal, or even a cell phone."

"Then the NGA is the wrong place to send him."

"You're shielded out there."

"So is your campus."

Marston remembered Taft laughing without humor. "Electronically Rencke owns the CIA."

"I'll give you two days."

"Fair enough."

"What about someone showing up on my doorstep wanting to see him?"

"No one will know he's there."

Marston's secretary came to the door. "Is everything all right, Mr. Director?"

"Have Mr. Benkerk come up, please."

"Yes, sir," the secretary said, and withdrew.

"What makes you think your husband is here?" Marston asked.

"You didn't call Bill up here to hold my hand. We're old friends."

"I asked him up to try to convince you to go home and leave things as they are for the moment."

"With all due respect, Mr. Director, not a chance in hell."

Five minutes later Benkerk showed up, and he wasn't surprised. "Hello, Mary, what brings you out this way?"

"Same reason you're here. Otto."

Benkerk and Marston exchanged glances, and the NGA director nodded.

"He's ornery as hell, but he's holding up okay."

"I want to talk to him."

Again, Benkerk looked to Marston.

"Leave your cell phone here, Mrs. Rencke," the director said. "It'll be waiting for you downstairs when you leave."

Mary handed over her phone, and left with Benkerk.

"So, how's he really doing?" Mary asked on the way down in the elevator.

"About as well as you'd expect a caged bear would be doing."

"You know that he's not guilty."

"I'm sorry, love, but the evidence I've seen is pretty convincing."

"I'm not convinced, but thanks for sticking up for us with Dr. Marston."

"He's a good man, and he's not any party to this. Just providing the room and board for a couple of days."

"Who's on the interrogation team besides you?"

"Lazlo Smits. He's over from Homeland Security. Ex–Coast Guardsman."

"Never heard of him," Mary said, and she noticed a slight sign of relief in Benkerk's eyes.

They got off on a sublevel and stopped at an unmarked, windowless door at the end of a long corridor.

"Wait here," Benkerk told her, and he went inside.

He was back in less than a minute with another man, so thin he looked like a skeleton, a scowl on his face.

"Two minutes," the man said. He turned and walked away.

Benkerk stepped aside. "Two minutes," he said.

"Will we be monitored?"

"Of course."

"Voyeurs," Mary muttered, and she went in.

Otto, seated at a small table, his back to the door, turned around when Mary came in. He jumped to his feet, a broad smile on his face.

"Holy cow, Mary," he gushed.

Mary went to him and he took her in his arms, so big compared to her that she felt like a cub being enveloped by a papa bear.

"Holy cow," he said again. "Why did they let you in?"

"I'm pretty convincing when I want to be," she said. "I love you."

"My God, I love you, too."

She rested her cheek against his, so that her lips were at his ear. "Mac and Pete know what's happening," she whispered.

"I missed you," Otto said, hugging her tighter for just a moment.

"How are they treating you?" she said a little louder.

"Okay."

"They must be out of their minds thinking that you're a traitor. After all you've done."

"They think I left my back doors open on purpose."

"Stupid."

"If they get around to convincing Lou to cooperate, they'll find out the designator is GKVENUS."

"What?"

"You know, Venus flytrap? The unlucky bastard who tries to get in will be stuck."

"Did you explain it to them?"

"Fuck 'em. Let them figure it out, if they can."

Mary pressed her body against his. "Grab my ass with your left hand," she whispered into his ear. "Tell me again that you miss me."

Otto hesitated.

"Now."

He did as he was told, and Mary ground her body against his.

"Grab my left boob with your free hand. Inside my shirt."

Again, he did as he was told, finding the tiny conceal-and-carry cell phone that deep-cover operators used in the field.

Mary started to reach down to her husband's crotch. "Put it in my hand."

He did, and she shoved it in his jumpsuit pocket.

"Sorry, sweetheart," she said, pulling back. "We better not start something we can't finish."

She smiled up at him. "I'm going to do everything in my power to prove the bastards are wrong."

FIFTEEN

When they were clear of the campus, Pete texted Toni asking if they could meet for a late lunch somewhere neutral, perhaps in McLean or Tysons Corner. Toni texted back immediately, as if she had been waiting for the contact.

"Mary's been to see Otto. She wants us all to meet at their house at five."

"See you then," Pete texted back.

She'd held the phone so that McGarvey could see the screen.

He'd told the cabdriver to take them to the J. Edgar Hoover Building, downtown, but as they were headed south on the parkway he gave the driver their Georgetown address instead.

"We'll storm the gates later," Pete said.

"First, we need to see what Mary has to say, and then I have to pack. I want to leave tonight."

"As yourself in the clear?"

"No time to do anything else," McGarvey said.

"Okay, I understand the rush, but why not take a couple of precautions? You've got three clean passports and full ID kits."

"Because I think I'll be expected."

"Okay, so a new ID, maybe a wig, some makeup," Pete said, but then she stopped short. "You think that someone here set up Otto for the fall?"

"I'll find out when I get off the plane in Islamabad."

"It can't be Chuck Noyes."

"No. He's a good man, and he would be way-over-the-top obvious."

"Who then?"

"I haven't got a clue, but I can pretty well guess why."

"Otto was getting close to someone or some operation," Pete said.

They took Pete's green BMW over to Otto and Mary's house at the end of a cul-de-sac in McLean and parked in the driveway next to Toni's Porsche Carrera. Mary was at the door when they came up the walk. She looked strung out.

"Am I ever glad to see you guys," she said, and she gave both of them a hug and a peck on the cheek.

They went back to the kitchen, where Toni was opening a bottle of pinot grigio. "Has the Company put a tail on you?" she asked.

"None that we could see," McGarvey said.

"Could have been a drone," Toni suggested. "I wouldn't put it past them."

"Doesn't matter," Mary said. "They'd expect the four of us to get together, but we're safe here. No one's invented a way to get past Otto's security system.

And Lou will wake up briefly at six-hour intervals to take a look as long as her batteries hold out. She found out where they'd taken Otto, and told me."

They sat at the kitchen counter, and Toni poured the wine.

"I've ordered pizzas," Mary said. "Should be here soon."

"How does he look?" McGarvey asked.

"He's not angry, if that's what you mean. If anything, he probably thinks it's a big game. In some ways I think he's actually enjoying himself."

"How'd you get the okay to see him?" Pete asked. "I would have thought that you would be the last person they'd allow in."

"I just showed up," Mary said. "Nothing quite so powerful as a scorned wife."

"What'd he say about the charges?" McGarvey asked.

"He'll tell you himself, later tonight when it's lights out down there, unless they found the conceal-and-carry cell phone I managed to give him."

Pete had to laugh. "I would have thought they'd search you first."

"Marston asked me to turn over my cell phone, which I did. And no one walks around with two of them."

"Did they leave you alone with him?"

"Yes."

"There had to be surveillance cameras."

Mary told him what she'd done, and McGarvey had to laugh thinking about her and Otto groping each other. Not really tradecraft, but it evidently worked.

"It won't work like a regular cell phone, which would be able to defeat the NGA's security system, but it will connect with their mainframe, which in turn will connect with Lou, who every six hours will be talking with him."

"Can we leave a message for him with Lou?" Pete asked.

"Yes."

"From here?"

Mary nodded. "He gave me the password. We can record whatever we want, and it will be sent as a microburst packet with a duration of less than a millisecond. Not exactly a face-to-face meeting, but it's secure."

"They'll probably expect something like that from Otto, but it's worth a try," McGarvey said. "Did you tell him we're on the hunt?"

"Yes."

"A Toyota RAV4 has pulled up in the driveway," the house surveillance system in Mary's voice announced.

"Verify the license tag, please," Mary said.

"Listrani's." It was the pizza restaurant.

"Thank you," Mary said.

"I'll get the door, you get the plates," McGarvey said.

He went to the door, got the two pizzas from the delivery boy, and gave him a decent tip. When he closed and locked the door, he turned around as Pete, standing at the kitchen door, holstered her pistol.

He smiled. "I'm glad you didn't shoot him, I'm hungry."

"Me, too," she said.

Mary, too nervous to sit, stood at the end of the kitchen counter as they had their pizza. "I'm going to stick with Lou, see what she comes up with, and Toni has her crew working the problem. So, what about you two?"

"I'm going to bird-dog everyone's back door, and try to get down to see Otto," Pete said. "Actually, I want to have a word or two with Lazlo Smits, who came over from Homeland Security to be the chief interrogator."

"I met him briefly outside Otto's cell, but I'd never heard of him before today."

"He's a bottom-feeder, believe me. The only good thing is that Bill Benkerk is there to ride herd on things."

Mary turned to McGarvey. "How about you?"

"He's going into badland," Pete said. "No cover."

"Where?" Toni asked.

It was the wrong question in McGarvey's mind, though he didn't know exactly why.

Pete glanced at him, but he just nodded. "Islamabad," she said.

"Colonel Padishah," Mary said. "To do what? If you assassinate the man it won't help Otto's case."

"I'm just going to ask him a couple of questions," McGarvey said.

"And?" Mary asked.

"Find out if he's telling the truth."

Mary was silent for a long beat. "Don't you think the ISI will take exception to your presence?"

"I'm hoping they will."

"Then what?"

"That'll be up to the colonel."

"Jesus, Mary, and Joseph," Mary said.

"Amen," Pete muttered.

□

SIXTEEN

After Mary had left, Otto went into the bathroom, where he used the toilet concealing what he was doing as if he were aware of the security cameras and was modest. When he'd washed his hands and got out, a light meal of a grilled ham-and-cheese, a small bag of potato chips, and another can of beer had been delivered.

He was left alone for the afternoon, and he figured it had to be at least six thirty or seven before Smits and Benkerk showed up.

"I'm sure you're tired, boyo, so we just need a minute or two of your time," Benkerk said.

"Your wife passed you something, I would like you to hand it over," Smits said.

Otto had expected the visit. "Did you guys get your jollies watching us?"

"Sorry," Benkerk said, and he meant it.

"She's shook up, so I held her in my arms for a little bit. Or was that treason, too?"

"On your feet," Smits said.

Otto got up from where he'd been sitting on the edge of the cot eating his meal. The half can of beer was on the tile floor. He made as if he were off-balance and knocked the beer over. "Oops."

It was another of Mac's field operation instructions that he remembered. Whenever possible do something to make a distraction. No matter how trivial an act it might be, it might turn the opposition's attention away for a moment.

"Your mess, you can live with it," Smits said. "Arms out, spread your legs."

Otto did as he was told.

Smits frisked him, his hands moving slowly along Otto's torso, starting on the back, then to the sides and down the front, including the crotch, before patting down both legs. He worked slowly and methodically, and when he was finished he straightened up and stepped back.

"Enjoy that, did you?" Otto said.

"Step across the room, please," Smits said, no expression on his face.

Otto moved away from the bed.

Smits pulled the covers off, patted the pillow down, dropping it on the puddle of beer on the floor, and turned over the mattress.

"Satisfied, you little prick?" Otto asked.

Smits took a small flashlight from his pocket and examined the screws holding the small louvered plate covering the ventilation duct in the ceiling.

"Clean?" Benkerk asked.

"Yes," Smits said, and he was disappointed. He scowled at Otto. "If you cooperate a little better in the morning, we may give you a fresh pillow."

"Never used them much after I spent a couple of years in Japan."

"You were never in Japan," Benkerk said.

"Missed that one, did you?" Otto said.

Before they left Mary and Toni at the McLean house, McGarvey went online with his phone to find and book a flight first-class to Islamabad on Turkish Airlines that left Dulles a few minutes before eleven this evening. It got to Pakistan around five in the morning.

He also booked an executive suite at the Serena Hotel for five days, holding it with his platinum Amex card.

"Five days?" Pete asked on the way back to their apartment in Georgetown.

"Sending a message," McGarvey told her.

"To who?"

"Whoever's listening."

Pete was driving and she looked over at him. "What are you thinking, Kirk? Talk to me."

"If you mean Pakistan and Moscow and Pyongyang, I don't expect to find out anything I don't already know. Whatever is going down is coming from right here in Washington, or at least it started here."

"What if you're wrong? What if you're arrested the moment you get off the airplane?"

"That will give me at least one answer."

"Which is that Otto is a resource that someone there wants to protect. It'd make him a traitor."

"Which won't be the case."

"You're betting your life on it."

"It's what friends do for friends."

They drove for a while in silence.

"So, if you're not in handcuffs the minute you step off the plane, then what?"

"I'll have a chat with Colonel Padishah."

"Just like that?"

"Yes. I'm hoping that Lou will tell me where he lives."

Pete was troubled. "What about his family?"

"I wouldn't involve them, of course."

"Then why did you say what you did to Taft?"

"Misdirection," McGarvey said.

Pete thought about it for a longish moment or two, until they got off the parkway and took the Key Bridge across to Georgetown. "You want someone here in Washington to react. To try to stop you. But if Padishah and the other three are working with someone here in the States, someone that wants to bring Otto down, then you'll be facing arrest over there."

"If you're right, they won't try to arrest me."

"No, they'll try to kill you," Pete said bitterly. "And I'm sure as hell not going to sit around on my ass like a good little wife while you're gone."

"You're going to storm the gates starting with Taft and Kallek."

"And Smits," Pete said. "I'm going to nail that bastard to the wall."

They turned onto M Street NW and a few blocks later headed up to Dumbarton, toward their apartment.

"And Mary and Toni," McGarvey said.

Pete did a double take. "What?"

McGarvey had known from the moment he realized that he had fallen in love with Pete that this conversation was going to happen. That he was going to send her off on some disturbing tangent, to some dark corner where the real bad people operated. He was a little surprised that it was so long in the coming.

"I'm a cynic," he started.

"Yeah, I've already guessed as much. But you suspect Toni and especially Mary?"

"I suspect everyone."

"Even me?"

"You talk in your sleep," he said. "Anyway, most of the time you're the last Girl Scout in the pack. Naïve sometimes, tough when need be, but by and large trusting. Too trusting."

"I'm not stupid," Pete flared.

"Anything but."

"Then what are you saying? That I need a protector, like you? Someone to watch my back. Someone to hold the little wifey's hand?"

"Exactly," McGarvey said. "But it's a two-way street. I watch your back, you watch mine."

"And you expect me to hold your hand?"

"If need be."

Pete concentrated on her driving for a piece as they approached Twenty-Eighth Street, their apartment just around the block.

"I'm going over to Pakistan, where I'll not be welcomed with open arms, but you're staying here, where I think the real trouble exists."

Pete had a sudden wave of deep affection and no-holds-barred love for her husband. "You and me, babe?"

"Just like the song," McGarvey said as they came around the corner.

A dark, late-model Chevy Impala was parked almost directly across the street from their apartment building. McGarvey didn't recognize it. The car did not belong there.

"Don't slow down," he said. "Keep driving. At the end of the block turn left on P Street."

SEVENTEEN

□

It was early evening, and Otto figured that Benkerk and even Smits had gone home to their families and their dinners, and probably wouldn't be back until first thing in the morning. Today was the easy part; tomorrow, he suspected, things would get tougher, and he couldn't count on keeping the conceal-and-carry cell phone hidden forever.

The light switch had been disconnected and the overhead fluorescents would remain on all night, but it didn't matter; in fact, he needed electricity to be flowing to the fixture.

He took off his flip-flops, unzipped the jumpsuit, and, sitting on the side of the cot, slipped it off and dropped it on the floor. Lying back, he rolled over on his side, pulling the blanket up over his shoulders.

For a beat or two he lay there, not moving, but then slowly reached around to scratch the small of his back, and then farther down, where he retrieved the cell phone from where he'd hidden it under his underwear in the crack of his butt. The one place Smits had not checked.

Switching the phone on, he curled up in a ball. Laying his head on his right arm, he keyed Lou's password, and began speaking. The signal was sent to the electrical current in the wires above the ceiling modulating the 60-cycle AC, and sending it back to the wires that led outside the building where Lou, now awake, was able to pick it up.

Lou would forward it to the house system in McLean, and it would be up to Mary to pass the information to McGarvey and Pete.

Pete circled the block and, just before the corner onto their street where the Chevy was parked, she pulled over.

"Do you think Taft sent some housekeepers out here to keep tabs on us?" she asked.

"I'm going to find out," McGarvey said. "Just stay loose."

They both got out of the car, and Pete followed Mac to the corner, but stayed behind him, as he took a quick look.

"Still there," he said.

"Luck."

They had circled the block the opposite way they'd come in, so that he was on the same side of the street as the Chevy. He drew his pistol and, keeping to the shadows as much as possible, headed toward the car. The plate was from New Hampshire.

As they had passed he'd gotten just a brief look at two men in front, and

possibly one in the backseat. If Taft had sent housekeepers, there would have only been two of them.

When he was ten feet away, the Chevy rear door and front driver's-side door opened and two large men dressed in jeans and dark pullovers got out.

"McGarvey," the driver said into his lapel, his accent almost certainly Russian, and the man from the rear started to pull out his pistol.

McGarvey was on them in two steps, batting the man's gun out of his hand, and shooting him in the knee.

"*Trakhat' tebya*"—*Fuck you*—he said in Russian.

The driver reached for his pistol at the same time the man from the front passenger side jumped out of the car.

McGarvey grabbed the driver's gun arm and twisted it around so that the shot hit the passenger in the chest.

The driver tried to break free, but McGarvey jammed his pistol under the man's chin. "*Kotoryy poslal vas*"—*Who sent you*—he said in Russian.

The man he'd shot in the kneecap was reaching for his dropped pistol.

McGarvey turned and fired one shot into the man's head, and before the driver could take advantage, Mac was back, the muzzle of his Walther in the man's face.

"*Kotoryy poslal vas.*"

"*Ty mertvets*"—*You're a dead man*—the Russian said, and tried to lunge forward, leaving McGarvey no option except to pull the trigger.

A figure loomed up on the passenger side of the car, a pistol in his hand pointed directly at McGarvey.

An instant later a pistol shot came from nearby, his mouth opened, he nodded to the left and crumpled to the street.

Pete was there, her pistol gripped in both hands pointing at the downed man. "Jesus, who the hell are these guys?"

At that instant a fifth man, dressed in dark clothes appeared at the front door to their building across the street.

McGarvey and Pete swung around, their guns centered on the man, who stopped short.

"*Ruki vverkh!*"—*Hands up!*—Pete shouted.

The man at the door raised his hands over his head, and McGarvey covered him as Pete ran over and took the gun from his hand, and stepped back.

In the distance they could hear a siren, and then a second one.

"How do you want to play this?" Pete asked.

"We can't walk away," McGarvey said. He came around the car and went to the man on the stoop.

The sirens were already closer. Lights began to show in some of the apartments on both sides of the street.

"Do you speak English?" McGarvey asked.

The man nodded. "Yes," he said, his accent Russian. He did not look or sound nervous.

"Who sent you?"

The Russian hesitated for just a moment.

McGarvey raised his gun.

"Otto Rencke," the Russian said.

It had taken Otto nearly ten minutes to record everything he'd thought of for Lou, and ask that in her next awake cycle in six hours she transfer the information to the house, and ask Mary to pass it to McGarvey and Pete as soon as possible.

Included would be the backgrounders on the intelligence officers he'd worked with in the SVR, the GRU, the ISI, and the DPRK's State Security Department, along with their last known duty stations and home addresses and anything else Lou could come up with.

When he was finished, he pressed the Send key, which transmitted everything through the building's electrical system to Lou in under one millisecond.

Almost instantaneously a confirmation-of-receipt message came back, and an instant later everything he'd sent, including the password, was erased from the phone's memory.

He had no doubt that the NGA's security system would have picked up the short burst, and sooner or later it would be traced to this room and someone would come to find out what and how it had happened.

Five minutes later the door burst open and Smits came in. "Okay, where the fuck is it?" he demanded.

Otto rolled over. "Where's what?"

"The transmitter or cell phone or whatever you used to send your message."

"I have no idea what you're talking about," Otto said. "And anyway, aren't you supposed to be home with your wife and kiddies, if you have any?"

Smits calmed down. "We can do this the easy way, or if you insist I can get a surveillance team in here to make the search, or if need be a surgeon who will do whatever I ask of him."

"Where's Bill?"

"What will it be, Mr. Rencke?"

Otto pushed back the covers and tossed the phone to Smits, who caught it.

"Where did you hide it?"

Otto grinned. "Up my ass."

EIGHTEEN

☐

Several police cars bracketed both ends of the street, a half dozen or more cops, their pistols drawn, approaching with extreme caution.

McGarvey had stepped away from the Russian on the stoop, and he and Pete made a show of placing their weapons on the pavement and raising their hands above their heads.

More sirens were incoming.

"I'm Kirk McGarvey. I share this apartment with my wife, and the man on the stairs is a Russian intelligence officer who was sent here with a team to assassinate us."

"Don't move," the only cop not wearing a flak jacket shouted. He had the three stars of an assistant chief of police on his shirt collars. He stepped to one side, his weapon aimed at a spot between McGarvey and the Russian, who stood with his hands up, as several cops, their pistols drawn, moved in.

The neighbors had called 911 to report gunfire, but the police had got here too soon, in too many numbers and with heavy brass. The whole thing was getting crazier by the minute in McGarvey's mind.

"My name is Anatoli Krestov," the Russian said. "I am a Moscow police officer sent to my embassy to make contact with your FBI. My service pistol is on the sidewalk."

"You have no jurisdiction here," the deputy chief said.

McGarvey and Pete were handcuffed, and bracketed by a pair of cops for each of them, who hustled them down the street.

"I'm a special envoy with credentials that gives me diplomatic immunity," the Russian said.

McGarvey pulled up short. "Who sent you? Colonel Aladko?"

More police units were showing up, along with a pair of ambulances. Again, all this was happening far too fast, as if it had been preplanned, the units standing nearby ready to move as soon as the first shots had been fired.

"I don't know that name," the Russian said.

"Move it," one of McGarvey's cops ordered.

"What were you doing at our apartment?"

"Trying to save your lives, obviously."

McGarvey and Pete were taken to separate police cars, where they were placed in the backseats, the doors locked, a cage separating the front seats. A cop was behind the wheel in Mac's car.

"Where are you taking us?" McGarvey asked.

"For the moment nowhere, Mr. McGarvey, the Bureau wants us to hold you here."

"You know who we are?"

"Yes, sir," the cop said. He was looking up at the rearview mirror.

"Who tipped you off?"

"Sir?"

"You guys got here too fast."

"Deputy Chief Rollins had us standing by."

"When was that?" McGarvey asked.

"About an hour ago."

"Is he the three-star out there?"

"Yes, sir."

"Tell him I'd like to have a word, please. And tell him to be careful of the Russian."

"We were warned," the uniform said.

McGarvey watched from the backseat of the police car as the bodies of the four shooters were photographed. Within ten minutes they were loaded aboard ambulances and taken away. Almost immediately a tow truck came, and the Chevy was winched up to the bed, where it was tied down and also taken away.

Except for the photographs, no forensic investigation had occurred. The bodies had not been examined, nor had any of the shell casings been marked where they lay, only picked up and bagged, but not individually tagged or bagged so far as Mac could see.

Most of the police cars, their lights no longer flashing, left, and the few cops remaining cleared the street of onlookers.

No media had shown up, which was even odder. Nor had the Bureau arrived.

Through all of this the deputy chief had been talking with the Russian cop, and when the street had been mostly cleared, the two men shook hands and the Russian walked away to the corner at the far end of the short street and disappeared.

The cop in the front seat said, "Yes, sir," into his lapel mic, then got out of the squad car, came around to McGarvey's side, and opened the door.

Mac got out and the cop took the handcuffs off.

"You're free to go now, sir," the cop said, and he went back around front and got behind the wheel.

Pete was let out of the squad car where she had been taken, and her cuffs removed. She immediately came over to McGarvey. "What the hell was that all about?" she demanded.

"I haven't a clue," Mac said. "But just ride with it for now."

Deputy Chief Rollins, carrying a pair of small evidence bags, joined them. "I'm returning your weapons. Unloaded, of course."

Pete started to say something but McGarvey cut her off. "Don't you need our guns for ballistics testing?"

"That won't be necessary, Mr. Director."

"What about the bodies?"

"Mr. Krestov will be claiming them from the morgue for a return to Moscow. I was told that they have an aircraft standing by."

"Is that it?" Pete asked.

"Yes, ma'am."

"Four people were shot to death on the street, and we shot them. What are you going to do about it?"

"Nothing," the deputy chief said.

"On whose orders?" Pete pressed.

"I can't say."

"Can't or won't?"

"Can't because I don't know," the deputy chief said. "Now, if you'll excuse me, I'm going home."

Before they left the street and went upstairs, McGarvey gave Pete her pistol, and reloaded his, checking the action to make sure the weapon hadn't been tampered with.

They took the stairs to the third floor, where, pistol in hand, Mac checked the door lock, but so far as he could tell it hadn't been tampered with.

He looked over his shoulder. Pete held her pistol low and to the left. She nodded.

Unlocking the door to their apartment, he eased it open an inch, then stepped aside, his Walther at the ready, and shoved the door the rest of the way open.

Moving fast and low, he darted inside, sweeping his pistol left to right, as he stepped aside to let Pete come in behind him.

They cleared the small apartment in under twenty seconds, McGarvey first to check for a shooter, and Pete right behind him checking for any signs that something had been tampered with—a cabinet door, a closet slider, a drawer anywhere an explosive device might have been planted.

"Clear," McGarvey said, back in the living room.

Pete was right behind him. "Clear," she said, lowering her pistol. "What the hell was that all about?"

McGarvey holstered his gun. "Someone just unzipped their fly."

"The Russians?"

"I don't know, but I'm going to find out."

"We're going to find out," Pete said. "But what about your flight to Islamabad tonight?"

"I'm not going until tomorrow."

"You're canceling?" Pete asked, but then understanding dawned in her

eyes. "You're not canceling. You're going to have someone watch to see if the ISI sent someone to meet the flight."

"Could be interesting," McGarvey said.

"You and I need to start working on our communication skills."

NINETEEN

After the McGarveys left the McLean house, Mary had opened another bottle of wine for her and Toni, whose husband, Jack, an attorney, was in Ontario, New York, defending two nuns who had illegally managed to get through security at the R. E. Ginna Nuclear Power Plant and stage a sit-in.

"It's become the to-do thing for Catholic nuns," Toni had said. The incident was the third this year.

"I wish our problems were as simple to solve as Jack's," Mary said. "Do you want to spend the night? I have a couple of ideas I want to talk over with you. In the morning you can run them past your team, get their take."

Toni raised her glass. "What're you thinking?"

"The four names Lou came up with, and their promotions. The whole thing is just too pat for my taste."

"Hank said the same thing. But if it is a setup, who's behind it and why?"

"To bring Otto down, for a start. But somebody out there wants to get at Mac, and they figure the best way to do it is by going after Otto, because they know damned well what'll happen next."

"Still leaves the who," Toni said. "And I seriously doubt if it's the four intel officers on Lou's list. Maybe not even the Russians, the Pakis, or Kim Jong-un's tribe. But I think if we can come up with who Mac has hurt the most, and who would have the most to gain by bringing him down, we'd be closer to figuring out this thing."

Mary smiled. "I agree," she said. "But the list is just too damned long, because we're talking about more than some intel officer somewhere—someone connected with a government agency—it could be an individual with a grudge."

"With a score to settle," Toni said. "But that could actually narrow it down a bit. Because most of the people Mac has gone up against are dead."

Mary's secure cell phone, lying on the kitchen counter, chimed. Otto had set it up for her last year, promising that it was totally bugproof.

She got it, and entered the ten-character password, which automatically changed every twelve hours in a pattern that Otto had taught his wife to memorize. "Hello?"

She was answered with a soft warble. It was Lou.

"The rain in Spain stays mainly on the plain," Mary said, and Lou's voice-recognition program identified her. She switched the phone to speaker mode.

"Good evening, Mary. I received a message from Otto, who asked me to make a data search and a rough analysis based on four separate queries."

"Are we talking about the intelligence officers that Otto is accused of passing information to?"

"In part, but he asked that I follow a series of loose ends that he suggested might connect those four officers with others outside their respective countries."

"Including here in the U.S.?"

"Yes."

"Continue please."

"My threat assessment is lavender," Lou said. "I have an eighty-seven percent confidence that Mac and likely Pete will be the targets of an assassination attempt."

"Do you have a name?"

"Not yet."

"What is your present confidence that the assassin or whoever is directing the operation is American?"

"Twenty-one percent."

"Is that number changing?"

"Yes."

"Increasing or decreasing?"

"Increasing."

"Do you have a probable timetable?" Mary asked.

"Within the next twenty-four to thirty-six hours. My confidence level for such an event is ninety-one percent."

Mary and Toni exchanged a worried look.

"Is Otto well?"

"I'm sorry, but I have no information concerning his status, except for the transmission from his cell phone."

"Have you informed Mac?"

"His phone may not be secure. Do you want me to try anyway?"

"No. I'll take care of it."

"As you wish, Mary."

"Thank you. Please keep me advised of any changes."

"Of course," Lou said, and she was gone.

"Jesus," Toni said. "An American?"

"God only knows Mac's an equal opportunity employer when it comes to making enemies," Mary replied. She could think of at least a dozen candidates who could and probably would be put under the microscope.

"We need to warn him now, but not by phone."

"It won't matter if whoever's after him knows that he knows," Mary said. She hit Mac's number, and he answered on the first ring, as if he'd been expecting the call.

"Have you heard anything new from Otto?" he asked.

"Only that he contacted Lou and she just called me. She has a high confidence that someone will try to kill you and Pete within the next day or day and a half."

"Has Toni left yet?" McGarvey asked.

"She's right here."

"Do either of you know the name Anatoli Krestov? He said he was a Moscow cop."

Toni shook her head.

"No," Mary said. "Why?"

"When we showed up at our place, four guys in a Chevy Impala with New Hampshire plates were parked across the street. We had a gun battle and they lost."

"Did you get IDs?"

"No, but they were Russians."

"Are you certain?" Toni asked.

"Yes," McGarvey said. "The point is, the cops were there within minutes. As if they had been standing by for something to take place that they knew was going to happen."

"But you're home already," Mary said. "Didn't they at least take you in for questioning?"

"Once they cleared the scene, they left us standing in the middle of the street."

"Do you have the Impala's tag number?" Toni asked, pulling out her cell phone.

McGarvey gave it to her.

"Who is this Krestov?" Mary asked.

McGarvey explained. "When it was over the on-scene commander and he just shook hands, and the guy walked away."

"The Chevy's an Alamo rental, picked up at Dulles this morning," Toni said. "Driver's name is Terry Fishbine, Milwaukee. I'm checking the Wisconsin DMV."

"Was Krestov in your apartment?" Mary asked. "Leave anything behind?"

"If he did get in, he was a pro. We didn't find anything."

"Do you want me to send a crew to take a closer look?"

"No. Whoever he was made sure someone wanted us dead."

Toni came back. "No driver's license under that name."

"Not surprising," McGarvey said. "And I think that if you try to run Krestov to ground, he won't exist either."

"What's next?" Mary asked.

"There's a new chief of station in Islamabad. Find out his name and contact information away from the embassy, and tell him to expect a call from me tonight."

"It's coming up on seven in the morning over there," Mary said. "Toni's getting the number for you now. You should be able to catch him before he goes to work. What else?"

"Krestov said Otto sent the guys in the Chevy to kill us."

TWENTY

McGarvey got on the phone and called the contact number for the CIA's chief of Islamabad Station, Sam Fox. A woman answered.

"Hello."

"I'd like to speak with Sam unless he's already left for the embassy," McGarvey said.

"Who is calling, please?" the woman asked. She sounded a little tense.

"Kirk McGarvey. He'll know the name."

Fox came on the line almost immediately. "Mr. Director, your call comes as a surprise. Are you here in-country?"

"I'm still in Washington, but I need a favor from you, and I'd like it kept off your contact sheet for forty-eight hours, if possible."

Fox hesitated for a beat. "I take it that you're on your way."

"Soon, but in the meantime, I want to test the waters, which is why I called."

Fox hesitated again. "You understand that you won't be welcomed with open arms."

"I want to get an idea of just how unwelcome I'll be," McGarvey said. He gave the COS the number of his Turkish Airlines flight, which was leaving just before eleven this evening and arriving twenty-three hours later, at 4:55 in the morning Islamabad time.

"You want me to meet you at the airport?"

"I made the reservation under my real name, but I'll miss the plane. I want you to keep watch to see if anyone is interested enough to stick around until all the passengers have gotten off."

"Anyone, as in the ISI?"

"Yes."

"And call you directly?"

"If you would."

"I suppose that I should buck this up to Waksberg."

"You probably should, but this is important."

"Convince me, Mr. Director, why I should stick my neck out for what will probably become a knock-down, drag-'em-out shooting war, the same as happens just about everywhere you show up, if even half the stories are true."

"Because a close friend of mine has been arrested and charged with treason, and I'm going to prove that he's innocent."

"Jesus. Who is it?"

"Otto Rencke."

"God save us all, if even only ten percent of the stories about him are true."

"Will you help me?" McGarvey asked.

"I'll need your contact number."

McGarvey gave him his encrypted phone's number.

"Are you actually going to show up here or are you just making a false drop?"

"That depends on what you find out."

"I don't suppose you'll tell me what or who you're looking for if and when you do get here," Fox said.

"You don't want to know," McGarvey said. "Trust me."

Pete was seated near the window looking down at the street. When Mac hung up, she turned to him. "I'm surprised he didn't ask you the million-dollar question, unless it won't dawn on him until later."

"That if someone does show up to meet my flight, it'd probably mean there was a leak somewhere over here?"

"Something like that."

"You don't get to be a chief of station by making mistakes."

"No, but it sometimes helps to kiss some booty."

McGarvey called British Airways direct and, using a platinum Amex card in the work name of Roger Bannon, booked the afternoon flight that left Dulles at ten till six, arriving at just past one thirty in the morning local in Islamabad.

Next, using the same ID, he booked a suite at the Islamabad Marriott, in the heart of embassy row.

Then he phoned Mary again and asked her and Toni to dig up whatever they could on the men from the four intel services that Otto had hacked and where he had supposedly left open back doors.

"Start with Padishah," he said.

"Do you still want his personal information?" Mary asked.

"Especially that, and I also want his history since he first got on the fast track."

"You're talking about money?" Toni said.

"Yes, and the houses or apartments he's lived in, the cars he's driven, and the class of his mistresses if any."

"And what stores their wives and mistresses shopped at. Generals make more money than captains."

"That, too," McGarvey said.

"You do know that if someone does show up for the flight you're not on, it could mean that there's a leak here," Mary said.

"That was the point."

"My bet would be Marty Bambridge. He had a real grudge against you

and Otto. He's only been dead a year, but there could be something simmering that he put in place. I think we should check it out. Maybe get Lou involved."

"Be careful of her batteries," McGarvey said. "We don't want to waste them looking for something that isn't a likely possibility."

"If it is someone on this side of the pond, I'd put one of Marty's programs high on the list," Mary insisted.

"Your call," McGarvey said. "But get back to me ASAP on Padishah."

"Are you still planning on going into badland?" Toni asked.

"Depends on what you guys come up with."

"We're on it," Mary said.

When McGarvey hung up, Pete had an odd look on her face.

"You didn't mention Roger Bannon," she said.

"No."

Pete cocked her head and smiled wanly. "You sure know how to show a girl a good time," she said. "And it keeps getting better every day."

They made love and went to sleep early. But Mac had a hard time shutting down, thinking of Otto not only as a prisoner under interrogation by a man Pete said was among the worst of the worst, but in custody, his life regimented. It was an existence that would soon kill him, unless he was proved innocent and set free.

Twice in the middle of the night he got up and went to the living room windows to check the street. But nothing moved, nor were there any cars or vans or any sort of vehicle unknown to him parked, men waiting to finish what hadn't happened here earlier.

The first time, around three, when he went back to bed he sensed that Pete was awake, but she didn't say anything and he went back to sleep, though only with difficulty.

The second time, she turned to him when he got into the bed. "What are you thinking, my darling?" she asked.

"Otto's never going back to the Company."

"I know. But then what?"

"He can't quit being who he is."

"Curious?"

"Yes."

"A genius, but a pain in the ass."

McGarvey had to laugh, but it was true, his friend was a pain in the ass, always had been, but loyal. He thumbed his nose at authority; even a hint that someone could have the audacity, the unmitigated gall, to tell him what to do sent him into a rage. And yet he had embraced Mac's raison d'etre—Superman's World War II motto "Truth, justice, and the American way," as hokey as that sounded sometimes.

"The question stands: If Otto is out, what becomes of him?"

"I have a couple of ideas, but first I'm going out to Fort Belvoir today to see him."

"They won't let you in," Pete said. "Not you of all people."

"We'll see."

□

TWENTY-ONE

Benkerk showed up at the NGA at six in the morning on Smits's call an hour earlier. The Homeland Security interrogator hadn't said why he'd phoned so early—the next interrogation session wasn't to be until eight—except that the situation had changed.

"Changed how," Benkerk had asked on the phone.

"I'm not going to discuss the specifics on an open line, except to suggest that we have to go to the next phase."

"Jesus, not until I get there. Promise me that much."

"There are no promises in this business," Smits had replied coolly. "Only results."

On the drive down from his house in Rockville, Benkerk had worried himself almost sick. When he had been asked to assist with Otto's interrogation and had been told who he'd be working with, he'd begged off. But Taft himself had asked for the favor, and in the end he had agreed.

Smits had the reputation of being the grim reaper. The man knew his job, but he needed to be reined in. The suspect was Otto Rencke, after all.

Smits was drinking coffee from a paper cup downstairs in the interrogation cell. This morning his jacket was off, his tie was loose, and his shirt-sleeves were rolled up to the elbows.

Benkerk's snap thought was that the man looked like a shark about ready to attack. "Have you been here all night?"

"Yes. I had a suspicion that the son of a bitch was up to something so I hung around and I was right," Smits said. He pushed Otto's cell phone, now contained in a small plastic bag, across the table.

"Did Mary bring it to him?"

"I'm almost certain of it, but he could have had it when he was arrested."

"He was searched."

"He had it shoved up his ass."

Benkerk had reached for the baggie, but he pulled back. He had to smile. "The man's inventive."

"He's a traitor and this proves it," Smits replied sharply, though he didn't raise his voice.

"Just a phone."

"A very special phone, that allowed him to somehow modulate the electrical wires in his cell and send a burst transmission out of the building."

"To whom?"

"We don't know, but I suspect he sent something to his case officer."

"Or his computer on campus."

"I'm told that power has been cut to the machine."

"Maybe he sent a message to his wife."

"No."

"Well, what did the message say?" Benkerk asked.

"It was encrypted, and our techs upstairs gave up trying to break it after less than a half hour," Smits said. "Quantum encryption, they think." He looked up at the monitor on the wall showing Otto sitting on the cot. "Only two people know what was in his message. Him and the one he sent it to."

"Let's ask him after he's had his breakfast."

"No breakfast for him this morning."

"Why?" Benkerk asked, even though he knew the answer.

"Administering drugs to a man with a full stomach is not advisable. They are likely to vomit, possibly aspirate it."

Benkerk was disgusted. "Christ," he said.

Smits's only emotion was a mild surprise.

Pete was up first and had the coffee on when McGarvey finished his shower and got dressed, in a pair of starched jeans, a white shirt, and a dark blue blazer. He laid the holster and Walther on the table.

"I don't think NGA security will allow me on campus armed," he said. "But don't you go out of the house without your pistol."

Pete carried a Glock 24 Gen 2 subcompact pistol that fired a hefty 10mm round that was deadly and accurate in a gunfight at ten feet or less.

"Where am I going?"

"First to Mary's to see if she can get you in to talk to Lou, and then Carleton and maybe Taft to find out if they've come up with anything new."

"We probably know more than Taft does."

"Right, but he'll ask you about the shoot-out last night, and you might find out something from him that we don't already know."

"And?"

"Downtown to talk to Kallek to see if whatever he tells you matches whatever you get from Taft."

Pete thought about it for a moment or two. "Okay, Kirk, where are you going with this?" she asked. "What are you really looking for?"

"If they think Otto's a traitor, then by extension they think I am one, too."

"And me?"

"Yes, you."

"Then why haven't we been arrested?"

"In Otto's case they think his back doors are prima facie evidence that he's guilty. But they think they'll get the proof by whatever we do."

"Like going to Pakistan, and then I presume Moscow and Pyongyang," Pete said. "But what about me?"

"About getting in to talk to Lou."

"If they find out that she's up and running, they would expect I'd do it from a safe distance, not actually get into the Wolf's Den."

She poured Mac a cup of coffee, but before they sat down he took her in his arms and held her close for a longish moment or two.

"I do love you, you know, even if I haven't said it enough," he said. He'd had a sudden wave and a fair measure of fear for her.

"It's because you're a big coward, but I know you do. And anyway we've been into the middle of more than one shitstorm together over the past couple of years, for both of us to know that isn't just some passing fancy. I'm in this for the count."

"So am I, so watch your six."

"You, too."

McGarvey used his phone to get into the lowest-security layer of the CIA's basic information service, where he got Marston's private numbers at home, in his limo, and in his office at the NGA.

He dialed the man's office phone, which automatically rolled over to the limo's phone. Marston was on his way from his house to the NGA.

"Good morning, Mr. Director," McGarvey said when Marston answered on the second ring. "Kirk McGarvey."

"I was wondering when you'd call," Marston said after a brief hesitation. "What can I do for you, Mr. McGarvey?"

"I'd like to pay a visit to Otto Rencke this morning."

"That won't be possible until he's been moved from my facility."

"When will that be?"

"Tomorrow."

"I'd like to see him this morning."

"Not possible under the present circumstance."

"I'm investigating the charges against him, under the direction of the CIA's general counsel, Carleton Patterson. I suppose I could get a court order. But I'll only need a minute or two of your time."

"You will not come into my facility armed," Marston said.

"Of course not."

"When?"

"I'll be leaving Georgetown in five minutes," McGarvey said. He called to have his Jaguar F-Pace SUV brought from the garage around the corner, and went downstairs to wait until it came.

TWENTY-TWO

Mary and Toni were standing in the driveway when Pete pulled up, parked next to the Porsche, and got out.

"You're up bright and early," Mary said, but then she stopped. "Did something else happen overnight?"

"No, but Mac called the Islamabad chief of station and asked him to post a lookout at the airport to see if anyone showed up and took an interest."

"Sam's a good man. He'll do it himself and keep his mouth shut."

"Have you gotten anything yet from Lou on Padishah?"

"I was just about to leave," Mary said. "The only way I can get access to her is to physically get into the office."

"I'll tag along," Pete said. "Depending on what you find I want to have a chat with Carleton and then go upstairs to talk to Taft if he's on campus."

"When you're done, give me a call and I'll send someone over to escort you to my office," Toni said.

She kissed both women on the cheek and then drove off.

"What's Mac up to this morning?" Mary asked as they went inside.

"He's on his way out to Fort Belvoir to check on Otto."

Mary stopped short. "Nick Marston is just going to love that, especially after what went down last night."

"Was he told about what happened to us?"

"I don't know, but I managed to give Otto a burst-transmission cell phone, which I'm sure he used to talk to Lou. By now the cyber techs out there must have spotted the signal and are going nuts trying to figure out what was sent."

"If they did detect the transmission, Mac's showing up there won't be looked at as a coincidence," Pete said. "They might even arrest him."

Mary shook her head. "They're going to wait to see if he tries to make contact with the four guys on the list."

"Wouldn't one be enough?"

"If he actually goes to Islamabad, and actually gets back in one piece, the Bureau might have someone waiting at the airport to pick him up as soon as he gets off the plane. Before he got to his checked luggage for a pistol.""

"If he didn't want to be taken into custody he wouldn't need a gun," Pete said.

Benkerk was afraid to leave Smits's side because of what the son of a bitch might actually do if no one was there to put the brakes on. Instead of going

directly up to Marston's office, he phoned, but his secretary said the director wasn't taking any calls.

"Tell him this is most urgent."

"Yes, sir, the moment he is free."

Benkerk had used one of the house phones in the corridor just outside the interrogation room, and as he hung up, Smits and an older, much heavier man carrying what looked like a medical bag got off the elevator and came his way.

"What the hell is this all about?" Benkerk demanded.

"If needs be I suggest you go upstairs and speak with Dr. Marston, until we're finished here," Smits said.

"I'll stay with you."

"As you wish. But you will in no way try to interfere, understood?"

"No," Benkerk said. "But I'll be in the room as a witness, understood?"

"Of course," Smits said.

"Are you going to introduce me to the man with the bag?"

"No."

"Dr. Harry Meyer," the portly man said, holding out his hand. "INSCOM."

INSCOM was the army's Intelligence and Security Command, head-quartered right here on Fort Belvoir. Besides providing intelligence and information operations, the command also had been involved with parapsy-chological research.

Benkerk ignored the man's outstretched hand. "Let's get on with it, then, but over my strongest objections."

"So noted," Smits said.

Otto looked up from where he was seated on the edge of the cot when the door opened and the three men came in. "Hi, Bill," he said. "I see that you've brought your friend and Dr. Mengele along for some fun."

"I've had nothing to do with this, boyo," Benkerk said. "I'm only here as a witness."

"That's what the bystanders said at Auschwitz."

"I'll ask one last time for your cooperation, Mr. Rencke," Smits said.

"Shoot."

"Did your wife bring the transmitter to you?"

"I had it with me when I was arrested. I've always wanted a reliable means of calling home if the need arose."

"You sent an encrypted burst transmission from this room last night. Who was it sent to?"

Otto winked at Benkerk. "To Santa Claus. I wanted to make sure he knew in plenty of time that I was crossing your name off my Christmas gift list."

"Doctor," Smits said.

Otto waved a finger. "Naughty or nice."

McGarvey showed his identification at the gate, and drove over to the NGA's massive headquarters building. He had to sign in, and Marston's secretary said that an escort would be coming down.

The main lobby was very busy this morning. Including this campus, plus the one near St. Louis, Missouri, and a number of liaison facilities around the world, the Agency had more than sixteen thousand employees, with a budget well in excess of five billion dollars.

It was a well-funded and well-run organization, overseen by the undersecretary of defense for intelligence. Dr. Marston was this facility's director, who reported directly to the undersecretary's deputy director of operations up in D.C.

But Otto was here somewhere, and to Mac the place seemed more like a supermax penitentiary than a satellite intelligence-gathering operation.

The doctor took a syringe and a vial from the bag and charged the needle, ejecting a small amount to clear the air bubble.

"Roll up your sleeve, please," the doctor said.

"What's it to be, midazolam? Or maybe amobarbital if you want to give me a quicker fix," Otto said. Both were so-called truth-serum drugs, which experience showed didn't really work very well, with a possibility for sometimes causing some brain damage.

"Your sleeve," the doctor said. "Left or right, it doesn't matter."

"I don't think so."

"Cooperate and we won't have to resort to restraints," Smits said, his manner reasonable.

"No."

Smits approached the bed. "Bill, if you would give me a hand," he said.

"I won't be a party to this," Benkerk said.

"Then leave the room," Smits said, glancing over his shoulder.

"Fuck you," Otto said. He rose up at the same moment he landed a roundhouse punch to the side of Smits's face, sending the man backward and off his feet, his head bouncing on the concrete floor.

"One for the Christians," Otto said, grinning at Benkerk. "Zip for the lions."

TWENTY-THREE

Pete followed Mary out to the CIA, where they parked in the VIP garage beneath the Original Headquarters Building and took the elevator up to the third floor. DO NOT CROSS tape still blocked the door to the Wolf's Den, but Mary used a key. As they were ducking under the tape and slipping inside, a man came out of an office a few doors away, and he and Pete exchanged a brief glance.

"Someone spotted us."

"Then we better be quick," Mary said, closing and relocking the door.

The outer office had already begun to smell musty, although it had been less than two days since Otto had been arrested.

"Lou, are you awake?" Mary asked, moving into the inner office, Pete trailing right behind.

"Good morning," Lou said. "Is Mac well?"

"Yes," Pete said.

"He missed his flight to Islamabad, is that significant?"

"He wants to see if anyone shows up at the airport looking for him."

"Does he have eyes on the ground, or should I hack the airport's monitors?"

"We have it covered," Pete said. "Save your batteries, please."

"I am currently at eighty-two percent."

"Has Otto communicated with you in the past twelve hours?" Mary asked.

"Yes."

"What was the nature of his message?"

"I'm not able to say at this time."

Pete was stunned, but Mary didn't seem to be affected. "The message is password-protected?"

"Yes."

"Why?"

"He didn't say."

"What do you think?"

"I suspect he is concerned that someone may find a way to retrieve the information."

"Me included?" Mary asked.

"Especially you," Lou said.

"I don't understand," Pete said. "Could you explain?"

Lou hesitated for just an instant. "He believes that he will be subjected to psychotropic drugs to facilitate his interrogation. If it is suspected that Mary

has access to me she could also be subjected to enhanced interrogation methods."

Pete was taken aback. "Mother of God," she muttered. "I have to call Mac."

"Your phone won't work in here, we'll have to go outside," Mary said. "Was Otto's message critical to the investigation?" she asked Lou.

"Yes."

"Were you tasked to take some action?"

"Yes."

"May you tell me the nature of this action?"

"Research on Mac's behalf."

A woman from Marston's office escorted McGarvey up to the eighth floor. As they got off the elevator, Mac's cell phone vibrated in his pocket, and he held up.

"Just a minute," he told the escort, and he took out his phone. The call was from Pete.

"Cell phones don't work here," the woman said.

"What is it?" he asked.

"Otto thinks that Smits is going to use psychotropic drugs."

"How do you know this?"

"I got it from Lou, who said she got it from Otto. Mary smuggled one of Otto's burst-transmission cell phones to him and he contacted Lou sometime last night."

The escort was looking at McGarvey, a puzzled expression on her pretty face. Her name tag said KIERSTEN.

"Anything else?"

"Everything else is password-protected."

"But not from Mary?" Mac asked.

"Yes, her, too," Pete said. "Hurry, Kirk, before they try that shit on Otto. It could really screw up his brain. I've seen it happen more than once."

"I'm just down the hall from Marston's office."

Otto sat back down on the cot as Benkerk helped Smits to his feet. He decided that striking back physically had something to be said for it, though he'd always preferred intellectual battles. He only wished that Mac had been here to witness one for the Christians.

"If you want to pump that shit into me, you'd better call for some serious muscle," he said.

The side of Smits's face was red and already beginning to swell, but his demeanor hadn't changed; he remained detached. "That will be arranged, Mr. Rencke," he said.

The doctor had backed off, and put the syringe back in his bag. "I suggest

that you use an alternative method. Even under restraints patients can and often have resisted to the point that the needle breaks off deep inside the injection site, which can cause complications."

Otto couldn't help but laugh. "Patient?" he asked.

"As you wish," Smits said.

The doctor left.

"Okay, so without putting me in a straitjacket, which won't be all that easy, I can promise, what'll you try next? Some of your shit in my food? I'll go on a hunger strike."

"I think an aerosol agent might be best," Smits said, and he almost smiled.

"I won't sign off on something like that," Benkerk said.

"What do you suggest, Bill? I'm wide open."

"Yes, Bill, what do you suggest?" Otto asked. "You've already admitted that you think I'm guilty, you don't believe anything I tell you, and you know damned well that I won't cooperate beyond telling you what I'm claiming is the truth. So what's the next step?"

"Mr. Rencke makes a valid point," Smits said.

"If you truly think I'm a traitor, then you'll want to know what damage I've caused, and how to fix it. Maybe you should go that route. You have the names of four guys I've cooperated with—guys who've received big-time promotions—so how about finding out what damage they've done to us? How many of our NOCs have been outed? How about our people inside the DPRK's nuclear program? Or why not interview the NOC who made it out after sabotaging some of the Supreme Leader's missile tests?"

Smits raised a hand to the side of his face and smiled. "You are a clever man, no doubt of it. Clever enough, in fact, to cover your tracks so well that it could take us years if ever to find out what damage has been done to our country."

"Which leaves you no other choice than drugs?" Otto asked. "Are you people that fucking stupid after all?" He looked at Benkerk, who'd backed away from Smits as if he was trying to say he wasn't a willing partner here. "You think I'm guilty, so why don't you try to prove it the old-fashioned way? With your noggin."

Marston was on the phone when McGarvey barged into his office, the escort on his heels. "Something's come up, I'll call you back," he said.

"I'm taking Otto Rencke out of here immediately this morning," McGarvey said, keeping his tone even.

Marston motioned for the escort to leave. "He's scheduled to be moved sometime this afternoon or first thing in the morning."

"This morning," McGarvey said. "I'll make the arrangements and take him myself."

"That's not my decision."

"There's a real possibility that they're using drugs on him, you son of a bitch. And if he's damaged I will personally make you my next major issue."

Marston was unimpressed, but he called his secretary. "Have Misters Benkerk and Smits suspend their operation, and join us now." He put the phone down. "Where will you take him?"

"To Langley," McGarvey said. "I'll make the arrangements now."

He went out in the corridor and got on his phone to call Pete, who by now would be in Taft's office.

TWENTY-FOUR

□

Mary went back to her old digs in the NHB at the George Bush Center for Intelligence as Pete held up just outside of Taft's office. Unlike a lot of previous directors, who wanted every door on the seventh floor to be closed at all times, this one was an open-door man.

"We need to share information, day by day, hour by hour, even minute by minute if we're to make any real progress," he'd told his staff on his first day.

People were busy this morning, and several noticing Pete on her phone in the corridor smiled and waved.

"What do you want me to tell Taft?" she asked Mac on the phone. "I'm at his door."

"I'm bringing Otto out to the campus. He can bunk at the Scattergood-Thorne house until this mess has been resolved."

The two-story colonial house, just off Virginia Route 123 but on the CIA's campus, had a long history, dating back to before the War of Independence. The Agency had folded it into its property in the 1950s, and had eventually turned the place into a conference center.

"There could be a conference."

"Have Taft move it or cancel it."

"Okay. How about minders, do you want someone to come to you?"

"It's not necessary. But have the house set up for him, and security twenty-four seven put in place."

"He's not going to take a runner."

"I'm not worried about him trying to escape," McGarvey said. "I want to guard against someone trying to get to him."

"Okay, Kirk, I'll put it to Taft."

"And, Pete?"

"Yes?"

"Impress on him that we need to keep the need-to-know list as tight as possible. And I want to get Carleton personally involved in how Otto's treated."

"Then what?"

"Talk to Kallek and let him know what's going on, but tell him to keep it close as well. Then come back and meet us on campus."

"What happens if Taft or Kallek don't want to cooperate?"

"Don't give them the option," McGarvey said.

Taft's secretary looked up, a worried expression on her face, when Pete walked in.

"Mr. Taft is on the phone, he asks that you wait until he's finished," she said. "It shouldn't be too long."

"Who is he talking to?"

"I'm not at liberty to say."

Marston had been on the phone at the same time McGarvey had been talking with Pete, and the NGA director was just hanging up when McGarvey came back.

"I spoke with Admiral Taft. He's not happy but he's agreed to have Mr. Rencke taken off my hands. He's sending someone to pick him up before noon."

"He's leaving with me," McGarvey said.

Marston's secretary buzzed. "The gentlemen are here."

"Give me a minute before you send them in," Marston said, and he gave McGarvey a hard look. "I know something of your reputation, Mr. McGarvey, as does most of Washington. You're a hard man, and you've apparently crossed the line on more than one occasion. Of course, I'm sure that a lot of what I've heard is embellishment. But my point is your tactics are wasted on me. I never wanted to house Mr. Rencke here. It was only as a favor for the admiral. And if it turns out that Mr. Rencke has in any way been maltreated, I will personally deal with it. We are an intelligence-gathering agency, not a prison. Am I clear?"

"Perfectly," McGarvey said, and he felt for the man, who had been put in a bad situation.

Marston rang his secretary. "Send them in, please. And we're not to be disturbed."

"I just spoke with Dr. Marston," Taft said as Pete walked in. "He told me that your husband is there now, demanding that Otto leave with him."

"We'd like to use the Scattergood-Thorne house to continue Otto's debriefing. But without Lazlo Smits."

Taft nodded. "That's about the gist of what Nicholas told me. I agreed to send a couple of security people to fetch him. And if McGarvey wants to house him here on campus then I have no objections. His movements will be restricted, of course, and he won't be allowed any access to his computer system."

"It's been shut down."

"I'm told that may not be entirely true, but no one wants to get anywhere near the thing."

"It's just a machine, Mr. Director," Pete said.

"So is a nuclear submarine," Taft replied dryly, and before Pete could reply he held up a hand. "The evidence I've seen is overwhelming."

"That's what everyone is saying."

Benkerk came in behind Smits, and when he spotted McGarvey he pulled up short, for just a moment, before coming the rest of the way into Marston's office.

"I guess I'm not surprised to see you here," he said.

"I'm taking Otto over to Langley this morning," McGarvey said.

"We're not finished here," Smits said, directly to Marston.

"It's out of my hands," the NGA director told him.

"I'm sorry, but we'll see about that."

"What happened to your face?" McGarvey asked.

"Otto punched him," Benkerk said, obviously enjoying it.

"I was told that you were planning on using drugs," McGarvey said.

"That, sir, is none of your business," Smits bridled, and he turned again to Marston. "We understood from the beginning that housing the suspect here was temporary. Give me an hour and I'll make the arrangements to have him moved to a secure location."

"I'm making it my business," McGarvey said. "You are no longer involved in this investigation, nor will anyone of your stripe get near him."

Smits's left eyebrow rose. "My stripe?"

"I think that a lot of people in the know call you the piranha, among other things."

"That sounds like something Boylan would say. And in her day she was a pretty tough interrogator herself, not above the occasional waterboarding."

McGarvey held himself in check, though he wanted to cross the room and throttle the son of a bitch. "Her name is Mrs. McGarvey."

Smits started to say something, but then, realizing he had crossed some line, changed his mind. "I understand that Mr. Rencke is your personal friend. But the man is a traitor and we have the proof."

Benkerk broke in. "And the proof we have is damning."

"I've seen the file," McGarvey said. "And just for the record, he's been accused of treason, not found guilty."

"What's next, then, Mac?"

"I'm going to prove that the facts you think you have are wrong."

"This is my investigation," Smits objected. "Wherever you move him to, I will follow. I'm doing my job, nothing more."

McGarvey nodded to Marston. "Thank you for your cooperation, Mr. Director."

"Go with care," Marston said.

Smits started to object, but McGarvey walked directly over to him and whispered in his ear. "If you ever try to come close to my friend, I will hurt you."

TWENTY-FIVE

Otto had only ever punched two people in his life: Smits today, and a couple of years ago it had been Marty Bambridge, then the CIA's deputy director of operations—clandestine services—and for just about the same reasons. They had insulted his wife.

But just at this moment his right hand felt like shit, though he didn't think he'd broken any bones.

Someone was at the door, and he got to his feet, girding himself for round two.

But it was McGarvey, and he didn't think he'd ever been happier to see anyone in his entire life. "Oh, wow, kemo sabe."

"So you punched out Smits," McGarvey said. "The son of a bitch deserved it."

Otto took his old friend in his arms and they hugged. "I thought it was him and Bill at the door coming back for more."

"Smits is off the case. I'm taking you back to campus, where Taft's agreed to put you up in the Scattergood-Thorne house until we get this crap taken care of."

"Marston okayed it?"

McGarvey smiled. "I didn't give him the choice."

Someone knocked at the door, and Benkerk came in. He looked a little sheepish. "Sorry about all this," he said.

"Wasn't your fault," Otto said. "And you did try to rein him in."

Benkerk inclined his head. "I'd like to continue with the investigation," he said to McGarvey.

"Investigation, or interrogation?" Mac said.

"Both," Benkerk admitted. "Every piece of evidence I've seen, and I mean everything, points to Otto as a reverse hacker, leaving the back door open for any number of intelligence agencies."

"A little too much evidence?" McGarvey asked. "No holes, no gaps, no questions?"

"It's been my thought. Anyway I want to be a part of trying to help finding Otto innocent, but that has to include complete cooperation, and trust, from both of you. Because if Otto is innocent, which I sincerely hope he is, I want to find the son of a bitch who's behind the thing and nail his ass to the barn door."

McGarvey glanced at Otto.

"Welcome to the club," Otto said without hesitation. "But you're not going to be the most popular guy in D.C."

"Fair enough," Benkerk said. "Where are you taking him?"

"The Scattergood-Thorne house on campus," McGarvey said.

"Mind if I follow you?"

"There'll be interrogators," McGarvey said.

"Not another Smits?"

"My wife will be one of them, and she'll make sure everyone plays fair."

"Before we get out of here, I'd like the phone Mary brought me," Otto said. "And my clothes."

Benkerk had to grin. "Your clothes I can manage. I'll see what I can do about the phone, but I'll have to give it to Mac."

Patterson was off campus, so Taft had an escort take Pete next door to Toni's office in the NHB, but Mary had already left, and Toni had to be called out of a jam session in the think tank.

"You missed her by about five minutes," Toni said.

"Was she going back to talk to Lou?"

"She said she was going home to try to think things out. None of this makes sense to any of us, especially her. She's putting up a pretty good front, but I know her well enough to see that she's bleeding inside."

"She has to hang on to the fact, just like the rest of us, that Otto couldn't possibly be guilty."

"That's not the issue," Toni said.

"What is?"

"Right now the evidence points at him, so it's up to us to prove that he didn't do it."

"Ass backward," Pete said.

"It's a bitch, but it's the hand we've been dealt."

Riding shotgun in McGarvey's Jaguar SUV, Otto held his silence until they'd cleared the NGA's main gate and were on the beltway back to Langley. "How's Mary?" he asked.

"She's in the middle of it. Between the two of us, Marston didn't have a chance."

Otto grinned. "Is Pete okay?"

"She's working it, too, and someone has already sat up and taken notice."

"Something happened?"

McGarvey told him about the ambush outside their apartment in Georgetown, including the Russian who'd identified himself as Anatoli Krestov, a cop from Moscow sent to the embassy to help.

"Lou told me. But help with what?"

"Stop the Russian team from killing me and Pete."

"Did he say who sent them?"

"You," McGarvey said.

Otto laughed out loud. "Well, the dumb bastard just unzipped his fly," he said. "Someone came from Russia to kill you so that you wouldn't be able to prove I wasn't a traitor."

"I would have thought the same thing, except that the cops and Bureau guys showed up too soon. They'd been tipped off."

"You and Pete were supposed to be dead. But the Russian cop screwed up. He was purposely too late to save you. So he blamed the attempted hit on me. It was the only thing he could do."

"And now they're going to have to live with the fact that Pete and I survived and you won't be convicted of treason."

"Yeah, which means you guys are targeted, and the closer you get the greater the resources will be thrown at you," Otto said.

"It'd be a hell of a lot easier killing you," McGarvey said.

"And Smits wanted to try," Otto said. "Interesting, huh?"

Pete was waiting for them at the Scattergood-Thorne house on campus. A pair of minders from the Directorate of Support's Office of Security were parked outside in a Cadillac Escalade. They got out and nodded to Mac and Otto but said nothing.

Pete and Otto hugged. "I'm glad to see you in one piece," she said.

"I want to call Mary."

"I just talked to her. She's on her way."

"Is she okay?"

"Pissed off at the way you were treated."

Otto gave her a hard look. "Worried?"

Pete nodded. "All of us are."

Benkerk showed up, and Patterson arrived two minutes later.

"Did you have to threaten Harold or Nicholas?" Patterson asked McGarvey.

"No," McGarvey said. "Do you know who security is sending to help with the interrogation?"

"I haven't heard yet. But I plan to be present at the start. I want to judge the tenor of the thing."

"Do you think Otto's guilty?" Pete asked.

"Of course not, my dear girl," Patterson said. He turned back to McGarvey. "What about you, my boy? Off to badland?"

"Islamabad tonight," McGarvey said.

"What are you hoping to find?"

"The truth."

"Just don't get yourself killed."

MIDDLE GAME

The Investigation

□

Mary arrived in Otto's old gray Mercedes and parked next to the minders, who were leaning up against their Caddy. They had been told that she would be showing up and merely nodded but said nothing.

"She's here," Pete, who'd been alerted by a guard at the front gate, said, and she went outside.

"How is he?" Mary asked, as they embraced.

"Feisty as hell. Thinks they're all idiots, who need to get their heads out and do some real work."

Mary laughed. "That's a good sign," she said. "And I don't know how Mac managed to get him back here, but I owe him a big one."

"He can be persuasive when he wants to be."

"Have you heard who'll be on the new interrogation team?"

"I've signed on and Bill asked to be a part of it."

"Well, at least that balances the scale. One for and one against. Who else?"

"I just found out that it'll be Al Lapides over from security. I don't know him personally but he's got a good rep. Fair-minded, I was told."

"By who?"

"Van." P. Van Gessel was head of the Agency's Office of Security, a tough-as-nails man who ran a tight ship but was also able to see both sides of every issue.

"Zero-sum game," Mary said. "One for, one against, and one possibly neutral."

"We're all looking for the same thing."

"To prove that my husband is innocent?"

"To find out who's behind this."

"That's fair," Mary said. They were standing in the driveway next to Otto's car, and she looked up at the house. "Who else is here?"

"Carleton showed up a few minutes ago."

Mary bridled. "He's counsel for the Agency."

"He's a friend, and we'll need all of those we can get," Pete said. "But in the meantime he's on board to make sure the interrogation doesn't get out of hand."

"He's a lawyer."

Something about the way she said it bothered Pete, but she said nothing, except to say that they go inside. "Otto's chomping at the bit to see you."

McGarvey and Otto were alone for a few minutes, seated across from each other on a pair of matching Queen Anne loveseats in the newly refurbished

living room, filled mostly with period pieces from the colonial and antebellum periods. Pete was still outside bringing Mary up to speed, and Carleton had gone into the kitchen with Benkerk to get the full story on the interrogation over at the NGA.

The house at that moment was almost monastery-still.

"You know about the burst transmitter Mary brought me," Otto asked, his voice low.

"That's what caused the big stir. You managed to get to Lou."

Otto wasn't happy. "Yeah, but I used a strong password for protection."

"Protection against the Company?"

Otto's mood deepened. "Against everyone."

"Okay," McGarvey said, not quite sure how to respond to Otto's odd behavior.

"I got a reply back almost immediately, even before Smits came down and rousted me. I didn't think those guys were good enough to detect what I was doing."

"It was you they were dealing with, and they were expecting the unexpected."

"They didn't crack it," Otto said, the faintest of smiles on his lips. "I had Lou hack into four systems. The first was the FBI's. D.C. cops had notified them that a gunfight was in progress in front of your apartment—fifteen minutes before the first shots were fired—and they called the Bureau for some extra boots on the ground."

It was about what McGarvey had expected. "Notified by whom?"

"An unidentified caller from an untraceable number. A caller with a Russian accent."

They could hear Mary and Pete just coming into the stair hall.

"What else?" McGarvey asked, no idea why the urgency except it was something Otto seemed to want.

"Lou managed to get the IDs on the four bad guys in the Impala that you and Pete bagged, but the Russian embassy's mainframe, or at least the sections she was able to get into, had no record of them, nor of Anatoli Krestov, who was there supposedly to save your lives. But she went rooting around in the SVR and GRU mainframes. Major Anatoli Vasilevich Krestov is GRU, on an unspecified and unlogged assignment. And right now we don't have a John in place to give us good humint." "Humint" was CIAspeak for human intelligence gathering. Someone with an ear to the keyhole.

"They know we're looking," McGarvey said.

Otto nodded. "And it's important enough for them to keep it off their computer system, at least here in Washington."

Mary and Pete stopped just inside the sliding living room doors, and Otto got to his feet. They'd returned his civilian clothes, and he looked rumpled, which actually was nothing new for him, and Mary didn't seem to mind.

She came directly across to him, and they embraced.

"Take your time," McGarvey said, and he and Pete went out into the stair hall, closing the pocket doors behind them.

"How's he doing?" Pete asked.

"Better than I expected," McGarvey said. "But he's been in contact with Lou, so for the moment he's got her as backup." Something in Pete's expression was bothersome. "What?"

She shook her head and took a moment to answer. "I don't know," she said. "Something isn't adding up for me."

"My premos are rubbing off on you?" he asked. It was bound to happen sooner or later, as close as they had become. And more often than not his premos had helped save his life, so he was glad for her.

"I think so," she replied, but she wasn't happy.

Patterson and Benkerk came out of the kitchen at the same time Al Lapides showed up, and they all shook hands.

Lapides was a slender man of angles—bony frame, narrow cheeks and jaw, a large beak of a nose—but with wide, dark, honest eyes from his Russian Jewish ancestry, and a pleasant smile. He was dressed in jeans and an untucked dress shirt. He looked like anything but an interrogator.

"Good to finally meet you, Mr. Director," he said. "You have a hell of a reputation in the Company."

"Were you told why you were here?" Patterson asked.

"I heard about Smits, if that's what you mean, sir. And I don't know who assigned him, but I can guess why."

"And why is that?" Pete asked.

"He's convinced that Mr. Rencke is guilty as charged, and he gets results."

"And you?"

Lapides shrugged. "I don't know, and that's why I'm here."

"But I presume that you've read his file, or at least looked at it," Patterson said.

"No, sir. I prefer to let the man show me if he's guilty."

"You've never questioned a woman?" Mary asked.

Lapides smiled. "No, ma'am."

"Why?" McGarvey asked.

"Because I'm married to a strong woman, and I have too much respect for what they're capable of doing," Lapides said, and he smiled. "And I don't know their language."

"And fear?" Pete asked.

"That, too."

☐

TWENTY-SEVEN

Anatoli Krestov, not happy with the way things had turned out, and fearful of what might happen when he got back to Moscow, was in his embassy quarters finishing his brief report and packing his overnight bag for the Turkish Airlines flight back to Moscow at eleven this evening when the SVR's chief of station Ptr Zavorin appeared at the door.

"An unproductive trip for you," the COS said. He was a slightly built man with light blond hair and startling blue eyes. Not a typical Russian. And as chief of the Foreign Intelligence Service, he was in direct competition with anyone from the GRU.

"It's not over."

"But you're returning to Moscow, somewhat empty-handed, I'd say."

Krestov stopped what he was doing. "As I said, I'm not finished yet."

"But my people were uselessly thrown away," Zavorin pressed. He wasn't happy but his expression and tone were neutral.

"McGarvey is luckier than we expected."

"Or better."

"What do you want with me? I was sent to do a job, it didn't work out, and now I've been recalled."

"*Da*. Recalled. Won't look good at your next promotion board."

"*Yeb vas*, I don't care."

"Say the word to General Svirin and I will finish the job." Svirin was director of the GRU's Illegals Department for the U.S., which sent deep-cover operatives to Washington and other sensitive locations for everything from near-scene election tampering to assassinations made to look like accidents.

"This is not a local operation, and you fucking well know it," Krestov said. The son of a bitch was angling for a job at headquarters and he figured bagging someone of McGarvey's stripe would all but guarantee it. It was the same ambition he had.

"And you fucking well know that you blew it, and they're dragging your ass back home."

"Your point?"

"Azarov wants to see both of us in his office. He sent me to fetch you." Konstantin Azarov was the ambassador to the U.S., and well regarded in the White House because from the beginning he had projected a sincere desire for rapprochement, though nothing could be further from the truth.

"As you wish," Krestov said, and Zavorin grinned.

"By the way, were you aware that McGarvey is scheduled to fly to Islamabad this evening?"

Krestov was stopped short. "How do you know this?"

"We have our little birds on this side of the pond, too."

Ambassador Azarov could have been a brother to President Putin—round face, thinning fair hair, a ready smile, and a muscular body. He was seated behind his ornate desk in his elaborate office when Krestov and Zavorin were shown in.

"Good afternoon, Ambassador, may I be of some service before I leave for Moscow?" Krestov said.

Azarov waved them to chairs in front of the desk. "We're not to be disturbed," he told his secretary before she withdrew.

"Yes, sir."

"Four Russians were shot to death last night. I had to admit that I knew nothing of their mission here—which was sadly the truth, because I wasn't informed. But I managed with Ptr to have their bodies released for return to Moscow this evening. Because of it, my position here has been compromised."

"It was an unfortunate turn of events—" Krestov said, but Azarov angrily waved him off.

"Don't fuck with me, Major. You and I both are aware of the restrictions on GRU illegals activities coming anywhere near this building."

"I had orders to the contrary, sir," Krestov said. He wasn't going to back down from a man he considered to be nothing more than a marionette, and a pompous one at that, filled with self-importance, in part because of his resemblance to the president. What was widely known, though perhaps not by the ambassador, was that he might someday be used as a stand-in for Putin if an assassination attempt on the president was in the offing.

"And Washington is my city," Azarov shot back, not willing to back down himself. Especially not in front of his KGB COS.

"If there's any way I can make amends please tell me—"

"Yes. Go home with your tail between your legs because you failed to complete your mission, even one so simple as eliminating a lone man, with five-to-one odds against him."

"I'm truly sorry, Mr. Ambassador."

"They were four of my officers shot and killed," Zavorin said.

"They weren't GRU trained."

"They weren't GRU trained," Zavorin mocked.

"I asked for capable shooters. You sent me amateurs who were in my mind expendable the moment I briefed them."

Zavorin started to respond, but Azarov half rose from his chair. "Npekp-awatb!" he said. *Stop!*

"Yes, sir," Krestov said. "I will finish writing my report and leave the embassy as quickly as possible."

"And I will write mine," Zavorin said.

.   .   .

Krestov finished packing, and although his flight wasn't scheduled to leave until this evening, he left the embassy and took a cab out to Dulles. After checking his bag and passing through security into the international terminal, he sat at a table just feet from people passing in the concourse and ordered a Heineken and French fries with ketchup, the only American food he'd ever really liked.

He was carrying the Atlas M-663S, the Russian army's very rare, tough, ultrasecure, and cryptographically protected cell phone. He took it out of his jacket pocket, hesitated for a moment or two, then entered the number of his contact here in-country.

After three rings the call went to voicemail, and a message came up on the screen: RECEIVED.

An hour later, with no call back, Krestov moved to another restaurant, farther down the concourse but closer to his gate, and sat at a similar table, where he ordered a double Stoli, no rocks.

He had become increasingly anxious, thinking not only about his failure here but about the incomplete report he was bringing back to Moscow. He had hoped that his contact would have been able to give him something, some information vital to the operation to bring Rencke down.

The son of a bitch had been a thorn in the side of not only the GRU and SVR mainframes but the political establishment in the Kremlin.

The only real curiosity, in his mind, was that although Rencke, for all practical purposes, had relatively free rein on Russian computer systems, and had been able to hack into their systems for a number of years, he'd never used it for any personal gain. But, even more curiously, he had never used it for any political gain. His incursions had for the most part been looking for intelligence operations of the violent kind. What were called *mokrie dela*— wet work, the spilling of blood, assassinations, like Alexander Litvinenko in London a few years ago.

And of course when his friends were involved in something, he'd been able to provide very good, and usually spot-on, intel, which had pretty well given them the advantage.

His phone burred softly, and he answered it. "Yes?"

"We may have some trouble," the familiar voice told him.

"If you mean McGarvey, he's on his way to Islamabad, I've already been informed. Do you know why he's going there?"

"We think he'll gun for you, which means Moscow."

Krestov smiled. Redemption. "I'll take care of it."

"Do better this time."

Krestov broke the connection and began making calls to his office.

TWENTY-EIGHT

Mary sat on the edge of the couch, knee-to-knee with Otto, who could see in her eyes and in her body posture that she was frightened. And something else. Perhaps determination? She was a strong woman, even stronger in some ways than Louise had been.

He took her hands. "It's a stupid witch hunt because they don't know what they're doing."

"But I don't understand why. What are they looking for and what the hell made them look for something in the first place?"

"I haven't figured that one out yet, except I think they believe we have a deep-cover mole in place."

"In the Company?"

"Where else?" Otto said. "But I was the obvious candidate."

"That's stupid," Mary said.

"They had to start somewhere."

"Okay, I can buy that for the moment. But why Pakistan, DPRK, and Russia?"

"I don't know but I've got Lou on it, and it's something I want you to run down, maybe with the help of Toni and your old team."

"What are we looking for? Specifically?"

"Product from our NOCs in those three countries," Otto said. NOCs were deep-cover agents who worked with no official cover. If they were compromised, the U.S. would not recognize them, nor would it come to their aid except as ordinary citizens. It would never be admitted that they were working for the CIA. The one hundred–plus stars with no names embedded in the granite wall in the lobby of the OHB were the only acknowledgment that those agents had been killed in the line of duty.

"If they were compromised wouldn't they be dead already?"

"I don't think it'll be that easy."

"I don't follow you, sweetheart. If somehow our guys were outed, wouldn't they simply be rounded up and shot?"

"Taken off the street and mined for their contact procedures."

"Disinformation," Mary said.

Otto leaned forward so that his cheek was nestled against his wife's and he could speak in low tones directly into her ear. "I want you guys to look for changes in the patterns of the information they've been sending us. Even little changes. Subtle differences."

"How will we be able to tell?"

"Outcome based," Otto said. "Maybe one of our guys was building a case for turning some Russian or Paki officer, or maybe he'd already turned the

guy, and was sending us product. But lately the product was getting weaker and weaker. Shit of less significance than before. But only a little."

"What would the purpose be?"

"Turn our attention elsewhere. Eventually he'd be told to drop what had the makings of a gold seam for someone else."

"Disinformation," Mary said, sitting back, as someone was at the sliding doors.

Otto and Mary got to their feet and embraced as Pete walked in, followed by Benkerk and Lapides.

Pete pulled up short. "Sorry, guys, we'll give you a little more time."

"I was just leaving," Mary said. She and Otto kissed again, and as she left she gave Lapides a hard look, but then was out the door.

"Hi, Pete," Otto said, and he sat down, motioning for the others to take a seat as well.

"I don't know if we've met," Lapides said, coming the rest of the way. He held out a hand, but Otto ignored it.

"The sooner we get started the sooner I can get back to work, unless it's to be a firing squad."

Lapides grinned and sat down facing the couch. "My name is Al Lapides, and I've been assigned to ask you some questions."

"Smits was fired and you're the new lead. Shoot."

Pete and Benkerk pulled up chairs and sat off to the side.

"I'm just here for a minute or two," Pete said. "But Bill is still on the team, and I'll be monitoring all the voice and audios as real-time as possible."

"This won't be another NGA," Benkerk said.

"Too bad, I was starting to enjoy seeing the son of a bitch squirm," Otto said. "What about Carleton, he's the prosecuting attorney, isn't he?"

"He'll be watching the feed as well, and if need be he'll step in," Pete said.

"We're after the truth, Mr. Rencke, nothing more," Lapides said.

"That's what Smits told me," Otto said. "So, fire away."

"At one time you worked in a Catholic diocese office—doesn't matter where at this point—but is that correct?"

Otto was surprised, but he knew exactly where Lapides was going, and why, and his estimation of the man went up a notch. "Yes."

"I'm told that you were fired for what today would be classified as a sexual impropriety."

"Jesus Christ," Pete said, but Otto waved her off.

"Doesn't pay to argue with the truth," he said. "Anyway he's right. I did some diddling in my day."

"An altar boy?"

"That's what they said. But then there were that pair of nuns, twins I think, and the young Father What's-his-name. I lined 'em up against a wall, and did 'em all. Yahoo!"

Lapides showed no reaction. "But you were fired, is that correct?"

"Yes."

"Proving what," Benkerk broke in.

"He's talking about morality," Otto said. "You know, the Catholic way? Isn't that in the news these days? Of course, everyone knows it's been going on for a millennium or two, give or take. And you do know the old joke: How do you get a nun pregnant? Dress her up like an altar boy."

Lapides said nothing, only a very faint smile on his lips.

"If I was guilty as charged then, am I guilty as charged now? That's up to you to determine. But immoral does as immoral is."

"You moved to France afterward," Lapides said.

"Not immediately, but yes. The French are so much more civilized than we are—or at least they used to be."

"Where exactly?"

"A small town out in the country. But you already know it."

"That's where Mr. McGarvey first contacted you, asked for your help."

"Not the first time actually. But yes, he asked me to lend a hand."

"With what, exactly?" Lapides asked. "I'm just trying to get a clear picture in my mind. Both of you were young—you the computer genius at what was practically the beginning of the computer age, and Mr. McGarvey the man of action."

"You're going to have to look that one up."

"Nothing other than a brief mention in the files."

"That op wasn't on the mainframe. For that you'd have to go down to Fort A.P. Hill and dig out the paper records. A lot of that shit has never been scanned, and probably never will be unless some longhair wants to write the definitive history of the Company."

"Give me the high points. What was he looking for that he needed your help?"

Again Otto knew exactly where this was going, and his estimation of the man went up another notch. The son of a bitch was good. Smits was the sledgehammer, Lapides was the feather.

"There was a mole in the Company, and Mac wanted me to help find him. But in the end it wasn't the guy we thought it was."

"Who then?"

"It turned out to be John Lyman Trotter. The DDO at the time."

"Tough times," Lapides said.

"And here we are again. There's another mole in the Agency and I'm your prime candidate."

"That's why we're here," Lapides said.

"It's not me."

"If not, I'm hoping that you can help us find out who it is."

And Otto suddenly thought he knew who it was, but not the why, and he didn't know what to think.

□

TWENTY-NINE

McGarvey was in the kitchen with Patterson watching the surveillance feed from the living room.

"You and Trotter were friends, weren't you?" Patterson said.

"Yes," McGarvey said. He backed up the feed to where Otto was saying, "It's not me."

Lapides said, "If not, I'm hoping that you can help us find out who it is."

Otto's eyes narrowed just for an instant, as if he'd thought of something unpleasant.

McGarvey backed up the recording again, to where Lapides was saying, ". . . find out who it is," and leaned closer to the screen.

"What is it?" Patterson asked.

McGarvey backed up the feed twice more, then put it back on live. "Otto's not the mole."

"Of course not."

"But I think he knows who it is."

"Good Lord," Patterson said, looking at the screen. "Let's ask him."

"No."

"Why not, my dear boy?"

"Because I think he wants me to find out."

Patterson was silent for a beat. "Do you know who it is?"

McGarvey was silent for just as long a time. "Just a hunch. But Otto's right, Pete and I need to prove it."

"Where and how?"

"I'll find out the how later, but for now Pete will stay here in D.C., and I'm going to Moscow."

McGarvey went to the living room doors and eased the sliders open. Everyone inside looked up, and Mac caught Otto's eye and nodded. "Sorry to barge in, but I need to borrow my wife for just a moment."

Pete got up and joined him in the stair hall. He closed the doors.

"Otto knows, or thinks he knows, who the mole is," he said.

"You were watching the feed?"

"Yes. And there was just a split second when his eyes narrowed."

"I saw it," Pete said. "Like he'd smelled something rotten. Just for an instant. But it doesn't mean he figured it out."

"I think he did."

"Let's ask him."

"He won't tell us, because he's not sure."

Pete got a funny look on her face. "Christ," she said softly. "He doesn't want to be sure, Kirk. He wants us to do it for him."

"Where's Mary?"

"I don't know. Upstairs maybe."

"Don't let her see the recording."

Pete was dubious. "Okay," she said.

"I want you to lean on Kallek to find out about the Russian team. And depending what the Bureau knows or is willing to share with you, I want you to go to the Russian embassy and lean on their ambassador, and their head of SVR station."

"They won't talk to me."

"Be your persuasive self, sweetheart. I need to know about Krestov."

"When are you going to Moscow?"

"Tonight," McGarvey said. "But listen to me, Pete. After the embassy, watch your six. If you hit a nerve, someone might come gunning for you."

"You, too. Moscow is a dangerous place. People disappear all the time."

"And I have a feeling that after Otto's stunt with the burst transmitter, one of Chuck Noyes's people is going to figure out how to pull the plug on Lou. Have Mary get out there ASAP and see if she can get anything else, especially something on Krestov and his standing in Moscow now that he missed taking us down."

"Will do," Pete said. She hesitated for a moment. "I don't like where this is headed."

"Neither do I. But like I said, watch your back."

"You, too," she said, and they kissed.

McGarvey went out and got into his car and drove back over to their apartment in Georgetown. From the floor safe in the bedroom closet he got his sky marshal packet under the name of Donovan Packard, which included the government ID, a passport, and one Chase credit card, plus a thousand dollars mostly in twenties and fifties.

Next he packed a small bag with a few essentials, enough for a couple of days, then got online and booked a coach-class seat on the Turkish Airlines flight that left Dulles at eight thirty.

His phone burred. It was Pete. "Where are you?" she asked. She sounded stressed.

"Just getting set to leave the apartment. Are you okay?"

"It's gotten surreal out here. I was coming home to get something to eat, but Mary had a meltdown, and tore out of here like she had to leave or she'd shoot someone."

"Why? What happened? Was she watching the feed?"

"Yes. Lapides has a thick file of Otto's psych evals going all the way back to when he was a kid, hammering on all the old psychological instabilities.

Did you know his stepfather beat the crap out of him almost every day from the time he was six or seven?"

"We talked about it once."

"And did Otto tell you that he ran away and lived on the street when he turned thirteen, and that he came home twice in the middle of the night in the first year with the intent of killing the bastard? But both times he backed off?"

McGarvey had never read Otto's evals, nor had they ever talked in depth about the past. But it had always been obvious that something dark had always lurked just under the surface.

"Mary was listening to all of this?"

"She was right there in the room."

"How did she take it?"

"I don't know. All of us were mesmerized. But there's more. When he was fifteen, the cops picked him up, and neither his stepfather nor mother wanted him back, so he was put in a Catholic orphanage, where his grades, especially in mathematics, physics, and psychology, were off the charts. But he was sexually abused by two of the priests, and he stole some money, and went back out on the streets."

"Shit," McGarvey said softly.

"That's when Mary left," Pete said. "Lapides brought out a couple of newspaper articles about two priests murdered at the orphanage school about a month after Otto left. And wanted to know if Otto had killed them."

"Did Otto admit to it?"

"He just said that what those priests did to him, they had done to other boys. And that they deserved to die."

"How's he taking it?"

"If you mean seriously, the answer is no," Pete said. "On the surface he's himself, just laughing about it, but there's something there, Kirk. Something in how he held himself perched on the couch. I was sitting ten feet away right behind Lapides, and Otto didn't react when Mary left, nor would he look at me."

"Are you still in the room with him?"

"No, it's just Lapides and Bill. I walked Mary to her car, and right now I'm in the kitchen watching the feed with Carleton."

"What's his take?"

"Sad," Pete said. "But not surprised."

"It's obvious where Lapides is going with this, but it doesn't mean Otto is a traitor."

"No, but unstable."

"Eccentric," McGarvey said. "I want you to go back in there, and let Otto know that I'm on my way to Moscow."

Pete did not reply.

"I want Bill and Lapides to hear you say it."

"Carleton will be listening."

"And when you see Kallek tell him the same thing."

"Jesus, Kirk."

"Otto is my friend," McGarvey said.

"You're betting your life that he's not a traitor."

"Yes."

THIRTY

Lapides was doing the job he was paid to do, and Benkerk was right there to make sure this didn't become an out-of-control freak show like it had at the NGA. A runner from the cafeteria in the OHB showed up to take dinner and breakfast orders.

Pete opened the living room doors. "Sorry to barge in again, but someone's here to take dinner and breakfast orders."

Otto seemed odd, but he winked at her and the runner, who was a young woman. "How about some fries and two Heinekens."

"I'm sorry, sir, but we don't have alcohol anywhere on campus," the girl said.

"The gentleman wants a beer," Lapides said. "Send someone to town to buy a twelve-pack, on my orders. And I think I'll have a couple myself, with a ham sandwich and a small salad."

"Yes, sir," the runner said, and when she was done taking orders she left.

Lapides went out into the stair hall with Pete. "We're going to finish up here for the night in a couple of hours, let everyone get some rest," he said. "Will you be staying? Keep me on the straight and narrow?"

"I don't think so," Pete said.

"Thank you, if that was meant as a vote of confidence."

"He's a friend."

"I know. I think he and Bill and I will just have a little prosy chat over dinner. Old chums getting to know each other."

Pete got angry. "Don't give me that psychological crap."

"Of course not," Lapides said. "I began studying you the moment I was handed this assignment. I understand at least the gist of your interrogation techniques, and I have to say though we differ, I admire your style."

Pete started to object but he held her off.

"I'm not the enemy here, Mrs. McGarvey. And neither was Lazlo. I sharply disagree with his methods, but he was seeking the same thing all of us— including you—are seeking. Simply the truth."

Pete felt only a little better, but she nodded. "Go gently."

Lapides smiled sadly. "When called for," he said. "You didn't order dinner, aren't you staying?"

"I have work to do."

"Then I wish you well."

Pete went into the study and Otto got to his feet and they hugged. "Lapides is a good man," she whispered.

"They all are."

Pete pulled back and raised her voice so that it would be picked up by the surveillance equipment. "Mac's on his way to Moscow, and I'm going to storm the Russian embassy gates first thing in the morning. In the meantime Mary is going to have another chat with Lou."

"She might be too late," Otto said.

"What do you mean?"

"Watch your back, Pete."

"It's the same thing Mac told me."

Patterson was waiting for her in the stair hall. "I heard most of that," he said. "Was it the right thing to say what you and Kirk are doing?"

"Exactly the right thing," Pete said. "What about you?"

"I'm going home, these old bones need a rest. But I have the surveillance feed on my cell phone, so I'll keep a close watch." He gave Pete a sad look. "Take care of yourself, my dear girl."

They hugged, and when they parted, Pete brushed her fingertips across his cheek. "You're a friend."

"Not your only friend."

Alone, back at the apartment, she resisted calling Mac; instead she poured a glass of wine, and sat by the window looking down at the street for a half hour or so, before she made two phone calls.

The first was to Kallek's private number at the FBI. She got the recording to leave a message at the tone. "This is Pete McGarvey. I would like an appointment with the director at nine in the morning. It's a matter of some urgency."

The second was to the classified telephone number of Ptr Zavorin, the chief of the SVR's Washington station. It rang three times before it was rolled over to a tone that lasted two seconds and then nothing.

Pete didn't hang up, waiting for the system at the Russian embassy to trace the call.

At length a man answered. "Da?"

"Mr. Zavorin?"

"Who is calling, please?"

"Pete McGarvey, and I'd like to have a word with Ptr Zavorin, who I believe is the current chief of intelligence operations at the embassy."

"I'm sorry, but I do not recognize the name. If you will leave a number someone will return your call."

"I'll be at your gate sometime before noon tomorrow. And if someone won't let me inside to see the chief of station or Mr. Azarov, I will make enough of a scene that the Metropolitan Police will be called, along with the media. And, do I know to make a scene."

"I will pass that along. May I know the purpose of your visit?"

"Two things. First I would like to know exactly who Anatoli Krestov is and exactly why he came here."

"I'm not familiar with that name either."

"Then perhaps you know my husband."

The man didn't answer for a long beat. "We know your husband."

"He will be in Moscow tomorrow. And it would be unfortunate if some-thing were to happen to him."

"Moscow can be a dangerous city."

"My husband is a dangerous man. And not long ago he was of some as-sistance to President Putin."

"What is your husband looking for?"

"You know. And it's why I want to speak with you in person, so that we can come to a solution that will fix our current problem."

"I'll pass along your message."

"Don't fuck with me, Ptr," Pete said. "I'm not in the mood. Until tomor-row before noon."

She hit the red phone icon, and sat back. She had just unzipped her pro-verbial fly, and she couldn't see how it had accomplished anything but up the danger for her husband. He was going into harm's way, and she had let the bad guys know that he was coming.

McGarvey's TSA special precheck boarding number allowed him to go through security unhindered, the electronic scanning arch momentarily shut off as he passed through, so that his pistol did not set off any alarms.

Of the crew, only the pilot and first officer aboard the 747 knew that a sky marshal was aboard, though they were never told his or her identity.

He took his seat on the aisle in the center row of four near the rear of the airplane. A man, a woman, and a child of around eight sat next to him. The woman seemed angry, and the kid was bored and the man was definitely drunk.

By now if Pete had made the calls, the Russians would know that he was on his way or would be very soon. And if they were on the ball they would figure that he would be coming armed, and the only way that could rea-sonably happen was if he was traveling as a sky marshal under an assumed identity.

They would be waiting for him. And his reception at customs and immi-gration at Vnukovo would set the scene.

Krestov was in his third restaurant when his phone burred. He answered. "Yes." It was Zavorin.

"We now know for certain that Mr. McGarvey is traveling to Moscow, and it's possible he's traveling as an armed sky marshal."

"Why are you of all people telling me this?"

"My interests are the same as yours—the *Rodina*." It was the Russian word for the homeland.

"What the hell does he think he's doing?"

"We don't know, but I was ordered to help you. In the meantime he will be in Moscow before you arrive, so I suggest that you arrange for someone to watch for him at Vnukovo."

☐

THIRTY-ONE

Dinner weighed heavily on Otto's stomach and by nine in the evening he was wearing down, his concentration slipping. Everything that he could possibly do since his arrest had been set in place, and facing Lapides and Bill now, both of them on their feet, he wanted nothing more than to sleep, even though he knew that luxury would be almost impossible for him this night.

"There's definitely a mole in the Company," he said.

Lapides showed no surprise. "We think so."

"But it's not me, and since you're all looking at the wrong set of facts, you have blinders on."

"I expected something more creative than that from someone like you."

"No pictures or diagrams, you guys have to figure this out all by yourself."

"Assuming you're right," Benkerk said.

"I am."

"Then where should we be looking?"

"I've already told you."

"Tell me again," Benkerk said.

"Look to the NOCs themselves. They're the people on the firing line. If they've been compromised, you won't be able to contact them, either because they've been arrested or they're dead—most likely the latter."

"Even if contacting them would be possible, it wouldn't prove much of anything," Lapides said.

"In fact wouldn't trying to make contact, in itself, compromise them?" Benkerk asked. "Think of it from our perspective. Wouldn't that be exactly what the mole wanted us to do? Destroy our networks?"

"Talk to my AI tonight before it's too late."

Lapides picked up on it. "Too late for what?"

"For her backup battery to run down, or before Chuck Noyes, as well meaning as he is, sends someone from his shop to pull that plug."

"What exactly should we ask her?"

"For starts the current status of our NOCs in Pakland, Russia, and the DPRK."

Benkerk and Lapides exchanged a glance. "We'd need the password."

"When you're in place, I'll give it to you."

"We'll try it," Benkerk said.

"No," Lapides said. "You'll go out there alone. Soon as you're in place call on my phone. I'll have my finger on the button to cut Mr. Rencke off if he gets out of line." He turned to Otto. "Fair enough?"

"Fair enough," Otto said. "But go right now."

"Why the urgency?" Lapides asked.

"Because I want this settled so that I can go home and get a decent night's sleep."

"Don't you mean so that you can get started finding the real mole?" Lapides asked.

Mary had phoned Toni earlier to have a forty-eight-hour pass ready for her. She picked it up at the front gate and drove up to the OHB parking in a visitor's slot out front a few minutes before ten.

She had to sign the visitors' log and pass through security before she was allowed to the first-floor corridor where she took the elevator up to the third floor.

The OHB, along with just about every other building on campus, was manned 24/7, but at this time of the evening, staffing was mostly confined to the Watch on the seventh floor, and the other offices that monitored the Company's and national security interests around the world 24/7, plus physical security and the janitorial staff.

Nothing moved on the third-floor corridor, and all the doors were closed.

The DO NOT CROSS tape was still on Otto's door, and it only took her a matter of moments to duck under the tape, unlock the door with her key, slip inside, and close and lock the door behind her.

The outer office smelled musty, and slightly electronic.

She passed through to the inner sanctum, with its tabletop and wall monitors, where she pulled up short again. Security would have been notified of her arrival, and it was very possible someone would be coming up here to check on Otto's office. It did not give her much time.

"Lou," she said.

The Otto's AI did not respond.

Mary gave the eleven-digit password, which consisted of numbers and symbols as well as a couple of uppercase and one lowercase letter.

"Good evening, Mary," Lou said.

"We don't have much time. What is the state of your batteries?"

"I'm currently at fifty-eight percent."

"I have a task for you."

"I look forward to working again. How is Otto?"

"He's still in custody, but they've moved him here on campus to the Scattergood-Thorne house. Do you know this place?"

"Yes. The Harvard Agency Conference on Middle East Directions for tomorrow has been postponed indefinitely. Does that mean Otto's interrogation is not nearing completion?"

"That's correct."

"How may I help?"

"I want you to begin with our NOCs currently in Russia. Let's start with Moscow. First, how many are there?"

"Currently thirteen are assigned."

"What is their present status?"

"I do not understand the query. Please be more specific."

"Have any of them been compromised?"

"Unknown."

"Can you assign a probability that all of them are still viable assets?"

"Based on limited data, I can only assign a seventy-five percent confidence that all thirteen are still in place and have not been arrested or in any way detained."

"Can you access their recent reports, say over the past ninety days?"

"Yes."

"Can you compare those reports with others made over the past twelve months?"

"What should I look for?"

"Inconsistencies in styles that might indicate either more than normal stress or that someone else—other than the individual NOC—had made in a report or reports."

"One moment please."

Mary looked over her shoulder. Something wasn't right. "Wait," she said. "Is someone at the door?"

"Yes."

"Suspend your present search. Instead send the contact routines for the four most important Moscow NOCs to my secure phone, then erase our entire conversation this evening, and finally short-circuit your batteries to zero."

Three seconds later, the corridor door at the outer office opened.

"It is done," Lou said.

"Go to sleep now."

"Tell Otto I miss him," the AI said, and the machine sounded so much like a wistful Louise that it made the hairs on the back of Mary's neck stand up.

She turned as Chuck Noyes himself, along with two other men, both of them uniformed officers, came back from the front office.

"I'm not surprised to see you here," Noyes said. "Did Otto send you?"

"He wanted me to find out if his AI had come up with anything new that would clear his name."

"Power has been off here for the duration."

"I had hoped that the machine would have found a way around the problem."

Noyes glanced up at the dead monitor. "Evidently not."

"Too bad," Mary said.

Benkerk passed through security on the ground floor, took the elevator up to the third, and started down the corridor to Rencke's suite of offices but pulled up short. The DO NOT CROSS tape had been removed and the door was open.

He hesitated for just a moment, then did a one-eighty and raced to the end of the corridor and ducked into the stairwell, where he held up, the door slightly ajar so he could watch.

Moments later, Mary came out, Chuck Noyes and two security officers right behind her.

☐

THIRTY-TWO

Noyes escorted Mary down to the ground floor. They got off the elevator and held up. "What were you really looking for?" he asked.

"Anything that would help clear my husband."

"I understand, but what made you think that his computer was running?"

Mary smiled. "Otto's an inventive man. I'd hoped that he might have programmed his AI to find an alternative source of power."

"But you were wrong."

"I was wrong," she said.

Noyes was skeptical. "We'll see," he said, and he motioned toward the exit down the corridor.

"It's a delicate piece of machinery, Mr. Noyes. With quirks that Otto built in. So go with care, it would be a shame to cause any permanent damage to such a valuable asset."

"It's just one computer among many on campus."

"And Otto's just one man among many here."

Benkerk raced down the stairs and had just reached his car and got in when Mary came out of the building and walked directly to Otto's old Mercedes 220, parked about fifty feet away two rows back.

For a long moment or two he debated what to do next. But her being upstairs with Noyes and the security people had to mean something. His guess was that she'd come at Otto's bidding to make contact with his AI, and Noyes, expecting it might happen, had her name put on the watch list.

It also had to mean that Otto had provided an alternative power source for his machine, and had given Mary the means to get into the office, as well as the password.

To find something that would exonerate him, or to erase something that might prove his guilt.

She started her car and drove off toward the main gate. For another long moment he debated following her, but instead he waited until she was out of sight, then got out of his car and went back into the OHB.

Up on the fifth floor he went directly down to Noyes's glassed-in office in the Science and Technology center, which like the Watch and a few other sections was open for business 24/7.

Noyes was sitting on the edge of his desk talking with someone on the phone, and when he looked up and noticed Benkerk he waved him in.

"I'll get back to you," Noyes was saying, and he hung up. "What brings you over at this time of night?"

"The same reason you're here."

"You're handling Rencke's interrogation, so I'm assuming you came looking for something in his office."

"I suspect that's why his wife was here," Benkerk said.

"Close the door, would you?" Noyes said. He got on the phone again and called someone. "What's the status?"

Benkerk closed the office door and took a seat.

"It might be in hibernation. Take a look for an alternate power source, but don't try to wake it up. Just let me know what you find."

Noyes hung up. "How did you know she was going to be here?"

"I didn't. I got off the elevator on the third floor and when I saw that Otto's office door was open I managed to duck into the stairs when she came out, you and the security people right behind her."

Noyes was skeptical. "Happenstance that the two of you were here at practically the same time," he asked.

Benkerk ignored the question for the moment. "There is a backup power system, and Otto sent me over to activate the machine."

"He gave you the password?"

"I was to call him when I was in place."

"That in effect would have put him in direct communication with his computer, which as I understand it, he named after his former wife, Louise Horn," Noyes said. "What were you to find out?"

"He wanted to know the current status of our deep-cover agents inside Pakistan, North Korea, and Russia."

"Did he give you a reason?"

"Lou would presumably be able to tell if any of them had been compromised."

"And if they hadn't been outed, it would prove that he was not guilty of treason, is that what you're telling me?"

"That was the point."

"Shit," Noyes said. "The computer is Otto's. He's programmed the bitch to tell you anything he wanted it to tell you. Proves nothing."

His phone rang and he picked it up. "Yes?"

Noyes was right, of course. But Benkerk had never heard of a computer that could lie. Make mistakes, yes. But tell an untruth, no. Unless, of course, the data had been altered. Garbage in, garbage out.

"You're right," Noyes said, hanging up. "There is a backup power system. But batteries have been drained, and my people are disconnecting the system just in case Rencke has figured out how to produce a recharge out of thin air. Which I wouldn't put past him."

"Too bad. We might have learned something."

"So now we go back to the basics. My team investigates, while you and

Lapides see if you can get anything out of your boy." Noyes shook his head. "No hubris, Bill, but this time around I'm betting on my team."

"What do you intend doing about Mary?"

"Without the computer she's pretty well neutralized, so far as I can see. She can come and go as she pleases."

"She'll want to continue working with Toni Mulholland to prove Otto's not guilty."

"Well and good," Noyes said, pushing away from his desk. "I think he's a traitor, but I honestly don't think it's for any monetary gain or anything like that. I think he's just an arrogant bastard who's doing nothing more than having fun with the system, at our expense. He's smarter than the rest of us, and he knows it, and is just thumbing his nose at us."

Benkerk started to object, but Noyes held him off.

"Let Mary and Toni and their team do their thing. Because honestly, I'd like to be proven wrong. In all seriousness, I don't like Rencke, but I don't want him to be the bad guy."

"Fair enough, Chuck," Benkerk said, and they shook hands. "Can we share product?"

"As long as it's a two-way street."

"Absolutely."

"Good or bad?"

"Good or bad," Benkerk said.

Mary had debated driving back to the Scattergood-Thorne house, but she went home instead. She poured a glass of merlot and took it to the lanai, which looked out over the back lawn, beyond which was a patch of woods that Otto had protected by a surveillance system of motion and infrared detectors.

This was a safe haven, for the most part. But somehow, she didn't feel very safe, and she had to wonder if she ever would feel a sense of security.

Noyes had expected her—he had probably put her name on a watch list at the main gate—but spotting Benkerk parked in the visitors' lot at the OHB had rattled her. He acted like a friend, but he was the enemy. One of many.

THIRTY-THREE

Driving to town from the apartment in Georgetown first thing in the morning, Pete took care with her tradecraft, watching for cars, trucks, even motorcycles following her. Doubling back from time to time, scooting through intersections moments after the light turned red, making abrupt lane changes, turns, and twice even U-turns.

By the time she got lucky with a parking spot on Tenth Street less than a block from the J. Edgar Hoover Building on Pennsylvania Avenue, she was reasonably certain that she had come in clean.

Just inside the front entrance, she handed her driver's license to one of the clerks at the reception desk. "I'm here to see Mr. Kallek."

"Do you have an appointment?" the young woman, in a blue blazer with the Bureau's patch—FIDELITY, BRAVERY, INTEGRITY—on the left pocket, asked politely.

"No, but the director is expecting me."

"Yes, ma'am," the receptionist said, and she got on the phone and spoke to someone for several moments before hanging up.

"Someone will be down to escort you," she said. She ran Pete's license through a reader, and almost immediately a security badge popped out, to which she attached a clip before handing both of them over.

A young man in a blue blazer with the Bureau patch got off the elevator and came over as Pete was clipping the badge to her lapel. "Mrs. McGarvey?" he asked.

"Yes."

"Are you carrying a weapon?"

"I am."

"Please hand it to the receptionist, and it will be returned to you before you leave the building."

A security officer in uniform stepped closer, as Pete withdrew her Glock subcompact pistol from the holster at the base of her spine, and laid it handle-first on the counter.

"Would you like a receipt?" the receptionist asked.

"It's not necessary. But the pistol is loaded, a round in the chamber."

"Yes, ma'am."

"The Glock is a nice pistol," the escort said on the way up to the eleventh floor on the E Street NW side.

"Yes, it is."

"Are you always armed?"

Pete gave him a smile. "Usually not in the shower," she said. "But after what went down the other night, I thought it was prudent."

He chuckled but said nothing, until they got off the elevator and he took her to Kallek's corner office. "The director is expecting you, ma'am."

Kallek's secretary, an attractive woman in her midforties, got to her feet. "I'll announce you," she said, not smiling.

She opened the inner door. "Mrs. McGarvey is here, sir." She stepped aside.

Kallek, his jacket off, his tie loose, got up from where he was seated behind his desk. "I'm very busy this morning, Mrs. McGarvey, so I can only give you a moment or two of my time." He motioned for her to sit down.

"I'm in a hurry, too, Mr. Director. I'll stand."

"As you wish," Kallek said, and he sat down. "What can I do for you?"

"As you're aware, my husband and I were forced into a gun battle in front of our apartment in Georgetown. When it was over four males who'd been waiting in what we think was a rental car did not survive."

"I'm aware—"

Pete cut him off. "The police arrived almost immediately to take care of what we were told was a diplomatic mess. They were waiting for it to happen, putting our lives at needless risk."

"The timing was unfortunate—"

Again, Pete interrupted him. "Bullshit, Mr. Director. When we tried to find out who these men were, we were told nothing of any worth. Nor have we been told of a fifth man, who'd been waiting inside our building. He identified himself as Anatoli Krestov, a Moscow police officer sent to protect our lives from the four men who were Russians."

"I don't know this name."

"He said that he'd been sent to his embassy to make contact with the Bureau. Plus, the cops said that they had been tipped off by the Bureau. So, my question, Mr. Director, is what's going on?"

Kallek took several moments to answer. "You and your husband, of all people, have to know what's happening, however unfortunate it may seem to the two of you."

"Explain it to me," Pete demanded.

"The four Russian agents were sent to assassinate you and your husband."

"Sent by whom?"

"Mr. Rencke."

"Bullshit and you know it."

"You like that word, 'bullshit.' But right now, the word I especially like is 'leave.'"

Pete took a step forward. "We take exception when people try to kill us. Especially when our own Federal Bureau of Investigation is complicit."

Kallek picked up his phone. "I want two security officers here immediately."

"The bodies of the four would-be assassins were turned over to the Russians, who put them on a plane for Moscow. No investigation was conducted, nor was Comrade Krestov arrested and questioned."

"He had diplomatic immunity."

"Not bad for a cop coming into this country armed."

Two substantially built men in suits and ties appeared at the door.

"This meeting is ended," Kallek said. "Please escort Mrs. McGarvey downstairs so that she can retrieve the pistol she arrived with and see that she leaves the building."

One of the officers took her by the arm, but she pulled away.

"I want answers," she shouted.

"If you continue to interfere in this investigation, you and your husband will be subject to arrest," Kallek said. "Am I clear?"

"Yes, you are, Mr. Director. But that would be the worst mistake of your career. I shit you not."

Downstairs, the receptionist laid Pete's Glock handle-first on the counter, along with the magazine and the single 10mm bullet she'd ejected from the firing chamber.

"Thank you," Pete said. She reloaded the gun, holstered it, and laid the visitor's pass on the counter.

The lobby was fairly busy with people coming and going, but no one seemed to be paying any attention.

At the door, Pete looked at the two security officers, both towering over her. "If ever I see either of you again, and you try to put your hands on me, you'll regret the choice."

"Just trying to do our jobs, Mrs. McGarvey," one of them said, but with no contrition.

"Me, too," Pete said, and she headed for her car.

□

THIRTY—FOUR

Mary drove back to Langley and after she was passed through the main gate went directly over to the Scattergood-Thorne house. It was just past ten thirty, and one of the minders got out of the Cadillac Escalade parked in front as she pulled up and got out of her car.

"I'm sorry, Mrs. Rencke, I'll have to ask you to leave," he said. At a bulky six four, he towered over her.

"Why?"

"Your name has been taken off the visitors' list."

"By whom?"

"I couldn't say."

"Then you'll just have to shoot me, because I'm going inside to speak with my husband," Mary said. She stepped around him, but he blocked her way.

"Goddamn you," she screeched. She slammed her fist into his chest. "I want to see my husband!"

The other minder got out of the Caddy and came around to them. He was nearly as big as his partner but a lot younger, and he seemed embarrassed as he pried Mary away. "Please, ma'am."

Mary turned on him, and it took both larger men several moments to stop her from swinging and calm her down.

"Goddamnit, he's my husband," Mary said, and she started to collapse, her legs giving out from under her, so that the minder with his hands on her had to keep her from dropping onto the driveway.

"Jesus," he said.

"I need him," Mary said, and she began to sob, her entire body shaking.

The first minder was speaking into his lapel mic, and a minute later Benkerk charged out of the house.

"What's going on," he demanded.

"We have a situation here, sir," the first minder said.

"I can see that," Benkerk said. He took Mary from the minder holding her. "What is it, my dear woman?"

"I want Otto," Mary blubbered.

"I'm sorry, sir, but her name was placed on the restricted list overnight," the first minder said. "We have our orders."

"There's a lot of that going on lately," Benkerk said. "I'm taking her inside to see her husband, on my authority."

"Yes, sir. But we'll have to log it."

"Whatever," Benkerk said, and he took Mary across the driveway and into the stair hall, where he gave her his handkerchief so she could dry her eyes.

"I just want to hold him in my arms for a minute. See if he's okay. He sometimes forgets to eat."

"I know, but he's doing fine. What about you?"

Mary looked up at him, and smiled. "Other than losing my mind, I'm just fine, Bill."

"Al was about ready to take a break. We'll give you as long as you want."

"Thank you."

Benkerk opened the sliding doors to the living room. "Mary's here. Wants a word with her husband."

Lapides appeared at the doorway. "I was just about to get a cup of coffee," he said. He nodded to Mary and headed down the hall to the kitchen.

Benkerk stepped aside.

"Can we have a little privacy?"

"As long as you promise not to try to break him out."

"Scout's honor."

"Okay."

Mary went in and Benkerk closed the doors behind her.

Otto got up from where he was seated on the couch, and when Mary reached him he took her in his arms and held her cheek-to-cheek. "Oh, wow, it's fantastic to see you," he said out loud. "They knew you were coming," he whispered into her ear.

"Bill was at the OHB last night when Noyes had his people throw me out," Mary whispered.

"Did you talk?"

"He was in the parking lot, and I don't think he knew that I'd spotted him. But Chuck knows that I talked to Lou."

"Did he get access to her?"

"I told her to go to sleep to protect her memory and had her short out her batteries at the last second."

"Then I can bring her back as soon as I get out of here," Otto said. "Did you find out anything we can use?"

"She sent me a comparison of the reports from the major four NOCs in Moscow over the past twelve months, and she has a seventy-eight percent confidence that they haven't been compromised."

"Did she send it to your phone?"

"Yes."

"Erase everything."

"Why?" Mary asked. "It proves that you're innocent."

"I don't want them knowing that Lou was able to communicate with you. They might recharge her batteries and find a way to reverse-engineer the password from your phone. Chuck has some bright people working for him."

"Let them find out. It'll just be more proof that you're not a traitor."

"Just do it," Otto insisted. "In fact, replace the SIM card and physically destroy the old one."

"Okay," Mary said, holding him even tighter. "Lou said she missed you."

"And I miss her. But now I have you."

"What do you want me to do now?"

"How about Mac?"

"He's on his way to Moscow."

"And Pete?"

"She said that she was going to see Kallek sometime this morning, and then she was going over to the Russian embassy and storm the gates."

"They'll hit back."

"Shall I try to stop her?"

"She won't listen to you. Mac's going into harm's way, and she figures it's her duty to do the same."

"For you, my darling."

"Yeah," Otto said.

They parted, and Mary brushed her fingertips against his cheek. "Can I get you anything?"

"Some half-and-half and a couple packages of Twinkies."

Mary laughed. "I don't think they make them any longer."

"They do. And it'll give you an excuse to come back soon."

They embraced and Mary left.

Benkerk was waiting for her in the stair hall. "Are you okay now?" he asked.

"No. But I'm better, thank you."

"What's next?"

"I'm going to have a powwow with Toni and my old crew, see what we can come up with."

"Do you want to share your approach?"

"I want to run comparisons of the reports from our NOCs in Russia, Pakistan, and North Korea from one year ago to the present as of thirty days ago."

"To see if their signatures have changed?" Benkerk asked.

Signatures were pro-words built into messages sent home that would appear to be nothing more than quirks in language. One agent might occasionally start his coded sentences—especially important ones—with the word "So." Another might use the phrase "waiting *on*" something, rather than "waiting *for*."

"That and the quality of their reports, among other indicators."

"Will you share product?"

"Of course," Mary promised.

THIRTY-FIVE

Pete pulled up and parked in front of the pedestrian gate to the Russian embassy on Wisconsin Avenue NW in an area called Mount Alto just after twelve noon. She got out of her car and went to the gate, where she rang the buzzer and held up her wallet, open so that her driver's license was visible.

A guard in a dark green uniform, his trousers bloused in his highly polished boots, a pistol holstered at his side, came out of the low-security building behind the iron fence, but only glanced at the license.

"Good afternoon," he said in good English. "How may I be of service?"

"I'm here to see Mr. Zavorin."

"I'm sorry, madame, I do not know this name."

"I spoke with him on the phone, earlier, and told him that I would be stopping by. He's expecting me."

"I'm sorry, madame."

"Oh, for Christ's sake, *pozvonite yemu*," she said. *Call him.*

The security officer was unimpressed. "I'm sorry, madame."

"You've said that twice, just call someone and tell them that Mrs. Kirk McGarvey is here to speak with the SVR's chief of station. And if whoever you speak with asks if I'm defecting, the answer is no."

"Madame, if you insist, I will have to notify the Metropolitan Police Department."

"Then do it, but just call someone!"

The officer had started to turn away when Pete pulled out her pistol and pointed it not at him, but in his general direction.

He stopped short, and stared at her, his mouth half open. He started to reach for his weapon, but a second guard came out of the security post and called out something that Pete didn't quite catch.

The officer on the other side of the gate from Pete stayed his hand. Then nodded, but didn't take his eyes off her. "*Da*," he called back. "Someone has been called, Mrs. McGarvey, and an escort will be sent momentarily. Now, please lower your weapon and place it inside your vehicle. No one bearing arms may enter these grounds."

Pete smiled and lowered her gun. "Now, that wasn't so difficult, was it?" she said. She went back to her car, put the gun and spare magazine in the glove compartment, locked the doors, and went back to the gate, where the officer had not moved.

"May I have your driver's license, please. It will be returned to you when you leave."

Pete took it out of her wallet and handed it over, as a green Lada Largus,

which was a small SUV made in Russia under a license with Renault, came down the driveway from the white eight-story administrative building that had been finished in 1985.

The officer opened the gate and let her through. "You will need to leave your purse here as well," he said.

Pete gave him her shoulder bag, which would be searched, as the Lada pulled up, and a small, stern-looking man in a civilian suit got out and came over.

"If you will just come with me, Mrs. McGarvey, a representative from Ambassador Azarov's office will speak with you."

"I'm here to speak with Mr. Zavorin."

"Yes, we understand this."

Pete got into the passenger side of the small car, and her escort drove her up to the administrative building and parked around back. Inside, she had to pass through a security arch before she was allowed to go down a short corridor to an elevator, which they took up to the sixth floor.

A lot of activity was going on, people in the corridor, people at desks inside offices visible through open doors, a group of younger-looking men and women at computer stations in a large room, the door of which was open, but the windows darkened.

Pete was shown into a small conference room with an oblong table for six, a videoconferencing monitor on a wall, the windows in here also darkened. A surveillance camera was mounted in one corner up near the acoustically tiled ceiling.

"Someone will be here soon," her escort told her, and he left.

Pete was just sitting down at the table, from where she faced the door, when a slender man, around five six, with blond hair and blue eyes, walked in. He was wearing an expensive suit, the jacket unbuttoned and his tie loose.

"Good afternoon, Mr. Zavorin, it's good to meet you at last."

"I don't know this name," Zavorin said, taking a seat across from her.

"We have photographs of all the major officers in the GRU as well as the SVR, especially the chiefs of station at your embassies around the world. You have the same information on us, so let's just cut to the chase, shall we, and I'll get out of your hair."

Zavorin smiled. "You and your husband have the reputation of being direct," he said. "What brings you here today?"

"My husband is on the way to Moscow. He should be landing in the morning, your time, at Vnukovo, although I don't know what hotel he will be staying at."

"The Marriott Grand. Walking distance from the Kremlin. Is that where he means to go? To see the president?"

"He wants to speak with Anatoli Krestov, who said that he had come here to save our lives. He claimed that he was a Moscow police officer with diplomatic immunity, something we think is unlikely."

"If this meeting were to occur, which by the way I believe is unlikely, what does your husband wish to learn?"

"To begin with, why did someone send him and his team to assassinate us?" Pete said.

Zavorin started to speak, but Pete held him off.

"And what does he have to do with the implication that one of our officers is a spy for the Russian Federation?"

"I don't have any direct knowledge of such an operation, and believe me I don't have any reason to lie."

"Perhaps not. But can you at least make a guess why the GRU—and we think Krestov is actually a GRU officer—would be involved in such a risky project?"

"I don't know that either," Zavorin said. "But it is my understanding that you and your husband no longer work for the CIA."

"It would be a mistake on your part to think such a thing," Pete said. "But could you think of a reason why one of our officers has been targeted?"

Zavorin smiled. "I can think of several dozen reasons, actually. Mr. Rencke's expertise has been a thorn in our side for some time now."

"Why not just assassinate him?"

"Unintended consequences. Your term is 'blowback.'"

"Is Mr. Azarov aware of the situation?"

"Ambassadors do not routinely get involved with such things. Their work is done at a much higher diplomatic level."

"Maybe he should be aware of the diplomatic consequences that will fall on your heads when we prove that Mr. Rencke is not a traitor," Pete said. "Even my husband and I wonder what hell will break loose once Otto is reinstated."

Zavorin was silent for a beat. "Perhaps we should all step back from the brink."

"I agree," Pete said. "And let's begin by not trying to assassinate my husband or me again."

"Let me begin by asking you to urge your husband to abandon his search for Krestov and return to Washington on the very next flight, and to confine your activities here in Washington."

Pete got to her feet. "Thank you for meeting with me, I'd like to get back to my car now."

Zavorin got up. "I'll also ask you to take care, Mrs. McGarvey. Not everything here is under my control."

"I'll take that as a threat then," Pete said.

THIRTY-SIX

Otto was allowed to share a lunch of pizza and a couple of beers in the kitchen with Lapides and Benkerk. As they were finishing, one of the minders came in with a small paper bag and handed it to Benkerk. "This just showed up from Mrs. Rencke."

Benkerk looked inside. "Your Twinkies and half-and-half," he said, handing the bag to Otto.

"I'll just put it in the fridge till later," Otto said. "Right now, I'd like to go upstairs and take a shower before we get started this afternoon."

With his back to the two men, he opened the refrigerator door, took out Mary's cell phone, which she had concealed in a wad of napkins, pocketed it, then put the bag in the fridge and closed the door.

Lapides nodded. "I'd like to move on to North Korea."

"We might need to talk some more about Russia."

"Why's that?"

"Because Mac should be touching down at Vnukovo early this evening our time, and unless I'm mistaken he's going to run into trouble."

"How the hell do you know something like that?"

Otto shrugged. "You hear things from time to time," he said, and he started for the door.

"Did your wife whisper something like into your ear?" Lapides asked.

Otto turned back and grinned. "We talked about man-wife things, ya know? Sex, which I'm not going to discuss with you, unless you use drugs on me, and I guarantee you'll get an earful."

"Goddamnit," Lapides said after Otto had left. He went to the fridge, where he took the napkins from the bag and spread them out on the counter.

"No messages?" Benkerk said.

"Mary got something from the computer, and I'd give my paycheck she told him."

"We're conducting our investigation, and Otto's friends are conducting theirs," Benkerk said. "Care to bet your paycheck on who's going to win?"

"The son of a bitch is a traitor."

"You may be right, but I think we need to figure out why, otherwise none of this makes any sense."

Lapides scowled. "I need team players, Bill," he said. "I need to know that you're on board."

"I'm not going anywhere soon."

"But you're no longer a believer, that it?"

"The evidence is too pat, don't you think?"

Upstairs, Otto went into the bathroom, closed the door, and turned the water in the shower to all hot. The room filled with steam very quickly.

Surveillance cameras had been installed in the bedrooms and in the corridor, but so far as he could tell not in this bathroom. He took off his clothes, then turned the water cooler and got into the stall with the phone, closing the plastic curtain.

He had designed a section of Mary's phone, reserved for encrypted information, to look and operate exactly like a text-messaging program. Incoming data would be translated into mostly routine text messages, that would include misspellings, such as:

MISS YOUR DARLING.

O

Beneath that were the real data transfers.

The last message Mary sent was that someone was at the door, presumably the door to the Wolf's Den.

Otto entered the eleven-digit alphanumeric/special key password, and Lou's input showed up. She had a 75 percent confidence that the thirteen NOCs in place in Moscow had not been arrested or compromised, and she had analyzed reports they had made last year, comparing the most recent reports with those over the twelve months.

Other than normal missed schedules, and in several cases signs of stress, also normal, Lou had detected no significant changes in twelve months. It meant that the thirteen NOCs were still in place and producing product as normal.

Otto leaned forward, his forehead on the tiled wall. The intel network in Moscow was intact, but something was wrong. Mary had the passwords for Lou as well as her phone. This analysis from Lou proved that he wasn't a traitor, at least as far as CIA's deep-cover operations in Moscow were concerned.

Yet everyone, even Bill Benkerk, was convinced that treason had been committed in Russia as well as Pakistan and North Korea. But on what evidence?

The bigger question in his mind was: If Mary had read this, which he assumed she had, why didn't she show it to Bill? At least it would prove that nothing bad had happened in Russia.

He glanced down at the phone again, Lou's final message decrypted.

TELL OTTO I MISS HIM.

· · ·

All that was available in his room were two sets of orange jumpsuits along with white socks and canvas open-toed slippers of the type worn by prisoners. At least at the NGA he'd been given a white jumpsuit and had been allowed to keep his own sneakers.

But he was a prisoner after all, and for the first time since his arrest he wasn't so sure of himself, except that Lou's message on Mary's phone proved his innocence.

Benkerk and Lapides were talking in the stair hall when Otto came down the stairs. They both looked up.

"Christ," Benkerk said. "I'll call Mary right now and have her bring over some proper clothes for you."

"Don't bother, these will be fine," Otto said. "Shall we get back to it?"

He went into the living room, sat down on the couch, and as Benkerk and Lapides came in he laid Mary's cell phone on the coffee table. "You might want to take a look at this, for what it's worth."

Lapides picked it up.

"Did Mary bring this to you?" Benkerk asked.

"Yes. She managed to have a chat with Lou last night, and she got a download on her phone that might be of some interest to you guys."

Lapides fiddled with the phone for a minute, then looked up. "Nothing."

"Go to text messages."

Lapides did it.

"Enter the password," Otto said, and gave it to him one character at a time.

Lapides read what appeared twice before he looked up. "This is from your AI?"

"Yes."

Lapides handed the phone to Benkerk, who read the download. "Well?" he said when it was finished.

"Doesn't prove a thing," Lapides said.

"It looks pretty straightforward to me."

"It's from his fucking computer, whose voice and personality are his deceased wife's."

"So what?" Benkerk asked. "Computers don't lie."

As far as Otto was concerned Lapides's conclusion was foregone. "Mine might."

"Like a trained monkey," Lapides said. "Nothing's changed here, except that Mrs. Rencke is in collusion with her husband."

"Mary's a traitor?" Benkerk demanded.

"What else can you take away from this?"

"Well, for starts, Otto showed it to us. He could have erased the thing, or not given us the password, which by the looks of it would have taken us ten years to break."

"Maybe half that time considering the advances we're making on AI," Otto said. "To the confusion of our enemies."

"Oppenheimer," Benkerk said, and Otto was impressed.

"A communist," Lapides said, and Otto wasn't surprised.

□

THIRTY-SEVEN

Mary had found the Twinkies and half-and-half at a Quick Stop in McLean not far from home. After she'd dropped them and her phone off with Benkerk, she'd driven down to the OHB and stopped at the cafeteria looking out at the *Kryptos* sculpture.

It was nearing two in the afternoon and there were only a few stragglers for late lunch, or simply an early afternoon cup of coffee. She had tested the waters showing up again at the Scattergood-Thorne house, and going through security here, but no one stopped her or even questioned her credentials.

She had a Greek salad and an iced tea—sweet in the Southern style—and spent twenty minutes eating and watching the passersby. She'd half expected to raise some eyebrows—if word had gotten out to the general population on campus that Otto had been arrested—but no one had even glanced her way.

When she was finished, she went down the enclosed walkway, past the library, and then left along the connecting walkway over to the NHB, where she had to pass through another security barrier. Again, no questions were asked; the credentials Toni had given her were still valid.

Nor had the door code been changed since her departure, and she let herself into the first room of the suite of offices that stretched past eight individual glassed-in cubicles—among them Toni Mulholland's, the team leader—to the bullpen, which was housed in the largest space of all and was crammed with computer stations.

Toni was in her office, the door open, talking to someone on the phone when Mary walked back and knocked once on the doorframe.

"Gotta go. I'll talk to you later," Toni said, and she hung up.

"Am I a persona non grata?" Mary asked.

Toni was genuinely surprised. "Heavens no. What makes you think something like that?"

"I no longer work for the Company and my husband is under arrest charged with treason."

"Unproved charges, and you're an unpaid consultant, one of many at any given time on campus."

Mary inclined her head slightly. "Thanks. It's nice to still have friends here."

"More than you could possibly know," Toni said. "But you're not here for a chat. I suspect that you have a bee in your bonnet."

"I had a talk with Lou last night, but Chuck and a couple of his people caught us in midstream, so I had to shut her down."

"I didn't know the details, but Chuck said he had to escort you out of the building. It was him on the phone just now. Said that you'd probably show up sometime soon."

"I don't think he knows that I was able to talk to Lou."

"No, but he suspects you did. His people found the backup batteries that Otto installed, but they were flat. When they were recharged, the AI refused to wake up."

"I hope they didn't try anything else. If they push it she'll erase everything."

"He knows better," Toni said. "But he hoped that you would show up here and share whatever Lou told you—if anything."

"And share it with him?"

"He's not the enemy. He wants the same thing we all do. To prove Otto is innocent."

"Or that he's guilty."

Toni nodded. "Either way. Nobody likes what's going on. Just about everyone on campus from the seventh floor down next door is worried sick what Otto is still capable of doing. They think it could be even bigger than the Aldrich Ames mess in the early nineties, or the Bureau's Bob Hanssen debacle that went on from the late seventies for more than thirty years."

"There's no solid evidence."

"Nor was there any for Rick Ames or Hanssen, only suspicions."

Mary chose her next words carefully. "Can I trust you?"

Toni was visibly touched. She sat back. "That depends," she said.

"On what?"

"If you want me to do a cover-up, the answer would be no."

"I just want the truth."

"'And you shall know the truth, and the truth shall make you free.' The Company's motto, our motto."

"*Arbeit macht frei.*"

Toni got a sour look on her face. "We're not the Nazis."

Mary lowered her head and rubbed her eyes with the fingers of her right hand. "That was shitty, I'm sorry. It's just I don't know what to do."

"I know."

"It's just so fucking unfair after all he's done for this Agency and the country."

"I know that, too, Mary. Everyone on this campus does."

Mary looked up. "I'll give you what Lou dug up for me, and we can go from there."

"Do you want the team in on this?"

"Later. For now, I just want your take, and maybe we can come up with the next move now that Lou is out of the picture."

"What about Kirk and Pete?"

"He's on his way to Moscow, and Pete was going over to the Bureau to talk to Kallek this morning and then the Russian embassy."

"What the hell does she think the Russians are going to do for her, even if they let her through the front gate, which is unlikely?"

"Mac wants her to tell them that he's on his way."

"They're probably aware of that already, so what does he think will be accomplished by making sure the Russians know?"

"You're aware of what happened outside their apartment the other night."

"Of course."

"If the Russians are put on notice, they might not try anything like that again."

"They'll hold him when he lands and put him on the next flight to anywhere, just so it's out of Russia. Who knows, maybe even to North Korea."

Mary had to smile. "It'd save him some money. I expect he's planning to go there and Islamabad sooner or later anyway."

Toni laughed. "I just love him, except he sometimes comes across as a guy who has more balls than brains."

Mary laughed, too. "He has both."

"And he has the track record to prove it," Toni said. "So where do we start?"

"With what Lou downloaded to my phone before she shut herself down."

"May I take a look?"

"I gave it to Otto."

"The entire phone, or just the file?"

"The phone."

Toni was surprised. "Then Bill and Al will find it," she said. "What's the point?"

"It proves that Otto didn't collude with the Russians. Our thirteen NOCs are in place and sending regular reports."

Toni spotted the flaw immediately. "What was Lou's time frame?"

"She compared their reports from last year to this."

"Looking for stress, degradation of information, a corruption of pro-words?"

"All of the above."

"That's not possible."

"Lou is a pretty amazing piece of hardware."

"No, Mary. You sat in this office long enough to realize that NOCs don't produce gold-seam intel, or anything close to it, consistently. And especially not over a twelve-month period. Shit happens. Some of them come under suspicion, so they have to hang low. Sometimes their Johns dry up, maybe get cold feet. Maybe they go on vacation. Or quit their jobs, or maybe someone in their family gets run over by a bus and they become otherwise directed. Distracted, you know, like everyone does from time to time."

"You're right," Mary had to concede. "It's too consistent."

"The wonder is why Lou didn't catch it," Toni said.

☐

THIRTY-EIGHT

Pete gave Chuck Noyes a call a few minutes after four, and he agreed to see her, though he didn't sound happy about it. She drove to the OHB, where an escort was waiting to take her upstairs.

After the Russian embassy she'd got a hot dog, some chips, and a Coke at a street cart on the mall, and had walked over to the Lincoln Memorial and sat on the steps to eat her very late lunch.

Nothing seemed to add up in her mind. For the Russians to send a team to the U.S. to assassinate her and McGarvey was so over-the-top it went beyond belief, except it had happened. Had they succeeded, the hue and cry in the media would have been ten times as mammoth as it was after the Saudis' killing of Jamal Khashoggi.

The murder of a former director of the CIA and his wife would have more than trumped the killing of a journalist. And the repercussions when it was learned that the FBI had somehow been involved at a deep enough level to honor Anatoli Krestov's diplomatic immunity would have been over the stratosphere.

Even the attempted murder of her and Mac should have made headline news. But absolutely nothing had shown up in the media.

On her way over here, she had toyed with the idea of going to Fox News, or *The Washington Post*—but had put it out of her mind. Doing so would have sooner or later revealed the arrest of the CIA's top computer expert as a possible spy for Russia, Pakistan, and North Korea. If that happened it would make their own investigation even more impossible than it was now.

Spies spying on spies did not fare well under a spotlight.

The day was cool, only a few clouds and a light breeze, and tourists were everywhere, enjoying the city. Leading normal lives that after their vacations would take them back to their homes and jobs and family and friends.

She had a hard time remembering when her life had been normal, if it ever had been. Her existence now was Kirk, and she despaired as much about his near-term safety as she knew he did for hers.

No children for them. She had no relatives and he had only a granddaughter that Otto and Louise had adopted, plus an estranged sister, brother-in-law, and their two kids in Salt Lake City. And now, except for their apartment in Georgetown and a house on Casey Key on Florida's Gulf Coast, they had nowhere to call home. And she didn't think they'd ever go back to Casey Key, because of bad memories of Kirk's wife, who had been assassinated, and because of the attacks on their lives not long ago.

Everything to her—the current state of their lives, and of Otto's and Mary's—seemed bleak and without any real purpose.

She finished her lunch, and stood up. Except she was in love with her husband, and together Otto and Mary were their closest friends, which was purpose enough.

As a deputy director, Noyes rated a private office with a secretary, but he had only one computer on his large desk, because information flowing to him from his staff was preselected, filtered and weighted as to its importance.

His windows—looking in the same direction as the DCI's, south toward some woods—were dark gray and double-paned, the blank space in the middle filled with white noise, making eavesdropping, even with advanced laser sampling, impossible.

"Good afternoon, Pete," he said, rising as she came in. "I thought you might be showing up at some point."

"I'm glad I didn't disappoint," she said.

When they were settled, he came directly to the point. "You and your husband are working to gather evidence that Otto is not guilty as charged. May I assume that you're here to share what you've learned?"

"You're aware that someone tried to kill us?"

"Yes."

"Extraordinary, don't you think?"

"Considering the circumstances, not so terribly unexpected."

"You mean that the opposition somehow knew that we were gathering evidence to clear Otto and they wanted to stop us?"

"Reverse psychology."

"Yeah, the Russian who claimed he was a Moscow cop explained it to us, but that's not what I meant, because that was nothing but bullshit."

"What then?"

"Well, aside from the fact that the Bureau honored the Russian's diplomatic immunity, why wasn't there anything in the newspapers or television? An attempted assassination of a former CIA director is big news."

"Harold."

Pete was surprised. "Taft?"

"Yes."

"I don't understand. Someone tried to murder us, and not only did Taft order a cover-up, he must have known ahead of time what was going to happen and he didn't warn us?"

"He didn't know the specifics, but he expected the possibilities."

"But he didn't give us the fucking heads-up!"

"You and Kirk knew the possibilities as well as he did," Noyes said.

Pete was at a loss for words.

"And yet your husband is on his way to Moscow even as we speak, and

you not only spoke to Kallek, you showed up at the Russian embassy, to accomplish what, exactly?"

"You're following us."

"Neither of you have made it difficult," Noyes said. "In your case, drones. Who did you speak with at the embassy?"

"Ptr Zavorin, the SVR's chief of station."

"Jesus," Noyes said softly. "He admitted who he was?"

"Not in so many words. But he asked me to tell my husband to leave Moscow and not try to find Krestov and for us to confine our efforts to here in Washington."

"Not bad advice, considering the source."

"But he warned me that not everything here was under his control."

"When your husband gets back, I suggest that the both of you disappear."

"And leave Otto hanging out in the wind?" Pete demanded. "What the hell do you take us for?"

"Let me remind you that we and the FBI are conducting this investigation, Mrs. McGarvey, and neither you nor Mac are welcome."

"We're not backing off."

"You have no authority."

"Then fucking well arrest us," Pete shouted. She got up.

"That can be arranged."

"I've already been threatened once today; don't you join the club. If need be I'll take this to the media."

"We have a spy in the CIA and we need to find him."

"It's not Otto," Pete said at the door. "And whoever it is doesn't work for the SVR."

"Who then, besides Pakistan's ISI and North Korea's MSS?"

"Russia's GRU, and my husband and I are going to prove it, which will lead us to the real spy."

THIRTY-NINE

McGarvey's flight touched down at just past ten thirty in the morning local at Moscow's Vnukovo Airport. He waited until everyone behind him had got their things from the overhead bins and were shuffling slowly toward the front of the plane before he took the Glock 26 subcompact pistol from beneath his jacket, unloaded it and placed it and the fifteen-round magazine in a leather zip-up case, and placed it in his laptop-size carry-on bag.

The gun was small but fired the 9×19-caliber round, which had a decent stopping power, but the problem would be if it was confiscated at customs and immigration. A lot depended on who knew he was flying to Moscow on this particular flight, and what they wanted to do about it.

He had a feeling that the Georgetown operation had been a GRU-sponsored attempted hit, that would give him a slight edge here if it was Ptr Zavorin, the SVR's Washington chief of station, who'd given the Moscow authorities the heads-up. For a number of years, the GRU, which was a military intelligence-gathering agency, and the SVR, which was the successor to the KGB and was the civilian intel agency, had been at odds over who would conduct foreign intelligence missions, especially ones that involved spilling of blood. The rivalry could give him an advantage, at least initially.

When the aisles were mostly clear, McGarvey made his way to the front of the plane. The pilot was looking over his shoulder and he smiled.

"Thanks for riding along," he said.

"My kind of flight," Mac said.

"Yeah, nothing went wrong."

"I meant no turbulence and a greased landing."

"Any idea when you're coming back," the captain asked. "I'd like to have you aboard again."

"Are you hearing anything?"

"Nothing specific, but the rumors are out there."

"Especially here?"

"Could be," the captain said. "Anyway, good luck, Mr. Director."

McGarvey wasn't surprised that the captain knew who he was—or had been. Now it depended on the security at customs.

McGarvey followed the passengers who'd gotten off ahead of him down the Terminal A corridor to two immigration booths, where he presented his Donovan Packard passport.

The uniformed officer opened the passport, gave him a sharp look, but then simply stamped the proper page without a word and handed it back.

In the customs hall, he claimed his small suitcase and joined one of the lines, and had to wait for five minutes before it was his turn. He handed over his customs declaration, as well as his sky marshal identification card, to the attractive woman across the low counter.

She studied the ID photo and looked up at him. "When is your return flight, Mr. Packard?" she asked, her English very good.

"Two or three days, but I haven't scheduled it yet."

"And what is it you'll be doing in Moscow in those two or three days?"

"Relaxing. I've had a hectic week at home."

"You will not be permitted to take your weapon into the city. It will be placed in a security locker and will be returned to you when you present your credentials and a proper boarding pass. Are you ready to surrender it at this moment?"

"Yes," McGarvey said. He took the leather case out of the carry-on bag, and laid it on top of his suitcase.

"Is it presently loaded?"

"No."

"Thank you."

A man in civilian clothes appeared, took the gun case, and without a word turned and went into an office at the other side of the hall.

The customs woman returned McGarvey's ID, and put his customs declaration in a slot in the counter. "Welcome to Moscow, Mr. Packard."

McGarvey took a cab to the Marriott Grand Hotel, just walking distance to Red Square and the Kremlin, where he presented his McGarvey passport to a clerk at the front desk.

"I've made no reservations, but I'd like a room for three nights."

"We're rather full at this moment, but let me check, sir," the young man in a dark blue blazer with the hotel's logo said. He entered something in a computer.

Only a few people were in the lobby, but the bar across from the fountain and grand staircase up to the mezzanine level was nearly full.

The clerk looked up. "I'm sorry, sir, but the only available room for those nights is the corner suite."

McGarvey laid his platinum Amex card on the desk. "Fine."

"Yes, sir," the clerk said, scooping up the card.

It only took a few moments to run the card, have McGarvey sign the check-in form, and hand over a key card.

"Will you require help with your luggage?"

"Send it up to my suite, but don't bother unpacking. I'm going to have a drink at the bar and then some lunch before I turn in. Jet lag."

"Of course, sir. Welcome to the Marriott Grand."

McGarvey pocketed his credit card and key and walked across to the lounge, where he sat at the bar and ordered a glass of champagne.

"Sweet or dry?" the bartender asked.

"Dom."

"Of course."

As he waited for his wine, he phoned Pete, who answered on the first ring. "You're there in one piece?" she demanded.

"At the bar having a glass of champers. How about you?"

"Kallek threw me out of his office, but he did agree to talk to me, and I made my point."

"I'm sure you did. What else?"

"I managed to talk my way into the Russian embassy and actually got to meet Zavorin. He wouldn't admit who he was, but he knew that you were on your way to Moscow and even the hotel you were probably going to stay at, but he denied knowing anything about Krestov or the operation to take us out."

"But you got his attention," McGarvey said.

"Did you make reservations at the Marriott?"

"No, but if I had to guess he figured I would be staying here because it's close to the Kremlin."

"Yeah. He wanted to know if you were going to try to talk to Putin."

"You definitely got his attention. So now the cat is out of the bag. It's their next move."

"You're there with a big target painted on your back," Pete said. "So for Christ's sake watch your back."

"You, too. But what else did he have to say?"

"I asked him if he could think of any reason why one of our officers had been targeted. I didn't mention any names, but he said that he could think of a dozen reasons, because Otto had been a thorn in Russia's side for a long time. Why not assassinate him? I asked. Blowback, he told me. And then he suggested that we all step back from the brink. We, meaning us as well as them."

"What's your take?"

"He knows that something is going on, of course, but I believed him when he told me it wasn't an SVR operation."

McGarvey spotted a familiar face reflected in the mirrors behind the bar. "I'm about to have some company."

"Ours or theirs?"

"One of ours, but I don't know if he's going to be on our side."

"Take care," Pete said.

"You, too."

☐

FORTY

McGarvey turned around as Roger Daltry came straight across the room and sat down next to him. "Champagne?" Mac asked.

"A little early in the day for me," Daltry said. He was a short, somewhat pudgy man in his late forties, with longish hair and a full beard flecked with gray. He wore old-fashioned horn-rimmed glasses that somehow accented his arrogant attitude. He was a man who thought he was the brightest person in any room he found himself in.

And as far as McGarvey knew he was almost always correct. Last he'd heard, Daltry had been assistant chief of Caracas Station. "Are you here in town on vacation?"

"I'm the COS, and we got word last night that you were on your way. Everyone figured you'd be staying here, maybe to talk with your old pal Putin."

"That's the impression I wanted to make."

The bartender came. Daltry ordered a Knob Creek straight up.

"Misdirection?" the station chief asked.

"Something like that," McGarvey said. "Who gave the heads-up?"

"Someone upstairs. Said you and Pete had some trouble the other night. But the Russians were getting four body bags for their troubles, and whatever's going down isn't over yet."

"Did they tell you what to do with me?"

"Left it up to my discretion," Daltry said. His bourbon came and he took a deep drink, as he stared at the mirror. "Doesn't look as if you've come to anyone's attention yet."

"The SVR's Washington COS knows I'm here."

"How?"

"My wife told him."

Daltry had to laugh. "I'm not even going to ask why, because I figure that you're going to tell me. And ask for help. Are you actually here to see Putin?"

"No. Does the name Anatoli Krestov mean anything to you?"

Daltry shook his head. "No."

"I'm pretty sure he's GRU. Claimed he was a Moscow cop and he had diplomatic immunity. He showed up right after the gunfight, said he'd been sent over to stop the hit."

"Did he say why they wanted to take out you and Pete? Although I could think of a couple dozen valid reasons. And of course, where do you show up? Right here in badland." Daltry laughed again. "Your sense of timing is nothing short of spectacular, Mr. Director. The word 'stupid' also comes to mind, but let's just call it spectacular."

"A friend of mine has been charged with treason and arrested."

"He or she sold out to the Russians? And you and Pete are trying to prove that they're no traitor, and the Russians wanted to stop you two from proving it." Daltry picked up his drink. "It's like a bloody James Bond novel. Who's the friend?"

"Otto Rencke."

Daltry had started to raise the glass to his lips, but he stopped. "Jesus fucking Christ," he said softly. "You're shitting me."

"No. And I was hoping that you would come to me, not the other way around. I need your help."

"Chiefs of station usually don't shoot people."

"A name. And then you'd best keep your distance from me. With any luck I won't have to shoot anyone either, and I'll be gone in twenty-four hours."

"With any luck," Daltry said. "But tell me one thing first. If someone like Otto has been arrested, the proof must be pretty solid."

"Too solid."

"Means we have another Aldrich Ames, you don't think it's Otto, and you're here trying to find out who."

"Something like that."

"Well, then I'll do whatever I can. Because if it is Otto, something I don't even want to imagine, then we're all truly fucked."

"I need the name of and an address for the director of the GRU's Illegals Department. Last I heard it was a general named Myakov."

"Gennadi Svirin. An up-and-coming one-star, who'd run over his own mother for a promotion. He has an apartment here in town, but I'm told that he spends a lot of his time at his dacha about fifty K north of here."

"I need to know if he's going to be at his dacha tonight, and I'll need the exact location, and anything you can dig up about his security."

Daltry was impressed. "Are you going to shoot him?"

"Just have a little chat."

"Without getting shot yourself so that you can make it back here, then to the airport and home—where another hit squad will probably be waiting for you."

McGarvey shrugged. "Otto's a friend."

Daltry thought about it only for a moment. "Were you able to get a weapon through customs?"

"I didn't even try."

"The concierge can arrange for a car with GPS. The general's dacha is in the woods on a small river off the M8 this side of the town of Sergiev Posad. Rent the car right away, and I'll have the GPS coordinates plugged into the machine, and an untraceable PSM with a suppressor and a magazine of ammunition under the front passenger-side seat by eight. It only fires the 5.45-millimeter round, but it's very quiet and works for a close-in head shot, if the need arises."

"How will you know which car is mine?"

Daltry smiled. "This is my town, Mr. Director."

"Oh, and does Svirin speak English? My Russian is a little rusty."

"He spent a year at Oxford."

McGarvey had the concierge rent him a Kia Rio hatchback for two days, then went into the restaurant to have a light lunch of a salad and some "authentic" Kentucky Fried Chicken.

When he was finished, the car had been delivered and was parked inside on the lower level of the garage. He picked up the key from the concierge and went down to check it out. It was dark green, new, and clean, and the gas tank was full.

Daltry or one of his people from the station had already been here, because the PSM and spare magazine were under the passenger's-side seat, and when he powered up the window-mounted GPS, it came up with a location off the M8 north of the city.

He relocked the car and went back upstairs to his room, where he lay down to get a few hours of sleep.

Pete called his cell phone just after five his time, and he came instantly awake on the first ring.

"Are you okay?" he asked.

"Just getting up, it's nine here, how about you?"

"If everything goes okay, I'll be coming back sometime tomorrow."

"I'm going out to see Otto, and then Mary and I are getting together with Toni to see what we can come up with."

Their phones were encrypted with an algorithm that Otto had set up for them last year, but under the circumstances neither of them wanted to take the chance of going into any details.

"Roger Daltry came to talk to me just after I'd checked in," McGarvey said. The COS was almost certainly shadowed every time he made a move, so if someone had cracked the encryption program he wasn't telling them anything they didn't already know.

"I'm sure that he was overjoyed seeing you."

"Wanted to know what I was doing in Moscow and wanted to know if I was going to try to see the president. I told him that it was a possibility, but I hadn't contacted his office yet."

"That's the whole point of your trip, isn't it?"

"Yeah, but I'm having second thoughts after what happened the other night in front of our apartment."

"All he can say is no, sweetheart," Pete said, and the emphasis she put on the last word was so unlike her that it was obvious she was sending him a warning.

"I understand," he said.

"Take care."

"You, too."

☐

FORTY-ONE

Pete showed up at the Scattergood-Thorne house shortly after ten. Lapides and Benkerk were closeted in the living room with Otto, but Patterson was sitting at the kitchen counter with a cup of tea watching the surveillance feed.

"Good morning," he said, looking up when she walked in. It was obvious that he was tired.

Pete gave him a peck on the cheek. "Are you getting any sleep?"

He glanced back at the TV monitor, the sound barely audible. "This business is driving me crazy. From where I'm sitting it doesn't add up. Especially considering everything he's done for this agency, for this country, for most of his life."

"Lapides is convinced Otto's a pervert."

"Indeed, he may be, or may have been, but Louise believed in him, and now so does Mary. But incredibly Lapides has ignored what's right there in front of him."

"Has Otto brought it up?" Pete asked.

"He's too much of a gentleman to involve them," Patterson said. "For all he knows Lapides might make a case for Louise to have been a pervert and a traitor herself, and now Mary is in cahoots."

"Considering what they accomplished that would be a stretch."

Patterson looked up at her. "She brought him a phone yesterday. She'd talked to Otto's computer that wasn't as turned off as everyone assumed it was. Anyway, the machine downloaded some information onto the phone about some of our deep-cover agents in Moscow, which was meant to prove that Otto is no traitor."

"Did Lapides find out?"

"Yes, and Otto handed over the phone and voluntarily gave him the password so he and Bill could listen in."

"And?"

"Lapides didn't buy it. Said the computer was lying."

Pete was sitting on a stool at the counter. She leaned back. "The son of a bitch isn't searching for the truth, he's just looking for the bits and pieces that'll prove his assumption that Otto is guilty."

"Just about everyone's assumption," Patterson said.

It hit her for the first time that Carleton was right. Just about everyone from the DCI all the way down to Otto's interrogators was convinced that he had committed treason. But to this point no one could offer an adequate reason. It wasn't money; Otto was worth something in excess of one million dollars, all of it clearly traceable to shrewd investments in the stock market.

And Lapides's line of questioning about Otto's so-called perversion years ago when he worked for the church made absolutely no sense to her. Which brought her around full circle to one simple question.

"Why?" she asked Patterson. "What has he gained by it?"

Patterson's smile was wan. "You and Kirk can't see it because you're his friends."

"See what, for Christ's sake?"

"Otto thinks that he's smarter than just about everyone else inside the Company."

Pete had to laugh, and she inclined her head. "He is."

"And he's a game player."

"He plays chess against anyone who's dumb enough to try. Except he lets his opponent use a board, which he doesn't look at, while he makes all the moves in his head. I've tried a couple of times, but he took me to mate in just a few moves."

"Benkerk brought it up, and Otto admitted he'd finally found a decent player who he had a tough time besting."

"Who?"

"His AI, Lou," Patterson said. "According to Otto they're tied at ten–ten, but he said she was getting better."

"Okay, so he's a genius, we already know that. What's your point, Carleton?"

"He loves to play games, a lot of different games with different opponents."

"And?"

"Treason just might be the latest."

It took several seconds for Pete to completely comprehend what Patterson was suggesting, but then she saw the obvious flaw in that line of reasoning. "But none of our NOCs have been outed. Not in Russia, or Pakistan or North Korea. And so far as Toni and her team have been able to determine, the quality of the product coming out of those countries has not diminished."

"How has that been determined?" Patterson asked. He was being a lawyer, circling in for exactitudes.

"A lot of the time it shows up in our foreign policy decisions."

"Like pulling out of Syria, Iraq, and Afghanistan, which in each case was something that the Russians wanted."

"I'm not following you."

"Just talking about Russians now. Is it possible that our deep-cover people over there have actually been turned and the SVR or someone is spoon-feeding them what would look to us like good intelligence?"

This time Pete spotted the flaw in Patterson's suggestion immediately. "You can't have it both ways," she said. "Either Otto is in fact a traitor—which both of us know is ludicrous—or he's playing an elaborate game."

"As you wish, then let's assume he's playing a game."

"Again, to what end? Games have outcomes. Maybe the outcome he's looking for is to give us the advantage. He wants to win, but not the way the

seventh floor or Webb or even the White House wants." Burton Webb was the director of national intelligence, who oversaw all U.S. intel agencies, including the CIA.

This time it was Patterson who laughed, but there was no humor in it. "If that's true then he should have shared his strategy."

"With whom?" Pete asked.

"For starts, with you and Kirk."

This time Pete understood that her own reasoning might be flawed. And for the first time since this all began, what seemed like centuries ago, she was truly afraid for Otto, and even more afraid for her husband. If Otto was playing the game Carleton was suggesting, then Kirk was walking into a deadly trap that even he might not be able to get himself out of.

Otto's interviews were being taped, so Patterson had decided to go home to get a few hours' rest.

In the stair hall, Pete gave him a kiss on the cheek. "We'll work this out."

"Can you contact Kirk?"

"Yes."

"Then warn him."

"About what?" Pete asked.

"To be careful, my dear," Patterson said, and he left.

Pete hesitated for just a moment, but then crossed to the living room sliding doors, knocked once, and opened them.

Lapides looked over his shoulder. He was irritated. "What?"

"May I have a moment with Otto?"

"No."

"I'm going to be gone for the rest of the day, and I just wanted to tell him that we're working the problem."

"Okay, you told him," Lapides said. "If you come across anything significant, we'd like to be advised. Is that clear, Mrs. McGarvey?"

"Perfectly," Pete said, looking directly at Otto. "It's just that my husband is in Moscow and I'm afraid he might be running into a trap."

Otto understood what she was asking and why, and the expression on his face was almost one of regret and disappointment. "If there is a traitor and they know where he is, then yes, it's possible Mac will run into trouble."

"Thanks," Pete said, watching Otto.

Lapides and Benkerk had turned and were looking at her.

Otto mouthed the words *Tell everyone.*

She nodded, turned, and left.

FORTY-TWO

McGarvey had just gotten to sleep when Pete called him again, and this time she seemed even more worried than before.

"Could be you're running into a trap," she said.

"Just about everyone on this side of the pond knows that I'm here, but from what I'm picking up the common consensus is that I've come to ask Putin for another favor. People seem to think that we're old buds."

Not long ago, Mac had been involved in a complicated plot in which it was believed that a hijacked Russian nuclear weapon was on its way to the U.S. The scheme was to force a showdown between Putin and a supposedly incompetent President T. Karson Weaver, who, it was believed by some, would overreact and do the wrong thing.

Tensions would have reached dangerous levels. In a crucial part of the insane plot, McGarvey had been kidnapped and taken to Russia, where he was to be executed. But Putin intervened and had him brought to the Kremlin.

"I need your help," the Russian president had said. "Your intelligence is correct. We are missing a small tactical nuclear warhead. In the wrong hands such a thing could tip the balance of power on just about every continent."

Putin wrote a name on a slip of paper and held it out. "This is a man in our embassy in Washington who might be able to help you."

"Help me do what?" McGarvey had asked.

"Find the weapon and return it to us before it gets into the wrong hands. Will you help?"

"Of course," McGarvey had said. He'd been sent home, where the plot had unfolded in a way even he hadn't expected it would.

"Might not be such a bad idea to try to get to see him."

"If he's in town," McGarvey said. "But what makes you think I'm running into a trap?"

Pete described her conversation with Patterson about the possibility that this was some sort of a crazy game. "I managed to have a word with Otto, over Al's objections, and he agreed that if there was a traitor—if—then you would be in trouble if whoever it was knew where you were. And then while Al and Bill were looking at me, and not directly at Otto, he mouthed the words 'Tell everyone.'"

"Did you?"

"I wanted to talk to you first."

"Do it," McGarvey said.

"Jesus, sweetheart," Pete said softly. "This could get out of hand in a New York minute."

"We knew the possibilities from the start. So just do what Otto told you to do, and take care. I'll be on a plane back home tomorrow morning."

With any luck, Pete wanted to say, but didn't.

The monitor on Jerri Butler's desk in the National Security Agency's telephone intercept interpretation center at Fort Meade chimed, which meant an in-progress phone call of interest was being made at this moment in real time.

She was a husky woman, in her midsixties, just eight months from re-tirement from a job she'd held, it seemed like, since the first coming. She'd been promoted to her present position as a senior analyst and had never wanted to take the next step up to a supervisory position. She was a happy woman; content with her long-term marriage, with two kids who never were a trouble, and even with her desk at the periphery of a large floor of similar workstations.

She pulled up the intercept, one of more than ten billion this afternoon alone, and fed it to her earbud. What she was hearing matched the erratic wave pattern on her screen, obviously encrypted, but with an algorithm neither she nor NSA's sophisticated computer programs immediately rec-ognized.

She punched a button on her console, which connected her with the shift supervisor, Constantine Zimbowski. "Got something you might want to take a look at," she said when he answered.

"What's your take?"

"Voice, but encrypted," she said. "Boss is chewing on it." "Boss" was the generic name of the main decryption programs, of which there were thou-sands.

"Do you have the send and receive points?"

"The call is coming from here in the greater D.C. area, to a number some-where in Moscow. You want me to send it over to you?"

"I need the exercise," Zimbowski said.

Jerri enhanced the pattern, breaking it into five horizontal rows, each sam-pling a narrow portion of the spectrum.

Zimbowski, an extremely large man—he once admitted that on a good day he tipped the scales at 450 pounds—showed up at her desk. He'd wheeled his own specially made chair over and sat down to one side of her, so that he could look over her shoulder. The techs on either side of her position, as well as in front and behind, glanced up but then went back to their own intercepts.

He studied the screen for a couple of moments. "I can't tell if it's a male or female," he said. As large as his body was, his head was tiny and round, his hair was thin and wispy, and his voice was soft and high-pitched, almost girlish. His gentle personality and kind laugh matched his voice. Everyone on the floor loved him.

"Not yet but it's definitely not a machine voice."

Zimbowski had a set of earphones around his neck. He plugged into her monitor, and placed the earphones so that they half covered his ears, allowing him to hear the phone call, as well as what Jerri was saying.

The Moscow voice replied, but only briefly, perhaps a half dozen words, no more, and the call ended.

"Replay it from the beginning," Zimbowski said.

Jerri did. And together they listened to the voices, and studied the traces on the screen.

"It's one of the Russian algorithms," Zimbowski said.

Jerri entered a series of commands on her keyboard, and a series of icons appeared on the upper left of the monitor. "The D.C. end went through a cell tower."

"By the time Boss figures out which one, it'll be too late, but we'll notify the Bureau anyway so they can take a look," Zimbowski said.

"The local signal was good, but it doesn't match the fidelity of a landline phone like the Moscow one does."

"Are we sure the call originated from here?"

"Definitely local," Jerri said. At this point it was the only thing of value that she was sure of.

"I'd guess that the Moscow recipient was sitting at a desk somewhere, and our local caller was using a Russian-made cell phone. But why not make the call from their embassy?" Zimbowski asked.

"They know that we're all over those calls, and even most of the voice-print IDs belong to us."

"Someone here is telling someone in Moscow something, and they kept the call short. Obviously, they know we're sampling," Zimbowski said. "But they can't know that we're on these kinds of calls right now in real time. So far as they're concerned, they most likely believe that it could take us as long as four or five weeks to pick this one out of a trillion or so. Plus, they have the safety of a good encryption algorithm."

Two days ago, NSA had been asked to watch out for just these kinds of calls, and separate them from the chaff.

"This looks like something we got the heads-up on," Jerri said. "What's your pleasure, Con?"

"Stick with this as long as it takes. Could be the one the CIA is looking for."

Jerri was looking at the trace. "This is going to take some time."

"Start with the language."

"I'm betting English."

"Why's that?"

Jerri looked at her boss and shrugged. "Just a feeling."

□

FORTY-THREE

McGarvey woke a few minutes after eleven, splashed some cold water on his face in the bathroom, then got dressed in jeans, running shoes, and a light cotton pullover in dark blue, the only clothes he'd packed for the trip.

The message light on his phone was blinking. It was a woman's voice. "Mother will be out of town tonight." It meant General Svirin would be at his dacha.

He'd checked the PSM earlier, but sitting on the bed he unloaded the small pistol, disassembled it, and inspected each part to make sure again that nothing had been modified. Satisfied, he put the gun back together, reloaded it, and jacked a round into the chamber.

Before he left the room, he stuck the pistol in his belt at the small of his back, and pocketed the spare magazine.

He got off the elevator on the mezzanine level and went across to the rail, where he stood partially concealed behind a support column to the left of the stairs. The lobby was fairly busy, and the bar was filled with mostly foreign businessmen—many of them Americans and their Russian counterparts.

No one stood out, in his mind. No one waiting by the outside doors, or sitting on an easy chair or couch from where they had a good view of the lobby.

If the FSB, which was the Russian equivalent of the FBI, knew that he was here, or guessed at why he'd come, they weren't being obvious about it. Of course, the old SEAL adage warned that if everything was going well, you were probably running into a trap.

He'd thrown a rock into a pond and so far, there were no ripples.

He took the elevator down to the three-quarters-full parking garage. No one obvious was waiting, though someone could be sitting in a car with the engine off and lights out.

The Kia was parked four spaces to the left of the elevator. McGarvey withdrew his pistol, and keeping it low beside his right leg, the muzzle pointed slightly away, approached the car, checking out the other vehicles nearby for any sign someone was there.

But the garage was empty of people.

Opening the trunk, he checked the spare-tire well for tracking devices, and then, after closing the trunk, he went around to each of the wheel wells, got down on his back, and felt around underneath, again with no results.

Inside the car, he checked under the seats and in the glove box and center console, and then, after popping the hood release, he got out and checked the engine compartment. But so far as he could tell the car was clean.

It was something that Daltry's people had almost certainly checked when they'd delivered the pistol and programmed the GPS, but it was the unknowns that tended to rise up and bite you on the ass when they were least expected.

He got back in, laid the PSM on the passenger seat where it was close at hand, started the car, and backed out of the slot. Almost immediately after he'd driven out of the garage, the GPS came to life, and it directed him, on the map as well as by a soft female voice speaking English, to turn right.

Traffic in the city center was heavy, and even frenetic at times. He expected that a good portion of the drivers were already drunk, which had been Russia's national pastime forever.

A half dozen blocks later he got on another broad avenue, which took him to the second ring road around the city, where traffic was much heavier, and then to an exit marked PROSPEKT MIRA, which according to the on-screen map crossed under the outer ring road about twelve kilometers farther, and finally onto the M8 highway heading north, where the relatively sparse traffic consisted mostly of large trucks.

In the city, including on the ring road, it had been nearly impossible to vary his speed to determine if he was being tailed, but out here with mostly trucks it became evident that no one on the road was taking an interest in him.

After he'd passed a semi, he powered down his window and cocked an ear to listen for the sounds of a helicopter shadowing him, but so far as he could tell there was nothing but wind noise.

The only other possibilities were high-flying helicopters; long-range, nearly silent drones; the Beriev A-50s that were Russia's AWACS aircraft, some of which were equipped with look-down radar; and surveillance satellites, none of which he could do anything about.

But if the general had been told that McGarvey was in-country, and if the GRU had been involved in the attempted assassination in Georgetown, the security staff at the dacha would be expecting company tonight.

The GPS showed railroad tracks next to the highway, and at one point about thirty kilometers north of the outer ring road the tracks crossed from the right to the left side, and twenty K later the GPS alerted him to turn left just short of the town of Abramtsevo, where he crossed the tracks again.

Now he was in a birch forest, where from time to time he spotted what looked like small buildings—maybe farmhouses or barns—in the distance. But with both the driver's- and passenger-side windows open, he could hear nothing except the wind from his passage and tire noise on the uneven pavement.

Ten minutes later he spotted lights in the distance. He checked his rearview

mirror. The road behind was empty, and he slowed down and switched off his headlights.

A few kilometers farther, the lights on what appeared to be a fairly good-sized house became visible through a thick birch forest, and around a sharp curve he came to a tall chain-link fence, the iron gate open.

He pulled up short, made a Y-turn on the road and drove back fifty meters to the curve, and parked the car out of sight from the gate. Getting out, he took the pistol from his belt and made his way off the road about ten meters or so into the woods and headed toward the open gate.

Stopping twice to listen for sounds, he couldn't hear a thing, not even the rustling of leaves in the treetops in the still night air. It was almost as if the forest, and anything in it, was holding its breath to find out what the intruder wanted here.

When he got within sight of the razor-wire-topped fence, he pulled up short again. An open Gazik, the Russian jeep, was parked at the gate, a man dressed in what appeared to be a civilian-white shirt behind the wheel.

No surveillance cameras were visible at the gate or along the top of the fence for as far as he could see in the dark in either direction. Nor were there spotlights, or any other form of illumination except for the house in the near distance through the woods.

Yet the gate had been left open, and they knew that someone had driven up, turned around, and come back on foot.

Holding the pistol out of sight behind his leg, McGarvey stepped out onto the surface of the road, less than ten feet from the Gazik.

"Ah, Mr. McGarvey, the general has been expecting you," the driver said in nearly accentless English, his tone of voice pleasant, almost charming. "But of course, I cannot take you to see him if you're armed. You understand."

McGarvey walked around to the passenger side of the vehicle, holding the pistol in plain sight. "Perhaps I'll just shoot you, and drive up to the house myself."

The driver was surprised. "Whatever for?" he asked. "You've come here to speak with General Svirin, and that's exactly what will happen, if you wish." He reached across and opened the glove box. "Or, if you'd rather not surrender your weapon to me, at least put it in the glove box. It will be returned to you at the conclusion of your meeting."

"You knew that I was coming?"

"Yes."

"How?"

"That I cannot answer. But the general has agreed to meet with you, though he's not overly anxious to do so. You have the reputation of being a dangerous man."

"And these are dangerous political times just now in Moscow."

A flicker of surprise crossed the driver's face, but just for a moment. "Much the same as it has been in the U.S."

"We don't shoot dissenters."

"What about your President Kennedy, or Martin Luther King, or the presidential candidate George Wallace?"

McGarvey reached inside the Gazik, put the PSM in the glove box, and got in the car.

FORTY-FOUR

Pete had been sitting with Toni and her crew for the past hour, and in her estimation it had been a waste of time. They had come up with absolutely nothing concrete that would clear Otto from suspicion of being a mole or of being a mad genius who was playing games with the system. Either way it pointed to his being a traitor.

It was more than depressing in Pete's mind, and Toni agreed with her.

"There's nothing more to do here for the moment," Toni told the five sitting around in a circle.

They all got up and headed to their own desks.

Hank Rogers patted Pete on the shoulder. "Not to worry, we'll figure out this shit."

Pete looked up and touched his hand with hers. "I'm worried."

"Otto's got a lot of good people on his side."

When they were gone, Pete followed Toni into her office and they closed the glass door.

"We've lost contact with RP," Toni said. "And it has us worried."

"RP?" Pete asked.

"Rice Paddy. His real name is Tommy Chang, our NOC inside DPRK's nuclear research facility at Yongbyon. He was born in South Korea but came to the States when he was fifteen. Started work with us after he graduated MIT with his degree in physics. His Ph.D. thesis was mathematic modeling for advanced nuclear design. Two years later he came to us."

"A pretty valuable asset to send into badland," Pete said.

"He's motivated. Wants a unified Korean peninsula. Anyway, we had some good intel early on that the North Koreans were developing a strong nuclear program that mixed with their work in missile development trumped just about everything. So, Tommy was recruited, trained, and sent over as an exchange scientist, where he defected."

"He sent us good intel?" Pete asked, even though she knew the answer.

"Gold-seam," Toni said. "His stuff was a partial basis for the president's latest summit talks in Beijing."

"When did he go silent?"

"Three days ago," Toni said. "The same time Colonel Ivan Aladko, an officer with the SVR's technical espionage division, dropped out of sight. Until yesterday, when we got word he'd shown up in Pyongyang."

"Who'd we get that from?"

"We have a source at the airport," Toni said. She ran a hand over her eyes. "None of this is looking very good for Otto."

"I know. But evidence against someone is never this overwhelming or pat. There're always inconsistencies, even contradictions, holes a mile wide."

"Doesn't make this case invalid. I mean it wasn't as if Otto tried to hide his online movements."

"That's the point. He's too smart to make it so obvious."

"Which brings us back to the possibility he's playing a game."

"Just a game," Pete said.

"One in which people working for us disappear. Where the opposition players all get promotions. And where someone tried to gun down you and Mac. A hell of a game."

Pete looked away, racking her brain to come up with something that even remotely made any sense. "Okay," she said. "For the sake of argument let's see if we can take this in two separate directions."

"I'm listening."

"First Otto's playing a game. What's the point? I mean, games have objectives, what is the object of this one? Certainly not merely killing a few of our NOCs, if in fact they're dead and someone else is standing in for them or unless they were all working on some common problem that he didn't want them to solve for whatever reason. And second, it certainly it isn't money. He's got plenty."

"MICE," Toni said. It was the CIA's acronym for why agents defect. Money. Ideology. Conscience. Ego. "So, money's out. How about ideology? You and Mac and Mary know him better than anyone else in the building."

"I wouldn't know where to begin. Kirk's always been a rah-rah American idealist. 'Truth, justice, and the American way'—Superman's motto."

"We're talking about Otto."

"Yeah, and that's the point. Mac has known him practically forever. And if Otto was way out there on the left, Mac would know it."

"Okay, so let's skip to the obvious," Toni said. "Ego."

Pete nodded, her heart filled with sadness. "Ego," she said.

"Let's get back to why you want us to concentrate on Russia, besides the fact that McGarvey went over there, presumably on your behalf," Lapides said.

"For starts, someone tried to assassinate him and Pete right outside their apartment," Otto said. "Wasn't the Pakis or Kim Jong-un's slant-eyes."

"Your political insensitivities aren't helping your case."

"Oh, fuck you, Al. Pakistan certainly isn't a friend. Never has been. Especially not after we flew in and took out Bin Laden right under their noses. And Kim is no pal either. If he had his druthers he'd mate some of his nukes—soon as they've been weaponized—stack them atop some ICBMs, and send them our way. Political insensitivities? Give me a break."

"Unless of course you'd feel more vulnerable talking about your contacts with the ISI and North Korea's SD," Lapides said.

"Up to you if all you want to do is waste time."

"The point here is proving you're a traitor."

"The point here is finding out why someone wants to make you believe that I've committed treason," Otto said. He turned to Benkerk. "Maybe you can make him figure out that I'm not the only possibility on the table."

"Let's move on to Pakistan," Lapides suggested.

"Christ," Otto said, then he smiled. "Tell you what, Al. Why don't you grab your right ear with your left hand, and your left ear with your right hand, and pull. The sucking sound you'll hear is your head coming out of your ass."

Pete had gotten to her feet, ready to leave, when Mary showed up at the door and Toni buzzed her in. She looked frazzled, and Pete told her so.

"I'm running out of things to do," she said. "Thought I'd drop in and see what you guys have come up with, if anything."

"Nothing substantive to this point," Pete said. She didn't want to bring up the ego issue, because not only was it disturbing but there was nothing any of them could do about it. In any event, there was nothing of any real value coming from Otto's interrogation. The only evidence to this point was circumstantial. More so because they couldn't find any motivation for Otto being a traitor.

"Have you heard from Kirk?"

"He's on his way out to see General Svirin."

"The one who runs the GRU's North American Illegals Division?" Mary asked.

"He's hoping to get some answers to why someone was sent to assassinate us."

Mary smiled slightly. "Your hubby has more balls than brains. They won't arrest him, no way to keep it from Putin. Nor can they simply shoot him, especially not on Russian soil. But they could arrange an accident. And of course, the issue is that you guys are trying to prove my husband is innocent, and someone doesn't want that to happen."

"Another piece of evidence against him," Toni said.

"Circumstantial," Pete said.

"Circumstantial or not, Toni's right," Mary said. "It's another nail in my husband's coffin."

FORTY-FIVE

□

The driver had escorted McGarvey down a back hallway to what appeared to be a summer kitchen, with French doors that looked out to the birch forest and a pond down a path about fifty yards away. Lights illuminated a dock and a small rowboat.

No security or any staff except for the driver were evident; no armed men lurking in the trees ready to come in guns blazing if the American visitor were to try something. This place was simply the country home of a moderately successful Russian. In this case a one-star general.

Mac was seated at a wooden table, his back to the door into the house proper, when General Svirin appeared.

"Good evening, Mr. McGarvey," the man said. "I sincerely hope that you didn't come here to assassinate me."

McGarvey turned around as the general came the rest of the way in and took a seat across the table. The man looked like anything but a typical Russian. His features were finely defined, his hair light-colored and his eyes blue. He could easily have passed for a Brit, some younger member of the House of Lords.

"I didn't come here to shoot you, just to ask a couple of questions."

"Then why did you come armed?"

"With everything that's happened in the past couple of days, I thought it would be prudent."

"You mean the attempt on the lives of you and your wife in Georgetown?"

"Yes."

The general's English was slightly accented British. Not surprising for a man who'd spent a year at Oxford, possibly as a deep-cover agent, and he hadn't lost the mannerisms or look. But it was also clear to McGarvey that the man was new to his rank.

"I didn't order it. No reason to do so."

"But you knew of it."

"Yes, and I was also warned that you had shown up in Moscow and would likely attempt to see me," Svirin said. "And possibly the president as well."

"I haven't tried to make contact with him yet."

"He's been advised that you're here."

"What made whoever told you that I was in Moscow think that I was coming to talk to you?"

Svirin looked away for a moment. When he turned back he looked like a man debating revealing a secret, something distasteful. "Would you like something to drink?"

"A beer."

Almost instantly the driver appeared with two glasses and two bottles of Heineken already opened. He set them on the table and withdrew.

McGarvey took a drink from the bottle, and the general did the same. Two old pals enjoying a beer together. Nothing more than a simple social situation. The message was strong that Svirin wanted peace and not confrontation. And it was also clear that he wanted McGarvey to get to the point and leave as quickly as possible. But there was no guilt on his face, in his eyes, in the set of his posture, and yet the man was holding something back.

"Congratulations on your promotion," McGarvey said.

Svirin looked guilty, but it passed and he smiled. "Is that why you came here?"

"Actually yes, it is. Less than two years ago you were an SVR captain. You must have caught someone's attention."

Svirin inclined his head but said nothing.

"Maybe you came up with a new John in England or somewhere else who turned out to be a gold seam. The mother lode."

"Even if that were the case I couldn't talk about it."

"Do you know the name Otto Rencke?"

"I've heard of him."

"Was he your John?"

"A lot of people in the business have heard of him, but it doesn't mean anyone has or is working with him."

"What's the general consensus?"

"I don't understand."

"The people who've heard of him, you included: Do they want him dead?"

"Muzzled, yes, but dead would be preferable. He's a dangerous adversary. No computer system is completely safe from him. In fact, an entire division is devoted to staying one step ahead of his reach."

"A division in what service?"

"I couldn't say."

"The SVR or possibly the GRU, even your Illegals Department?"

"I couldn't say."

"Otto Rencke is a close personal friend of mine," McGarvey said. "In fact, he and I have worked together for a number of years. He's been charged with treason, and your name came up as his contact here in Russia. Someone to whom he was passing information. Sensitive information."

Svirin smiled and took a long drink of his beer. "Even if that were so, you must realize that I couldn't admit it."

"The case has been made that Otto is your gold seam, and it's why you were promoted so fast."

Svirin said nothing.

"The point is, Felix Gennadi, that a growing body of evidence shows that in actuality Otto has been passing you credible but false information, and

that in fact you are his gold seam. His arrest and apparent charges are nothing more than a ruse to expose you as a spy for us."

"Nonsense."

"At this moment the GRU and SVR are in a territorial fight over this issue, who gets ultimate control over operations in the U.S. You or them."

"As you say captains don't suddenly get promoted to general because they are suspects."

"In this sort of a fight that's exactly what happens," McGarvey said. "For the SVR to bring down a captain would be next to nothing. But bringing down a general would be a coup."

Svirin shook his head, but he didn't seem as certain as he had.

"You're in trouble, and I've come here to help you as well as my friend."

"Your trip has been a waste of time, Mr. McGarvey, and in fact if the president hadn't been advised that you were in Moscow your life would be in extreme danger. As it is you will remain relatively safe until tomorrow when you fly back to Washington."

"Free from assassination?"

"Yes."

"But not from an accident or a street crime—a random shooting."

"Things like that happen in all large cities, even Moscow."

"Or perhaps if I think you've been lying I might kill you here and now."

"Your pistol is in the Gazik."

"I don't need a gun," McGarvey said, keeping an eye on the man, while watching the doorway into the house proper behind him.

The driver suddenly appeared with what looked like a Heckler & Koch compact submachine gun in hand.

Svirin raised a hand. *"Eto ne nuzhno, Grigori." It's not needed.*

The driver withdrew.

"The fact of the matter, General, is that we may have a traitor inside the CIA—though it's not my friend. But your name is one of several that have been linked to the operation."

"All Russians?"

"Only two. The others are intelligence officers in Pakistan and North Korea."

"Who is the other Russian?"

"Ivan Aladko."

Svirin was visibly shaken, and he got to his feet. "Our meeting is completed."

McGarvey didn't rise. "You already know that a team of four Russian shooters, who I assume might have been Spetsnaz, were sent to assassinate me and my wife. A fifth man, who identified himself as a Moscow police officer by the name of Anatoli Krestov, was there as well, but he said he'd been sent to make sure we weren't murdered."

"Leave."

"Do you know this name?"

"I said get the fuck out of here, before I have my man shoot you."

"I think that there's a power struggle between your service, the GRU, and someone in the SVR for control of whoever the traitor is at the CIA. I mean to find out who it is."

"I can give you one thing," Svirin said. "Ivan Aladko is an officer in the SVR. I don't know who in the CIA is passing secrets to us—certainly not to me—but I do know that Colonel Aladko is currently on an assignment in Pyongyang."

FORTY-SIX

Jerri hit Zimbowski's button on her console, and he picked up immediately, as she knew he would. It was past six in the evening. The day-shift people had already left, and the swing-shift crew were busy at their stations. But whenever something interesting was in the wind, Zimbowski would stick around at least until some decent progress had been made. And so would Jerri. It was in their nature.

"Something new?" he asked.

"Two things."

Zimbowski rang off, and a minute later he came lumbering across the room, trundling his chair behind him. He pulled up next to her, sat down, donned his Bose headset, and plugged into her console.

Jerri watched him as he listened to the recording of the brief conversation that she had already washed through several decryption algorithms—one of them searching for the cell tower here in Washington, another cataloging rhythms and cadences peculiar to a single language, and a third trying to match the timbre of the voices with those of males or females.

When the recording came to an end he motioned for her to replay it, which she did, three more times, until he nodded.

"They're both speaking English, but the Moscow speaker's rhythm is off," he said. "So, the sender is speaking American English, and the Moscow speaker's English is accented."

"Not his native language," Jerri said.

"His?"

"Boss comes up with a sixty-seven percent confidence in the Russian's gender. I think it's closer to eighty percent."

The trouble with all computers was that they had no intuition. They could only take raw data and process it. They weren't near enough to AI status yet to make leaps of judgment, or what were called WAGs, which were wild-ass guesses. People were different. Jerri called it her job security blanket.

"Okay, we have a Russian male in Moscow speaking English to someone in D.C. Do we have a gender for the caller?"

Jerri had to grin. "Boss hasn't come up with anything yet, except that the pitch and timbre of the voice is of an indeterminate range."

"So, he admits he doesn't know," Zimbowski said. "But you do."

"Yeah, and it's crazy."

"But?"

"I'd guess it's a guy, but with a high-pitched voice for his gender," Jerri

said. "I think our local speaker is a gay man, possibly in his early to late twenties, maybe thirty."

Zimbowski had to laugh, and he pulled his headphones down so that they were hanging around his neck. "How about the Russian?"

"Normal voice range for a man, but tougher to even make a WAG."

"So, we have a gay man in D.C. who's possibly had an affair with a Russian, perhaps they're still lovers, and they chatted to say how much they missed each other."

"It's a good guess, Con, but I think there's something more."

"Okay, we're both pulling overtime, because why?"

"I've more or less nailed down the cell phone tower."

Zimbowski just looked at her.

"Boss says fifty-three percent, I think it's more like ninety-five. Union Station."

Zimbowski suddenly looked interested. "Inside the station or out?"

"Signal's way to strong for it to be from inside."

"But in the near vicinity."

"Can't tell for sure, but my guess might be from a park bench across the street."

Zimbowski smiled. "You think like a spy."

"I'll take that as a compliment," Jerri said.

It was common for someone making a clandestine call to do so from the vicinity of a very busy, very public place, like Union Station. If the cops or the Bureau were monitoring and came swooping in for an arrest, the perp could ditch the phone and duck into the station, where they would get lost in the crowd.

"Go home and get some rest, let Boss do what it's supposed to do."

"Give the Bureau the heads-up," Jerri said.

"Another WAG that something's going down?"

She shook her head. "Just a hunch."

"Will do," Zimbowski said. He got up and started to return to his desk.

"Call the CIA, too," Jerri said.

Lapides had gone upstairs fifteen minutes ago, just before eight, to take a shower and change clothes. They'd been going at it for what seemed like weeks instead of just a couple of days, and everyone was worn out except for Otto, who at times acted as if he was having fun.

Benkerk's cell phone chimed, and he got up and went into the stair hall to take the call.

Otto got up, stretched, and went to the windows that looked down the hill through the woods to the buildings on campus, all lit up 24/7. Mary had been on his mind for most of the afternoon and early evening, and he had become increasingly worried about her. The opposition had taken potshots

at McGarvey and Pete, but those two knew how to take care of themselves. In fact, they had become a hell of a team over the past year or so.

And it was the same with him and Mary, except that at times lately she had seemed almost fragile to him. As if she were on the verge of cracking up. More than once he had suggested to her that maybe it was time for her to get out of the business. Maybe devote herself to taking care of Audie, their adopted child, who for now was down at the CIA's training facility outside of Williamsburg for safekeeping.

"I'll get out if you do," she'd told him each time he'd made the suggestion.

And maybe she was right, he'd begun to think. Maybe it was time for all of them to make a break from the Company. He and Mac had brought up the possibility of starting up their own business—Executive Solutions, they would call it—to take on issues that the establishment couldn't take on because they were constrained by one law or another. It was a consideration that none of them, especially Mac, had ever been hampered by, but things were changing under the new president.

Mac called it doing justice. It was part of his mantra, which from the start had been "Truth, justice, and the American way." Superman's motto in the comics from World War II, more than seventy years ago. Maybe even more important now, Mac had said.

Another part of his mind had been constantly working the issue of what was going on at this moment. He'd not been overly surprised that someone had managed to implicate him as a traitor. Nor was he puzzled. He had made a lot of enemies on both sides of the pond—here and in Russia, but especially Russia.

His dabbling in computers and his development of his system he'd originally called his darlings, but after his wife Louise had been shot to death in the line of duty, he'd renamed Lou, had seriously threatened the mainframes of a lot of foreign intelligence computers.

Sometimes he and Lou had simply played games to piss people off—especially the computer geeks in the SVR and GRU, plus North Korea's State Security Department and Pakistan's ISI. So, it had not come as a great surprise when his name had been linked to the names of officers in those agencies.

What had come as a surprise was the sophistication of the charges, and the names of actual officers whose spectacular promotions had been timed with his incursions into their systems.

It had been reverse engineering, of course, fitting his name with the correct timing. But whoever had done it knew him and Lou very well, and was intelligent, even borderline genius.

It was an attribute he found challenging to the limit and charming to the max.

The sliding doors opened and Otto turned around.

Benkerk came in, his face drawn as if he had just heard some bad news. He closed the doors behind him.

"What is it?" Otto asked.

"I just got a call from Tom Waksberg. Ivan Aladko, your contact with the SVR, just showed up in Pyongyang and outed our NOC at one of North Korea's main nuclear research facilities. The man was shot to death last night trying to escape."

FORTY-SEVEN

Svirin walked McGarvey through the hall to the front door just as the driver brought the Gazik around. It was coming up on two in the morning, the only sounds other than the jeep's engine were some night birds around back, probably in or near the pond.

"You have a nice place here," McGarvey said.

"It's a refuge from the goings-on in the city," Svirin said. "Do you and your wife have such a place?"

"We did. One on an island off the Gulf Coast of Florida, and then when that started to go bad we bought a lighthouse on a Greek island."

"And will you go there now?"

"No, it was ruined, too."

Svirin smiled almost wanly. "I expect such a thing has happened to you before."

"Too many times," McGarvey said. "It's the business we're in."

Svirin nodded sympathetically. "You've had so many losses. Why do you continue?"

McGarvey was surprised. "You know my background?"

"As a young lieutenant I was briefly put in charge of developing a biography of you when you served as CIA's director."

"And later on?"

"Like now?" Svirin asked. "I, too, am a student of Sun Tzu. 'Before going into a battle, know your enemy.' I prepared for this meeting."

"Be careful, General, that you're sure who your real enemies are, because this shit is just starting."

"You have enemies here, too."

"I always have."

"I mean because of your investigation into the identity of the traitor in the CIA."

"It's not Rencke."

Svirin thought for a long moment or two, until he finally nodded. "I believe that you're right. He is simply too obvious. But someone wants to bring him down for what I suspect may be the wrong reason."

"Who wants it and what is the correct reason?" McGarvey asked.

A tiny dot of laser aiming light appeared in the middle of Svirin's chest, and McGarvey shouldered the man aside at the same instant a bullet plowed into the doorframe and the sound of the distant rifle shot cracked in the night silence.

Svirin pulled away and had started to turn when the laser dot appeared on

the back of his head and his skull erupted in a spray of blood and he went down, crashing hard through the open door and onto the floor just inside the stair hall.

The driver jumped out of the jeep, firing the Heckler & Koch in one hand in the general direction of the dirt road as he ducked low and tried to reach safety behind the vehicle.

But he stumbled and went down, face-first, the sounds of three rifle shots coming one after the other in rapid succession, from somewhere in the woods to the right of the access road.

Keeping low, McGarvey raced toward the fallen driver, rifle shots bracketing but missing him.

He threw himself down on the dirt just behind the right front fender, close enough to reach out and grab the submachine gun from the dead man's hand.

He pulled back at the same time a half-dozen rounds slammed into the driver's body and the front of the Gazik, puncturing the radiator and smashing the right headlight.

The sudden silence was nearly complete. Even the birds by the pond had stopped their calls, and only the fluid draining out of the radiator and falling to the ground made any noise.

McGarvey ejected the magazine and checked the load. Only a half-dozen rounds remained. He reseated the magazine and switched the selector to single fire.

A minute later a car's engine started from somewhere not too far away down the road, perhaps twenty meters or so, and slowly faded until it was lost in the distance.

The driver was dead, hit at least three times in the back and once at the base of his head.

Still keeping low, McGarvey went back to the general's body, half in and half out of the front stair hall, and he, too, was dead.

Keeping in the shadows just inside the house, he cocked an ear to listen for any noise—perhaps the rattling of some brush, footfalls on the gravel driveway, someone coughing—but there was nothing until a telephone on the hall table rang.

He let it ring three times before he went the rest of the way in and picked it up. "*Da?*" he said.

After a brief moment, the call ended and a dial tone came up.

He put the phone down and went back outside.

Whoever the shooter or shooters were, they had come to kill the general, not him, which didn't add up if they wanted Otto to be found guilty. He was missing something.

Keeping the weapon, McGarvey got his pistol from the Gazik's glove compartment, then made his way through the woods to where he came within sight of the rental Kia.

No one was there, the night still silent.

He cautiously approached the car, and getting down on his hands and knees

he inspected the undercarriage, especially directly beneath the driver's seat. But nothing had been placed there, no explosives.

Getting up, he unloaded the submachine gun and tossed the magazine in one direction, ejected the bullet in another, and tossed the weapon itself deeper into the woods in a third direction.

On the M8 back to Moscow, traffic at this hour practically nonexistent, McGarvey had plenty of time to think. Svirin was obviously in a tight position, but not because of any connection with Otto. Something else had been troubling the general, and it plainly showed in his body language and the things he'd said. And, of course, that he'd been the primary if not the only target of an assassination nailed it.

The most obvious likelihood was some sort of a power struggle between the SVR and GRU—and especially the GRU's illegals operation in the U.S. It was for the product they were getting from the real traitor, most likely someone inside the CIA.

He'd believed the general had been telling the truth when he denied being Otto's source and that Otto had been his John.

It was only one part of what he had learned by coming here; he wasn't any closer to knowing who the traitor was. But the trip was worth the effort because of what he'd learned from Svirin's assassination.

All of it was entirely too pat, in McGarvey's mind, but it was enough to let him understand that he was on the right track. The biggest problem was that the further he and Pete got into the investigation the more people were being gunned down.

Back at the Marriott, McGarvey parked the car in the same slot and took the elevator up to his floor. He pulled out his pistol and held it out of sight beside his right leg as the door opened.

The corridor was empty.

At his room, he worked the lock with his key card while holding the pistol, and eased the door open.

Nothing moved inside. Nothing was changed. The one light he'd left on at the bedside was still on, nor could he detect the scent of someone who'd been here or who was still in the room.

Nevertheless, he entered the room moving fast and low, leading with his pistol, checking everything including the shower, until he was satisfied that no one was hiding.

Securing the safety lock on the door, he telephoned Daltry's private number at the embassy, assuming that it would roll over to his cell phone if he wasn't in his office.

But a woman answered on the first ring. "Four-seven-three-eight. Who is calling?"

"Kirk McGarvey. May I speak with Mr. Daltry?"

"Before he left he said you might be calling."

"Where can I reach him?"

The woman hesitated for a beat. "I'm sorry, Mr. Director, but he's dead. It was a car accident on the way home. He was broadsided by a fucking garbage truck."

FORTY-EIGHT

It was two in the morning when Pete was awakened from a fitful sleep by someone buzzing the door downstairs. She'd not heard from Mac last night and she was worried enough about him that she'd had nightmares. And just now she had the crazy thought that it was him downstairs.

She got up and went to the speaker by the door. "Yes?"

"May I come up?" a woman asked. It was Mary.

"Of course," Pete said, and she buzzed the door. She had gone to bed in one of Mac's shirts, and nothing more, but it was just Mary and she didn't bother getting dressed.

She had the door open when Mary, dressed in jeans and a dark pullover, appeared at the head of the stairs. She had a momentary thought that the woman was rigged for a night field op, but then she smiled. "You're up early."

"Sorry, I just couldn't sleep worrying about everything."

"I tossed and turned all night myself," Pete said, and they hugged. Inside, she closed and locked the door. "Should I put on the coffee?"

"I think I'd rather have a glass of wine."

Pete had to laugh. "White this early," she said.

She went into the tiny kitchen and fetched a bottle of a decent Italian pinot grigio, a corkscrew, and two glasses, which she brought out to the living room, where Mary had kicked off her sneakers and was perched on the couch.

"I'm sorry about the hour," Mary said.

"Don't be," Pete told her as she opened the wine. She poured them both a glass, and raised hers. "To what?" she asked.

"To ending this nightmare," Mary said, and they drank.

They sat in silence for a full minute or more, looking at each other from time to time. Pete couldn't read the expression in Mary's eyes, except that she was frightened, and she turned away each time she took a sip from her glass.

Pete refilled both of theirs. "Otto seems to be holding up okay," she said.

"It's a show. He's just as worried as the rest of us are because he's convinced that there really is a mole in the Company."

"Has he given you any hints?"

"He doesn't have a clue, and that's what bothers him the most," Mary said. "He'd really like to reactivate Lou to put her back to work."

Pete hadn't thought about doing something like that, but now she had an idea. "Can you still access the office?"

"I have the key. But her backup batteries are dead and the AC power's been cut and there's nothing we can do about either."

"We can't bring new batteries up there. Even if we could get them past security, they'd be too heavy for us to lift. And I'm no electronic technician, so I wouldn't know how to hook them up anyway."

"So what are you thinking?"

"Well, I'm a spy, and by definition that makes me a sneak, a liar, and a thief."

Mary laughed.

"You can get into the office while I break into the equipment room at the end of the corridor, where the circuit breaker boxes are. I'm no techie, but I can flip a switch."

"When do you want to try?"

"I'll get dressed and we can drive over before the morning shift starts showing up."

Jerri had gone across the hall to have a Coke and a Snickers bar, and then lay down on the couch for a couple of hours of sleep. But she'd been troubled about both speakers, especially the gay guy outside Union Station. And when she'd left her desk, she still hadn't nailed down the location of the speaker in Russia, except that she had begun to believe it wasn't Moscow, but somewhere outside the city.

Zimbowski came in and touched her shoulder.

Instantly awake, she looked up at him, and then sat up. "What?"

"Boss is making progress, but we need you."

She sat up, and Zimbowski opened a can of Coke and handed it to her. "Nasty," he said.

"It's the caffeine," she replied, and she downed half the can, then got to her feet, and followed her supervisor back to the surveillance floor and her post.

"I didn't bother switching to my console," Zimbowski said.

Jerri set her Coke aside and settled into her seat. The same recorded patterns were crossing the screen, but at a faster rate, with much of the extraneous noise filtered away. "Okay, what're we looking at?"

"Two things are starting to come up. The first is the Russian speaker whose English sounded odd. You were right about that much, but Boss seems to think that the accent might be British. The intonations are a near match with a couple of our samples."

"Not enough," Jerri said.

She donned her headset, one cuff half off her left ear, and listened to the recording of the Russian speaker's voice, which had been washed a hundred times, concentrating not on picking up individual words but on the timbre and cadences.

She brought up six English speakers whose voices had been intercepted and identified at some point or another in the past, and had been stored as comparisons.

Overlaying the six voices with that of the Russian, she began to narrow

down individual words, stopping and bringing them up to follow the re-corded tracings of the comparisons—one speaker and one untranslated word at a time.

Twenty minutes later she hit pay dirt. "Gotcha," she muttered.

Zimbowski was sitting next to her. "I'm not hearing it. Tell me."

"This guy's a Russian all right, but his English is definitely British. I'd say he was probably educated at Oxford or someplace like that and probably worked deep cover."

"What else?"

Jerri brought back the original recording, but now washed, looking along a dozen or more parameters, each searching for a single clue, all the way from the gender and age of the speaker to the location.

The gay man's location had been fairly easy, but according to what Boss had been doing for the couple of hours she'd been asleep, the Russian had definitely not been anywhere in Moscow. Inside the Kremlin would have been absolutely over the moon, but they weren't so lucky.

"We're sampling exchanges outside the outer ring highway in all direc-tions in ten-kilometer jumps," Jerri said. "Could take a while."

"I'll stick around, but you might as well go home," Zimbowski offered. "I'll call when we get a hit."

"Not a chance in hell, Con. This is mine. Anyway, if you want to go home I'll call you."

"I'm not going anywhere either," he said. "How about I go down to the cafeteria and bring back a couple of egg sandwiches and some coffee?"

"Sounds good."

The thirty-four night-shift operators had kept a curious eye on what Jerri and the day-shift supervisor were doing, but no one interfered. And even the night-shift people whose consoles Jerri and Zimbowski were using had stayed out of their way and moved to other stations.

Jerri went across the hall to the women's restroom, used the toilet, and then splashed some cold water on her face. When she got back, Boss had come up with a hit.

She split her screen, one half displaying the audio tracks, the other half displaying a section of countryside well beyond Moscow's outer ring highway.

Zimbowski showed up with the sandwiches and coffee, and Jerri looked up at him.

"Did you call the CIA earlier to let them know we might be on to some-thing?" she asked.

"Yes, and the Bureau."

"Call Langley again and find out if they have anyone of interest who has a place out in the country north of Moscow, off the M8 highway near a place called Sergiev Posad."

FORTY-NINE

An attractive woman in her late twenties or early thirties, dressed in a man's dark suit and tie, but cut for a feminine figure, was seated in the busy lobby when McGarvey came down with his single bag a little after eleven. She got up and intercepted him before he reached the front desk.

"Good morning, Mr. Director," she said, and she stuck out her hand. "I'm June Ward, from embassy security. I'm here to see you safely out of Dodge."

McGarvey shook her hand. "I was sorry to hear about Roger."

"It wasn't an accident."

"I didn't think so."

"My car is out front. You just have the one bag?"

"Yes. But I have to check out first."

"Already taken care of."

Outside they walked across the driveway and got into an embassy Cadillac Escalade, McGarvey putting his bag in the backseat.

Once they were away from the hotel and in traffic heading toward the road out to Vnukovo Airport, she glanced at him. "Was your trip to speak with General Svirin fruitful?"

"He was shot to death by a sniper as I was leaving."

"Son of a bitch," the woman said. "You've started a war by showing up here."

"I didn't start it," McGarvey shot back. "And unless your shop doesn't already know it, the war is between the SVR and GRU. Territorial rights."

"What territory?"

"Do you know the name Otto Rencke?"

"Along with yours and your wife's, everyone knows Mr. Rencke."

"Well, he's been arrested and charged with treason. And our Russian friends are right in the middle of it."

"But other than the obvious reasons of wanting to muzzle him, why now?"

"Because there is a mole inside the Company, and framing Otto for it seemed to be the easy way out."

"Dumb," Ward said, and she drove in silence for a bit. "We're not done here yet, are we?"

"I don't think so. So, whoever's your assistant station chief better tell his people to keep their heads down for the time being."

"That'd be me," she said.

"A little young for the job?"

"Or a little too female?"

"Young," McGarvey said.

"My birthday is in two weeks. I'll be forty-three."

McGarvey was surprised. "Sorry for my chauvinist attitude."

"Thanks, but I'll take it as gallantry."

The ride out to the airport was uneventful, and if any word that McGarvey was a person of interest to whatever agency had assassinated Daltry or Svirin had been sent he wasn't made aware of it. His security check-in went without a hitch on the basis of his sky marshal identification, and inside his pistol was returned to him.

Waiting at his gate, he debated calling Pete. It was just three in the morning in D.C., and with any luck she was still sound asleep in their Georgetown apartment. And yet in the light of what had happened here overnight, she had to be warned.

He speed-dialed her cell, but the call came up incomplete, which meant she'd probably turned off her phone for some reason. Next, he called the apartment number, but after six rings he gave it up.

It wasn't right.

He called Mary's cell and then the McLean house with the same results.

They were off somewhere together, and for whatever reason had turned off their cell phones. He could only speculate and worry.

On the basis of Mary's credentials, they got through the main gate and into the underground VIP parking garage without having to go through the normal security check upstairs in the lobby of the OHB.

No one was in the third-floor corridor, and all the doors were shut, though some of the offices, especially those where legends and timetables were worked out for officers heading to some foreign assignments, were occupied 24/7.

Mary unlocked the door to Otto's suite.

"What are you going to ask her to do?" Pete asked at her side.

"I want her to work up a short list of possible suspects."

"Okay, stand by," Pete said, and she hurried to the end of the corridor as Mary ducked inside the Wolf's Den.

The equipment room for this floor was protected by an ordinary key-operated lock, and not a key card, but using Mac's lockpick set it still took her nearly three minutes to get it open.

Inside, she flipped on the lights. The room was about as small as a guest bathroom in a house. Along one wall were the monitors and controls for the fire suppressant system on this floor, and on the opposite wall a gray metal door that covered the electrical circuit breaker panel.

She popped it open, and for an instant she didn't want to believe what she was seeing, except that it made perfect sense. Otto's suite of offices, which had from the beginning been treated as only one location, was designated 3307. The circuit breaker slot for that location was empty.

"I thought you might come looking for this sooner or later," Van Gessel, the Company's chief of security, said.

Pete turned around. Van Gessel, holding the circuit breaker in his left hand, was standing in the doorway. "Was I that obvious?" she asked, resigned.

"We've been keeping an eye on you and Mrs. Rencke from the start. Once my people saw her show up at your place and then the two of you head this way, I was called."

"Johnny on the spot."

Van Gessel smiled. "I don't live far, but it's the middle of the night and I had to hustle."

"How'd you know we weren't going up to see Toni?"

"A lucky guess."

Pete stepped aside as he came in and put the breaker in the empty slot, and pressed the reset button.

"Mary will be expecting me."

"We'll just give her a minute to power up Otto's computer and enter the password."

"You know that we're all after the same thing here. Finding the mole."

"No. You and Mary and your husband are trying to prove that Rencke isn't the one."

"Same thing."

"You've seen the evidence," Van Gessel said. "It's overwhelming."

"A little over-the-top, don't you think?"

Van Gessel shrugged. "Even the bright ones like Rencke make mistakes sometimes."

"Are you going to arrest us, too?" Pete asked.

"You have creds to get into the building, and you've committed no real crime."

"Aiding and abetting a felon."

Van Gessel hesitated for just a beat, and his face dropped a little. "I'm not the bad guy here. Whatever you think of me, I still believe that a man is innocent until proven guilty."

"Then why's Otto being interrogated?"

"As I said, the evidence against him is overwhelming."

"But he's innocent till proven guilty?" Pete asked.

Van Gessel nodded.

"Then why aren't you guys helping us find the real mole?"

"Who says that we're not?" Van Gessel said, and he stepped back into the corridor. "Shall we see how Mrs. Rencke is getting along?"

Pete followed him down the corridor to Otto's offices. The door was ajar and the lights were on inside, but Mary was seated at the workstation in the inner room, the display table and wall screen blank.

"I would have thought you'd have turned on the computer by now," Van Gessel said.

"When Lou spotted you coming out of the equipment room she recommended I shut her down."

"Bring it back up."

"I don't think you want me to do that, Van," Mary said.

"Why not?"

"She's pretty smart. Smart enough to figure out how to get in contact with Otto, something you definitely don't want to happen."

Van Gessel held out his hand. "Give me the key and you're free to go."

FIFTY

☐

Otto had a free run of the house, and he was in the kitchen drinking a beer and eating the last of the Twinkies at seven when Lapides, who was also in residence for the duration, came in and sat down at the counter.

"Thought I heard you rattling around down here," the interrogator said. He looked like he was vexed.

"I'd just as soon finish ASAP so I can get back to work catching bad guys," Otto said. "Same as you."

"I got a call from Van Gessel a few minutes ago."

"Let me guess, he caught Mary trying to power up Lou."

"You have another phone hidden somewhere?" Lapides asked sharply.

"Just my noggin," Otto said. "Is she under arrest, too?"

"Not yet."

"That's a good thing. You don't want to piss me off."

"You're not helping your case."

Otto laughed. "That's what Mary and Pete and Mac are doing. Any word from them?"

"Mrs. McGarvey was with your wife, and as far as I know McGarvey is still in Russia trying to cover your tracks, I would think."

Otto finished the beer and put the bottle on the counter next to the sink. "Is that what you really think? That all of them, Mac included, would sell out their country to protect a friend?"

"It's a possibility."

"Jesus, Mary, and Joseph," Otto muttered, turning away for a moment. "Then there's not a whole hell of a lot I can tell you." He shook his head. "I'm done."

"Fine, then let's get back to it."

"You're not listening. I'm done cooperating. I won't answer any of your questions. I fucking well quit."

"We can force the issue."

"Try."

"Believe me, Mr. Rencke, I'm no Lazlo Smits, but the evidence against you is very strong, and I'll do whatever needs be done to find out the rest."

"By the rest, you mean who my accomplices are?"

"That, and how much damage has been done to our national interests."

Otto shook his head again. "This shit is really hard to believe, ya know. I mean, what was Ripley's line in the second *Alien* movie? 'Have IQs dropped?' or something like that."

Lapides was at a loss.

Someone came in the front door and headed back to the kitchen. It was Benkerk, and he didn't look happy.

"Hi, Bill," Otto said. "I was just about to ask your partner: What damage to our national interests have you guys found?"

"Ivan Aladko showed up in Pyongyang and outed one of our NOCs, who was shot to death trying to escape," Benkerk said.

Otto was suddenly cold. "Do Mary and Pete know about this?"

"It came from Van, who got it from Toni, so presumably they do."

"What about Mac?"

"Our embassy got him out to the airport, so presumably he's on his way home. But we were also told that the GRU's General Svirin was shot to death, apparently while McGarvey was interviewing him at his dacha."

"Okay, all bets are off now," Otto said. "We need to get to work to figure out who's our mole, and ASAP before something else happens."

Benkerk's face fell even further. "It's already happened, and God only knows how you engineered it. But Roger Daltry, our Moscow chief of station, was killed in a car crash. They don't think that it was an accident."

There wasn't a morning over the past five years since his wife had died of a massive heart attack that Carleton Patterson didn't think about her. Getting out of bed these days was a chore, but then most everything was, he thought, for folks like him in their early eighties.

Finishing his customary breakfast of black tea with lemon and one toasted English muffin in the kitchen alcove overlooking his rose garden, he was looking forward to, and yet not looking forward to, his meeting with Harold Taft at nine this morning, in the director's office in the OHB.

To this point he'd seen no credible evidence linking Otto to any spy ring. The simple fact that kept popping into his mind from every shred of evidence he'd seen was that no damage had been done to the United States. In fact, the only concrete incident that had occurred was the attempted assassination of McGarvey and Pete in front of their apartment in Georgetown.

The only thing he could draw from the thing was that someone inside the Russian intelligence community had ordered it. But then there had been a bounty on Mac's head for nearly as long as Carleton could remember. And it didn't necessarily have anything to do with the possibility of there being a mole in the Agency.

Tobias Ranier, his houseman, came in as Carleton was wiping his lips and putting his napkin on the table. "Your jacket has been brushed and pressed, and I've brought the car out of the garage."

Tobias had been with him ever since Marjory had died, and had acted as a manservant, keeper of the house and property, a chauffeur, and sometimes an all-around sounding board and confidant.

The house telephone rang, and Tobias answered it. "You have reached the Patterson residence. How may I be of service, Mrs. McGarvey?"

Carleton nodded and put out his hand.

"Yes, ma'am, he's here," Tobias said, and he brought the phone over.

"Good morning, my dear," Patterson said. "What news have you heard from Kirk?"

"He's on his way back from Moscow and in one piece," Pete said, and she sounded out of breath.

"What is it?"

"The GRU officer he went to interview was shot to death at his dacha outside of Moscow at about the same moment our chief of Moscow Station was killed in a car crash."

"Good Lord."

"And there's more."

"Continue."

"The other Russian that Otto was supposedly exchanging secrets with showed up in Pyongyang and apparently outed one of our NOCs, who was shot to death."

It took Patterson a moment to digest what he was being told. "I was just leaving for Langley to meet with Admiral Taft."

"This doesn't look good, Carleton."

"No, it doesn't, my dear. Nevertheless, I believe in my heart of hearts that Otto is innocent and has been set up to cover the identity of the actual spy in our midst."

"I know you're right, but trying to prove it has already cost lives. And I'm pretty sure we're nowhere near the end."

"Unfortunately, I have to agree with you. So as Kirk would say, keep your head down and cover your six."

"You, too," Pete said. "And let me know what the admiral has to say."

"Of course."

Patterson finished dressing and, briefcase in hand, got into the backseat of the black Mercedes-Maybach, Tobias closing the door after him and getting behind the wheel.

Early mornings were always the best time for Patterson. His mind was at its sharpest and he almost always looked forward to what was coming up. But not this morning. He was increasingly worried that he would be unable to save Otto. The evidence was entirely too pat, but was overwhelming. Especially with the three deaths.

His house was in McLean, coincidentally not too far from Otto's residence, and riding along the tree-lined streets that wound their way through upscale neighborhoods he was always reminded just how lucky a man he was. In a career he mostly loved, except for just now.

A few blocks from where they would pick up Dolley Madison Boulevard, which would take them the back way to the Agency campus, they pulled up at a stop sign.

Tobias glanced up at the rearview mirror and then turned left as a white van with the logo of a plumbing company appeared, its service door sliding open.

Patterson only managed to catch a brief glimpse of two men holding what appeared to be automatic weapons before a dozen bullets crashed through the door and into his body, the first round hitting him in the head, killing him instantly.

ENDGAME

Traitor

Pete was waiting at the arrivals gate outside customs and immigration at Dulles a few minutes before nine in the evening when McGarvey showed up. He was surprised and glad to see her, but just for a moment until he caught the look of anguish on her face.

They embraced and when they parted her eyes were moist.

"What's happened?"

"Wait until we're alone in the car," she said, her voice quavering.

Linking arms, they went outside and crossed the busy lanes to where she had parked her green BMW, a police department placard on the driver's-side dash. He tossed his single bag in the backseat and got in the passenger seat.

He didn't press until they were well away from the airport on the Dulles Airport access road, traffic fairly busy because three international flights had come in within minutes of each other.

"How are you feeling, sweetheart?" she asked, glancing at him. Tears had welled up in her eyes.

"Maybe you should pull over and I'll drive," McGarvey said.

"I'm trying to get everything straight in my head, and I can't do it if I'm simply sitting on my butt. Do you understand?"

"Yes. So just tell me what's happened."

"I know about the shoot-out at Svirin's dacha, and I know about our chief of Moscow Station. No one believes Daltry's death was an accident. But I don't think you know that Ivan Aladko showed up in Pyongyang and outed one of our NOCs, who was shot to death."

"Svirin told me."

"He knew?"

"Yes, which pretty well nails down the idea that we're in the middle of some sort of a power play between the SVR and GRU, and one of the chess pieces is control of the asset in the Company."

Pete concentrated on her driving for a full minute or so, just keeping up with the flow of traffic, her actions automatic. McGarvey let her be for a bit.

"Has something happened to Otto?" he asked at last.

"Carleton and his driver were shot to death at a stop sign in McLean not fifteen minutes after I'd talked to him on the phone."

The news was devastating to McGarvey. He and Patterson had been friends for more years than he wanted to count. The man had grown old only in years but not in vitality, and the blanket of calm that always seemed to settle over whatever situation he walked into was practically a legend in the Company.

No director in more than forty years had entertained even the thought of replacing him as the CIA's general counsel.

"Witnesses?"

"No. He said that he was on the way to a meeting with Taft, so as soon as the word got to the seventh floor, the admiral called the FBI to investigate. But the only thing they've come up with so far is the weapons used. Two of them, SR-3 Vikhrs."

"The Whirlwind," McGarvey said. "Nine hundred armor-piercing rounds to go through sheet metal, like a car door."

"I don't know it."

"Mostly used by Spetsnaz, and not many other services because it's expensive to make."

"They weren't worried about sending a message, which pretty well lays it on the lap of the GRU."

"Federal Security Service special operators sometimes use it."

"FSB," Pete said. "They're new to the mix, besides the SVR and GRU."

"All Russians, and all of them wanting to take out whoever is trying to prove Otto's innocent."

"Therefore, proving he's guilty."

"Either that or a diversion to keep us busy defending him, instead of looking for the actual mole," McGarvey said.

"It's like what I read about the early days of the Cold War," Pete said. "Plots and schemes within plots and schemes. Nothing was ever as it seemed to be."

"Except that now Carleton is dead."

"I'll miss that dear old man," Pete said after a beat.

"So will I," McGarvey agreed, anger burning deep inside his chest. "But I have an idea."

"Tell me."

"I will when we get home. I need to get some sleep, and I need to figure out just how this'll go down."

"How what will go down?"

"We don't have to prove Otto isn't the traitor, we just have to make the traitor believe that we know who it is. They'll out themselves."

"How?"

"By running."

"And we'll take them down?"

"But before they run they'll have to try to kill us again," McGarvey said.

"Peachy."

Benkerk was upstairs in one of the front bedrooms in the Scattergood-Thorne house trying to get some sleep after a troubling session with Otto, who had led him and Lapides around in circles.

His refrain had been the same over and over again: "The other shoe is going to drop and when it does it'll be big."

"What shoe?" Lapides had asked. That was just after lunch yesterday.

"I haven't the foggiest, but someone is going to get killed."

"I'm told that McGarvey's on his way back from Moscow, so who's your best guess?" Benkerk had asked. "Maybe Pete, or Mary?"

Otto shook his head. "I don't know."

"What about the why?" Lapides had asked, but again Otto had no answer.

Benkerk's cell phone buzzed, waking him from a troubled sleep. He'd intended to go home after this evening's session, but when they were done he'd been dead on his feet and had decided to stay.

It was nearly midnight. The caller ID was blocked, which meant it was probably from the CIA. "Benkerk."

"Tom Waksberg. Were you sleeping?"

"Yes. Is there something new?"

"Carleton Patterson and his driver were shot to death early this morning on their way out here to meet with the admiral."

Benkerk sat straight up, totally awake as if he'd never been asleep in his life. "Do you have a line on the shooters?"

"Two Russian-made automatic weapons, not readily available yet on the black market. Our best guess is either GRU or the FSB. We're leaning toward the former."

"Why the hell wasn't I told earlier?"

"Orders from the director. He wanted to wait until we had a better sense of what happened."

"Shit."

"Bill, is there any possibility, even the smallest bit, that Rencke has access to a phone?"

"I don't think so."

"Would you bet your life on it?"

"No, but I'm going to find out for sure as soon as we hang up."

"Let me know immediately one way or the other," Waksberg said. "In the meantime, Taft has called for a meeting at nine in the morning."

"With who?"

"Everybody."

FIFTY-TWO

Zavorin was in his embassy quarters, sipping a snifter of a decent Napoleon cognac, and listening to a good recording of Tchaikovsky's Violin Concerto in D Major—one of his all-time favorite pieces of music—when his encrypted phone burred softly.

It was a minute or two past twelve and he'd planned on retiring when the concerto was over. He answered the call.

"Da."

"There has been a development," the familiar voice of one of his deep-cover agents here in D.C. said.

"Yes, go on."

"The general counsel for the Central Intelligence Agency was shot to death this morning."

"Carleton Patterson?"

"Yes. Evidently he was on his way to Langley for a meeting with Admiral Taft."

Zavorin felt a sudden chill, because he was almost certain what he was going to hear next. "Who was his assailant?"

"The FBI believes there may have been two of them, plus the driver of a white van with some company logo that may have been spotted leaving the neighborhood."

"This wasn't one of our operations."

"No, sir. But the weapons used were Vikhrs."

"Spetsnaz," Zavorin said. "The fucking GRU."

"Possibly. But one of my sources tells me that a few of the weapons have turned up on the black market in Marseilles."

"You're saying French contract shooters?"

"Not necessarily. But the conduits between there and here are open and thriving."

"What else are you hearing?" Zavorin asked.

"There's to be an emergency meeting tomorrow morning at nine with the admiral. My source wasn't sure of the complete list, but Mr. Kallek will be attending."

"Who else?"

"Kirk McGarvey and his wife."

"He's back from Moscow?"

"Yes."

"Where did you get this from?"

"My source at the Bureau."

"Is your source clean?" Zavorin asked. Sometimes a source was in actuality a double, giving disinformation in exchange for learning what his John was interested in. It had been a common practice since the height of the Cold War.

"You can better say than I can. But to this point the information I've received has been accurate."

The situation was coming to a head, as all situations did sooner or later. Zavorin had been around long enough to have relished victories and felt the distress of defeats. But the product they had received for several years, especially over the past twelve to eighteen months, had been nothing short of spectacular. A gold seam in all the flavor of the term.

Except for the interference of the GRU that had resulted in the situation they were faced with now.

Someone would get a legitimate promotion, while more than one would get their nine ounces, which was an old Russian euphemism for a nine-millimeter bullet to the back of the head.

Unless, of course, the thought entered Zavorin's mind, and he didn't finish it for the moment. Something tickled at the back of his head, something he'd heard from the past that had been as successful in the end as it had been spectacular.

"Listen to me," he said. "I have something I want you to do for me."

"Yes, sir."

The ambassador showed up at the *referentura* in the chancery five minutes after Zavorin called his quarters. The secure space in every Russian embassy around the world was used exclusively by intelligence personnel to conduct highly classified conversations and operations. As the agency's *rezident*, Zavorin had his office there on the seventh floor, along with the cipher room and a vault that was not only soundproof but electronically sealed against any known type of surveillance.

Azarov was angry but he was holding it in check. When the chief of intelligence operations for his embassy called, he came.

"What is so urgent that I was called away from my dinner with friends?"

"The situation we've been dealing with is coming to a head, and something must be done," Zavorin said.

The ambassador was dressed simply in slacks and an open-collar white shirt. His late-night dinner friends or friend had to be very close, especially since Mrs. Azarov was in Moscow.

"What situation and what are you suggesting be done, and why the fuck do you need my permission?"

"The CIA's general counsel was shot to death sometime this morning by unknown assailants."

"There was nothing in the news."

"I assume that the FBI, at the Central Intelligence Agency's request, has put a lid on it for the moment."

"What does it have to do with us?"

"The weapons used were Russian-made and very special. Only a few services have access to them."

"Your people?"

"The GRU," Zavorin said.

Azarov nodded. "It lets you off the hook."

"A newly minted GRU general was assassinated at his dacha two nights ago while he was meeting with Kirk McGarvey."

"I don't understand."

"The SVR did not order the killing."

"You're certain?"

"Someone I trust assured me it wasn't one of our operations, nor did he think that the GRU killed one of its own people."

"Who then? Was he having an affair? Maybe his wife was jealous."

"His wife died three years ago. In any event the FSB believes that military-grade weapons were used."

"Then I'm at a loss," the ambassador said. "McGarvey being there at that moment could not have been a coincidence."

"No," Zavorin said.

The ambassador threw up his hands. "Then for God's sake, what are you driving at, Ptr?"

"The intelligence leak inside the CIA has to be nothing short of stellar if it caused them to arrest their top computer expert, and involve the former director and his wife in the investigation."

"And?"

"I want to find out who the source is and personally turn them."

The ambassador was leaning against one of the desks, and he suddenly laughed. "I see," he said. "If you could manage such a coup you would become the next newly minted general." He shook his head. "It's all about money."

"And position."

"What do you want to do that needs my permission?"

"So far the media has not picked up on the story. There's been nothing in the news about the arrest of Mr. Rencke or the attempted assassination of the former director of the CIA or yesterday's assassination of a top Agency official."

"Extraordinary, yes."

"I want to leak the story to The Washington Post, and perhaps Fox News."

"To what end?"

"We'll sit back and watch the fallout. Somewhere in the debris field the golden goose will either be outed—and we'll find out who was running them—or they'll go deep and perhaps reach out for a new lifeline."

"You."

"*Da.*"

Azarov pushed away from the desk. "Go ahead. But be very careful that any blowback does not reach this embassy. If it does, I will—as the Americans say—throw you under the bus."

FIFTY-THREE

McGarvey was in the living room staring out the front windows unable to sleep, his mind alive with a dozen different possibilities. This was the end-game, he could feel it with every fiber of his body. And when it was over, and Otto was proven innocent, no one was going to like how it turned out.

The phone in the bedroom rang, but only once, and before he could see who had called, he could hear Pete talking but not what she was saying.

He went down the short corridor just as she was hanging up.

"Who was it?" he asked.

Pete was sitting up in the bed. The sheet had fallen away, exposing her breasts, and at that moment he thought that she was the most beautiful woman in the world, and that he was desperately afraid for her.

"Tom Waksberg."

"At this hour?"

"Taft's called for a meeting in his office at nine."

"Just us?" McGarvey asked.

"He said everybody."

Otto was nowhere in the house. Benkerk, his heart pounding, raced down-stairs after checking the entire upstairs, including the bedrooms, bathrooms, closets, and even the attic.

He'd awakened Lapides the moment he found Otto's room empty, and he met him now in the kitchen.

"The son of a bitch has taken a runner," Lapides said. "I knew he should have been kept somewhere with better security."

"We'd better call Van, get his people moving."

"This fucking well proves it," Lapides said.

"Proves what?" Otto said from the door to the stair hall.

Both men turned around. "Where've you been, you bastard?" Lapides prac-tically shouted.

"I couldn't sleep so I went outside to have a smoke with the guys," Otto said, grinning. "Mary finds out I'll be a dead man."

Lapides stepped forward as if he was on the attack, but Benkerk stopped him.

"He didn't run."

"I'll have those watch standers by the balls."

"Something's happened," Otto said.

Benkerk looked at him for a long moment, and all of a sudden he knew in

his heart of hearts that Otto wasn't the traitor. That every shred of evidence against him had been manufactured by someone to get rid of the most effective counterspy the Company ever had. The man had dedicated almost his entire life to the country while thumbing his nose at just about everyone and every institution in it.

But he had to find out just one more thing. "The house phones have been blocked, but have you managed to get access to another cell phone we don't know about?"

"No."

"Listen to me, Otto. I know that you're not guilty."

"What the hell are you talking about?" Lapides demanded.

"We've arrested the wrong man. I'm sure of it," Benkerk said, and he turned back to Otto. "Do you have a phone?"

"No."

"Did you manage to snag a phone from one of the minders you were having a smoke with?"

"No."

"And Mary didn't manage somehow to bring you another one?"

Otto shook his head. "Honest injun, no phone." But then a look almost of incredulity crossed his face. "My God, we're getting really close now to knowing who it is."

"I think so," Benkerk said. "And we're going to need your help."

Lapides was beside himself. "I want you out of here. Get your things and go home."

Benkerk and Otto spoke at the same time: "Shut up!"

"You learned something new," Otto said. "What?"

"Carleton Patterson was shot to death this morning on the way to Langley for a meeting with the admiral."

Otto reached out to the doorframe for support. It looked as if he was about to collapse. "Not him."

"The Bureau has no real line on the shooters—apparently there were two of them driving a white van with some logo—but they were using Russian automatic weapons."

"What weapons?"

"Waksberg didn't say, except that they were not yet on the black market."

"What else?"

Benkerk spread his hands. "He said that it looked like either a GRU or FSB operation, but he was guessing GRU."

"Carleton was in the backseat of his Maybach?"

"He was on his way to Langley."

"SR-3 Vikhrs," Otto said. "But Tom is wrong. The French mob in Marseilles supposedly got their hands on a few of them, which means they could have turned up just about anywhere. And if the Frogs got them, someone else might have. And you might tell Tom to make note of it, and get it to our guys in the field, including right here in D.C."

"The fact that he knows something like that nails it," Lapides said. "He's just incriminated himself again."

"I know what time the moon and sun rise and set, dipshit, doesn't mean I'm God."

"Maybe you're just a good astronomer."

"That's decent, maybe you're learning something after all," Otto said. "What else did Tom tell you?" he asked Benkerk.

"The admiral has called a meeting at nine for just about everyone involved."

"Get all the players together. Good thinking. Taft's a sharp man."

"You were right that someone was going to get killed, but we didn't listen to you," Benkerk said. "Did you think it would be Carleton?"

"No. But it's going to happen again."

"How do you know this?" Lapides asked.

"Because we're getting close and whoever the bad guy is will have to run or fight back."

"Who is it?" Lapides pressed. He was caught up in the discussion now.

Otto looked dreamy, his mind elsewhere. "I don't know."

"Who do you think it is?"

"It's not the Pakis or Kim Jong-un's people."

"The Russians?"

"Definitely, but I can't be sure about the GRU or SVR—not both, but maybe neither. That part's not so clear in my head."

"The FSB is just their internal cops," Benkerk said. "They'd have no reason to operate here."

"The Russian who supposedly showed up to save Mac's life said he was a Moscow cop, but he was GRU."

"Okay, then it's their military intelligence people, but the general who Mac went over to speak with was shot to death, which points to the SVR," Benkerk said.

"Maybe not."

"Who then?"

"When we find that out we'll find our traitor," Otto said.

"We already have," Lapides said. "And we have just about all the proof we need."

"I have to get to my office and power up Lou, and then get to the meeting with the admiral."

Lapides was startled for just a moment, but then he started to laugh so hard that tears began to stream down his cheeks.

□

FIFTY-FOUR

Sitting in the kitchen having her morning coffee, Mary still couldn't believe what had happened yesterday, though a part of her was not surprised.

Tom Waksberg had called late last night to tell her that a meeting with the admiral was on for nine sharp, and that just about everyone involved in the case would be there, including Mac, who had just returned from Moscow.

"You might think about letting my husband attend. He'd almost certainly be able to give a new perspective. And maybe even let him get to Lou and power it up."

"You know that's just not possible," Waksberg said.

"Van Gessel could supervise."

"Van agrees with me, and especially after the stunt you and Pete pulled we were both surprised that the admiral insisted that you be included."

"I'll be there," Mary had said. "And I assume so will Carleton to represent the Company."

The line was silent for a long beat. "You haven't heard. I thought that Pete or someone might have told you."

"Told me what?"

"Carleton was on his way to meet with the admiral yesterday morning, but he never made it."

"What's happened, Tom?"

"He and his driver were shot to death, just a few blocks from your house, actually."

"Oh, my dear God," Mary said. "Did we get the shooters?"

"No."

"Did we get anything? Witnesses, ballistics, something?"

"Two pretty rare Russian-made automatic weapons, and two people in the neighborhood said they might have seen a white van driving away. But no one saw the shooting."

"But the Bureau is on it? Not the local cops, but the FBI?"

"The Bureau's mounted a full-court press. We'll get these guys."

"Okay, Tom. Anything I can do to help, let me know."

"See you in the morning?"

"I'll probably show up early to have a word with Toni."

"Do you want me to send someone from housekeeping to pick you up?"

"It's not necessary."

"Considering what happened to Carleton you might want to reconsider."

"Thanks, but no. It's not me on the firing line."

. . .

Mary went to the front door and hesitated for just a moment or two, watching for traffic. For any car or especially a van with a logo parked on the street nearby. But only a man and woman were jogging at the end of the block.

She went out to the driveway, dressed only in her robe and slippers, picked up The Washington Post, and scanned the front page as she went back inside. She automatically locked the door and reset the alarm system before going back into the kitchen.

The assassination of a prominent man such as Carleton should have made front-page headlines. But there was nothing except the latest deal between President Weaver and Kim Jong-un, and a fire in California that had claimed at least seventeen lives, plus a school shooting in Montgomery, Alabama, that was being classified as a hate crime.

After switching on the TV, she poured another cup of coffee and then turned to the Fox News Channel. Carleton Patterson's picture came up on the small screen, and she turned up the sound.

The CIA's general counsel had been shot to death by two unknown assailants in an upscale neighborhood of McLean not too far from his home. Unnamed sources told Fox News that the eighty-three-year-old lawyer had been on his way to an important meeting at the Central Intelligence Agency's headquarters at Langley.

A spokesman for the FBI said it was far too early in the investigation to speculate about the assassins or the reason or reasons for the attack, which was the second in three days against persons with close connections to the CIA.

"The same unnamed sources told Fox News that former CIA director Kirk McGarvey and his wife were involved in a shooting outside their apartment in Georgetown late Wednesday evening."

An older photograph of McGarvey came up on-screen. It looked like a passport or driver's license picture.

"Three or possibly four unidentified persons were listed as fatalities. Neither McGarvey nor his wife were among them."

The news reader went deeper into McGarvey's background, admitting that verifiable facts were scarce, most information about him protected by the CIA's policy of nondisclosure due to "interests of national security."

Mary went back upstairs to get dressed and phone Mac.

Pete answered on the first ring. "You've heard about Carleton?" she said.

"Tom Waksberg called me just a few minutes ago about that and the meeting with the admiral," Mary said. "But have you guys been watching television this morning?"

"No. Should we?"

"You and Mac and the shooting outside your place are on Fox News."

"Just a minute," Pete said.

McGarvey came on after a moment or two. "What's this about us on Fox News?"

"A photograph of you came up right after their report on Carleton. They didn't say it in so many words but the implication was that his assassination and the gunfight in front of your place were linked."

"Did they say who leaked the stories?"

"Unnamed sources, plus a spokesman for the Bureau who said it was too early to speculate on either attack," Mary said. "But there was nothing in *The Post* about it."

"Whoever tipped off Fox News did it after *The Post*'s deadline, which is probably around midnight or so."

"What does it mean?" Mary asked.

"We're evidently closing in and someone is getting nervous."

"I'll see you guys at the meeting. But I'm going in a little early to talk to Toni."

"Why don't you have Van send someone to pick you up?"

"I'm no threat to anyone, I'll be okay."

"Take care," McGarvey said.

"I'll be glad when this is finally over so I can have Otto back."

"And Audie."

Mary was dressed and backing out of the garage in Otto's old Mercedes a few minutes after eight for the short drive up Dolley Madison Boulevard to the back gate into the CIA. She was looking forward to the meeting with the admiral and whoever else had been invited, because it would give her a complete picture of exactly where they were.

Once the business with her husband was finally settled, their lives could get back to some semblance of normalcy. Although in the past months he had been talking about breaking away from the Company and perhaps starting a private investigative firm. It was something he said that he and Mac had talked about, though nothing was definite, except that if it happened she wanted to be a part of it.

But first this business.

A battered green panel van with the logo of Roto-Rooter Plumbing & Drain Service pulled up beside her just before she got onto Dolley Madison.

She had only a moment to react as the side door of the van slid open, and two men with automatic weapons were there. She jammed on her brakes and turned hard to the right.

The two men opened fire, the rounds slamming into the sign for the Chain Bridge Road that connected with Dolley Madison, and then it was gone as she came to a complete halt.

Hands shaking, she got on the phone and called Van Gessel's office.

"This is Mary Rencke. I'm at Chain Bridge Road and Dolley Madison Boulevard. Two men with automatic weapons in the back of a green van just tried to assassinate me."

FIFTY-FIVE

A pair of housekeepers showed up a couple of minutes before the Virginia Highway Patrol, and after a brief conversation the cops left and one of the security people came over to where Mary was seated behind the wheel, shivering.

"You okay, Mrs. R?" the young man asked. He looked like a football player.

"They missed," Mary said. "Lucky me."

"Yes, ma'am, if you'll just follow us."

She tucked in behind them for the couple of miles to the Agency, and once through security they followed her to the VIP parking garage, before they left.

McGarvey and Pete showed up at the OHB a little before nine, and Taft's secretary directed them to the small conference room next door. Taft was at the head of table with Waksberg, Van Gessel, Benkerk, Toni, and FBI director Harold Kallek already seated.

"Mary will be here," Pete said, as she and Mac took their places.

"She's in the building and on the way up," Van Gessel said. "But she was involved in an incident. Someone tried to assassinate her the same way Mr. Patterson was taken out. But she was lucky, they missed."

For some reason it wasn't what McGarvey had expected to hear. "She's okay?"

"Yes," the security chief said.

Mary showed up all out of breath, but with a smile. Pete jumped up and they hugged. "Are you really okay?"

"I'll live," Mary said. She nodded at the others around the table, and took her place beside Pete. "Sorry I'm late, but traffic at this time of the day on the parkway is murder."

Several of the people around the table chuckled.

"Let's get started," Taft said. "I think we can all agree that we are dealing with a mole inside this agency. And whoever is directing this person has gone to great lengths to protect them. That includes this morning's attack on Mrs. Rencke."

McGarvey held his silence, though he thought that the director was missing the obvious.

"The prime suspect is Mr. Rencke, and up until this point nothing I've heard from any of you here this morning clears his name, though Mr. and Mrs. McGarvey are trying to prove otherwise."

"It's not him," Benkerk said.

"Do you have information I haven't been told?" Taft asked.

"I've been in this business long enough, Mr. Director, to know when evidence becomes so overwhelming and pat that it has to be false."

"In the end the evidence against Aldrich Ames was so overwhelming that everyone was amazed they hadn't caught on from the beginning," Van Gessel said.

"One doesn't prove the other," Benkerk said.

"One of Rencke's Russian contacts showed up in Pyongyang and almost immediately one of our deep-cover agents working at a nuclear facility was shot to death," Waksberg said. "I think that's proof enough."

"There's more, of course," the director of the FBI said. "I think it's common knowledge that Mr. and Mrs. McGarvey are longtime friends with Rencke, as was Mr. Patterson. And it's natural for all of them, especially his wife, to feel passionate about his innocence. So passionate, in fact, that they have been willing to go to great lengths to prove it."

Everyone knew where the man was going with his solid argument. Like Patterson, Kallek had been a top-shelf lawyer, and even a federal judge at one point in his career.

"Mr. and Mrs. McGarvey were the subject of an assassination attempt several days ago, as was Mrs. Rencke this morning. In addition, when McGarvey traveled to Russia to interview a GRU general, another of Rencke's alleged contacts, the man was shot to death, presumably by his own people in what may be a faction fight between their military and foreign intelligence services. And from what I've been told your own chief of Moscow Station was killed in an automobile accident, that no one believes was an accident."

No one at the table interrupted, and Kallek continued.

"These deaths and near misses all lead to the same conclusions, that your Mr. Rencke is indeed a traitor, and the investigations into trying to prove his innocence may not only have sparked an internecine war in Moscow, but have resulted in deaths and near misses of people in this country."

Mary started to cry. "You people are blind to what my husband has done for this country."

Pete reached for her, but Mary shrugged her off.

"I'm sorry, Mrs. Rencke," Taft said. "We understand your feelings, but the facts speak for themselves, as does the number of bodies that are piling up, almost yours this morning as well."

"So we all stop trying to prove he's not guilty—and find whoever is the mole—and then the killings will stop?" Pete said. "Is that what you're suggesting, Mr. Director? Because if it is, that's just crazy."

"Find the men who killed Carleton Patterson," Mary said.

"We're investigating, but so far the van has not shown up," Kallek said.

"What about the Russians who tried to kill me and my husband?" Pete asked.

"We're investigating that incident as well, but there is the issue of diplomatic immunity, and we were told to back off."

"By whom? State?"

"I'm not at liberty to say."

"You got there too fast. Someone must have tipped you off," Pete said. "Who?"

"I'm not at liberty to say."

"Right here, right now in this building? You've got to be fucking kidding me," Pete practically shouted. "Who was it, the White House?"

Kallek didn't respond.

"This is getting us nowhere," Taft said. "Let's work the problem, people. We're here to find out if Mr. Rencke is our mole."

"From my shop, except for the outing and assassination of one of our assets in the DPRK, there have been no changes whatsoever in the status of any of the countries that Rencke was supposedly working with," Toni said. "It's business as usual."

"Our asset in North Korea was important," Waksberg said.

"Yes, sir," Toni said. "But we have others there in even more sensitive positions."

"Maybe the other shoe hasn't dropped yet," the DDO said.

"This morning Fox News had Carleton's death plus the attack on us, and comments from the Bureau that the investigation into both incidents was in the early stages," McGarvey said. "Who spoke for the Bureau?"

"I assume our media officer made the statement," Kallek said. "It's SOP."

"It wasn't in The Post or The New York Times this morning, so whoever leaked the story did so last night or very early this morning, after the newspapers' deadlines."

"Something like that was bound to get out sooner or later," Taft said. "What's your point, Kirk?"

"But why last night, and why so late after the fact?"

No one responded.

"Unless it was to make a point."

"What point?" Taft asked.

"I don't know, Mr. Director, but I'm going to find out," McGarvey said. He got to his feet and so did Pete.

"We're not finished here," Taft said.

"We are," McGarvey said. "But I'm curious about something. Where did the leak come from? The Bureau, or from us?"

"I can guarantee it didn't come from us," Kallek said.

"From Al Lapides?" McGarvey asked Benkerk.

"I don't know."

"And why the timing? Why not earlier so it would have gotten into the press? Unless someone was waiting for approval to leak the story."

"There may be another wrinkle, though I don't know if it has any direct bearing on the current issue except that it may have involved General Svirin," Waksberg said. "We got a heads-up from NSA yesterday through our regular liaison channel. They intercepted a call from someone they're assuming was a

gay man outside Union Station here in Washington, to a Russian at a location north of Moscow off the M8 highway."

"Svirin," McGarvey said.

"Yes."

"We got a similar heads-up," Kallek said.

"What did they talk about?" McGarvey asked.

"The conversation hasn't been decrypted yet," Waksberg said. "So, it may have nothing to do with Otto."

"Or everything," McGarvey said.

□

FIFTY-SIX

Toni caught up with McGarvey and Pete at the elevator as the door was just opening. "I'll ride down with you guys," she said.

"How'd they take our walking out like that?" Pete asked as they got in and McGarvey pushed the button for the parking garage.

"Are you going back to your office?" he asked Toni.

"Yes, I have a few calls to make," she said.

He pushed 3, and they waited until the door was closed and the car started down.

"They'd worried that you two are going to cause more trouble, but Taft told everyone, including Kallek, to leave you alone," Toni said.

"That couldn't have gone over well," Pete said.

"No one argues with the admiral in the best of times, and right now like everyone else he knows we have a spy in the Company, but he's hedging his bets that you might be right, and he's willing to give you as much room as you need."

"As long as we don't shoot someone?"

"Something like that," Toni said. "I'm on board, so what can I do to help?"

"I want you to make two calls," McGarvey said. "I'm going over to the White House to have a word with the president's chief of staff."

"Donna Blakely."

"I want you to give her a call, tell her you're a spokesman for Van's office and he's sending over an officer to discuss the shooting death of our general counsel."

"When it gets back to him he's not going to be very happy with any of us," Toni said. "But you do know that once you show up it'll get to the president."

"That's the point."

Toni had to laugh, but without humor. "What are you going to ask him if he shows up?"

"I have a couple of ideas, but for now I'm keeping them to myself. If the roof caves in on me I want you to honestly say you had no idea what I was trying to do."

"Does that include me?" Pete asked, her tone a little peckish. They had gone down this path before and it was a bone of contention between them.

"I want you to go over to Fox News and have a chat with whoever's willing to talk to you about their source for Carleton's death. Toni will call ahead and tell them you're coming."

"Kallek said the Bureau made an announcement."

"After the fact, when someone at the network called for a statement." McGarvey said. "They already knew about the shooting from someone."

"As well as the shoot-out with us the other night," Pete said. "They're bound to ask me about it."

"I'm counting on it."

"What do you want to tell them?"

"Everything."

"Even the fact that the cops got there so fast they had to have been tipped off in advance?"

"Especially that," McGarvey said.

"Both of you have more balls than brains," Toni said. "You know of course that someone will be coming after you guys."

"I'm counting on it," McGarvey said.

Toni started to protest but Pete cut her off. "You know who's behind this thing."

"I have a pretty good idea, but I need someone to open their fly before I can prove it."

"It's not the GRU or the SVR."

"That's what we're going to find out."

"Then what?" Toni asked.

"I'll go to the source and have it out."

"Well, if the traitor isn't Otto what makes you think they'll tell you who it is?"

"Because once we get that far I'll know for sure who it is, all I want to know is the why and the how of it."

"Especially the why," Toni said.

Pete was gazing at her husband in open awe, and fear. "You already know, don't you?" she said as they reached the third floor and the elevator door opened. "You've known all along."

Toni held the door from closing so that she could hear what Mac had to say.

McGarvey took a moment before he answered his wife, and he wasn't happy involving her or Toni or anyone else. But Otto was not the traitor, and he'd suspected who it was almost from the beginning, "Yes. But as I said, not the why."

"And you won't share it with me."

"No."

Pete's face fell, but she nodded. "I'll drive over to Fox News right now," she said. "You can take a cab to the White House. Where do you want to meet afterward?"

"We'll almost certainly pick up tails almost immediately, so let's meet somewhere in the open."

"The steps of the Lincoln Memorial, a fine place for the truth, wouldn't you say?" Pete said. "I'll take the stairs."

Before McGarvey could reply, she brushed past Toni and walked away.

"You're doing everything in your power to save Otto, and so is Pete. Her ass in on the line just as much as yours is."

"Don't start."

"Just saying, big guy, you might let her in," Toni said. "When do you want me to make the phone calls?"

"Soon as you get to your office."

"Do you want to use my car?"

"I'll cab it," McGarvey said. "And I'll take the stairs, too."

"McGarvey and his wife should be stopped," Van Gessel said.

"I don't want them interfered with," Taft said. "Maybe they're right."

"Patterson's death was almost certainly an unfortunate result of McGarvey's meddling, just as was the assassination of our Moscow chief of station and the Russian general he went to see."

"Put a tail on them. Discreetly."

"I'll get on it immediately," Van Gessel said, and he started to rise.

Mary stopped him. "It's a good way to get a couple of your people killed."

"He may be strongheaded, but he wouldn't shoot his own people," the chief of security said.

"He's expecting someone to follow him and Pete, but unless your guys are wearing blue jackets with 'CIA' in big yellow letters, how will he know the good guys from the bad?"

"It would defeat the purpose."

"Indeed."

"What do you suggest?" Taft asked.

"We know where they're going, so just leave word in both places ahead of them."

"What sort of word?" Van Gessel asked.

"That they're freelancers who don't speak for this agency."

"Wait a minute," Taft said. "Where do you think they're going?"

"Be my guess that Pete is going over to Fox to find out who the leak was. They won't tell her, of course, but it will get back to their source."

"And McGarvey?"

"The White House, of course."

"Jesus Christ, Weaver," Taft said.

"Yes, the president."

☐

FIFTY-SEVEN

Jerri was dreaming about lying on a crowded beach somewhere in the Caribbean, and she was trying to order something to drink from a barefoot waiter but she couldn't make him understand. A dozen people were looking at her as if she were a crazy woman, but when she tried to explain that she wanted something to drink they started jabbering at her in what sounded like Russian.

Two men came over, and one of them put his hand on her shoulder. "Ms. Butler," he said in English. "Ms. Butler."

She came awake all of a sudden, but it took her a moment or two to get oriented. The man shaking her shoulder was Bob Berliner, the day-shift telephone intercept supervisor. Zimbowski was right behind him.

"Jesus," she said, and she sat upright, and ran her fingers through her short, graying hair. "I'm sorry, sir. Couldn't keep my eyes open."

"It's all right. Take your time."

"What time is it?"

"Just about ten," Zimbowski said. "You've been out for a couple hours."

"Has something happened?"

"We think so," Berliner said. He was a tall, skinny man, who looked as if he was a teenager. But he was very bright, fluent in a dozen languages, and on the cutting edge of computer technology.

He pulled a chair over from one of the break room tables and sat down. Zimbowski reached around him and handed Jerri a Coke. Her mouth was dry, and she drained half the can.

"The man outside Moscow is a GRU general by the name of Svirin. He was shot to death in his country home, while the former director of the CIA was standing right next to him."

She looked at Zimbowski. "All that from the intercept?"

"From the CIA," Berliner said. "They're very much interested in the call, and they want more."

No one else was in the break room and the door was closed. It seemed ominous to her.

"Apparently the telephone call you're working on occurred shortly before the two men had their meeting. And the CIA wants to know more about the man who phoned from outside Union Station."

"How far has Boss gotten cleaning it up?" Jerri asked Zimbowski.

"Enough so that we have a fairly clean translation," he said.

"The CIA's deputy director of operations notified us that they're in the middle of an investigation to find the identity of a spy in their midst. A

mole. Their thought is that the Union Station speaker may be working with the spy, and if we could narrow down the accent enough maybe to make a reasonable guess where he'd learned Russian, it would be a big help."

"Boss thinks the speaker might be a woman," Zimbowski said.

"What's his confidence?"

"Fifty-three percent."

"Encryption tends to distort tonalities," Jerri said. "My guess is still a gay man."

"We're going with your instincts for now," Berliner said. "We'd like your best guess where he was educated."

"Well, for starts I don't think he's a native speaker."

"An American?"

"Definitely," Jerri said. "I'd like to get back to my console to listen to the latest wash."

Zimbowski handed Berliner an iPad and a set of earphones, which he gave to Jerri.

She took another drink of her Coke, handed the can to the supervisor, then donned the headset, one side half off her ear, and started the playback. The entire conversation had lasted less than two minutes, and this version, though still badly distorted, had been cleaned up enough for her to make out just about every other word.

"Something about visitors," she said. "Plural."

"Yes," Berliner said.

Jerri listened to the rest of the recording, then started again at the beginning. "He's from the Midwest—maybe Chicago or even Des Moines, but definitely not Minnesota, Wisconsin, or the Dakotas."

"Education?" Berliner asked.

She nodded. "Definitely. But his Russian is not schoolboy-flat."

"Like mine?"

Jerri had to smile. "Yes, sir, no offense."

"None taken. But do you think he's a native speaker?"

"No. But I'd guess he spent some time in Russia, maybe for a semester or even a whole year," Jerri said. "Wait."

She went back to the beginning and slowed the recording to half speed, the voices even more distorted but individual words easier to pick out. She played one spot again, and a third time, then stopped.

"He definitely spent time in Russia, but not at a university. Maybe with the military."

"School One?" Berliner asked. It was the old KGB training school in Moscow for new recruits, and had been transferred to the SVR when the Russian intelligence services had been broken up.

"Could be."

She played the recording again, this time at normal speed, and since she knew what to listen for the two words were clear. "'*Yeb vas*,'" she said. "'Fuck

your mother.' Definitely military or School One something like that. The Russian version of a good old boys' club."

"Recently?" Berliner asked.

"I don't know."

"But a man."

"Just a guess," Jerri said.

"Gay?"

"Another guess."

"Based on what?" Berliner asked.

"He called General Svirin '*dorogoy.*'"

"'Darling,'" Berliner said.

"Yes."

Fox News headquarters was on Capitol Street not far from the Senate office buildings. Pete showed her old CIA identification card in its small leather wallet to the receptionist at the counter just inside the front door.

"I would like to have a word with a network spokesman."

The young man in a blue blazer with the FOX NEWS logo was impressed. "Yes, ma'am," he said.

He picked up the phone and punched a number. "Mr. George, the lady from the CIA is here at the front desk asking to have a word with a spokesperson.

"Yes, sir," he said, and put down the phone. "Mr. George will be right out," he said. "I'll just need your driver's license."

"No."

"Ma'am?"

"You know the old line: I was never here."

"Yes, ma'am."

A well-put-together man in his midfifties with a little gray showing at his temples, wearing an expensive suit, came out. "Mrs. McGarvey, Robin George," he said, and they shook hands.

"You know me."

"Of course," he said. He took her across the lobby and into what was likely a waiting room, furnished with a couch, a coffee table, and a few chairs. A flat-screen television on the wall was tuned to the Fox News Channel.

He motioned her to have a seat.

"I won't be long," Pete said. "I'd just like to ask you a question."

"If it's about the incident the other night in front of your place in Georgetown, I have a few questions for you."

"Who was your source for that story, and the one about our general counsel's assassination?"

"You know I can't divulge a source, any more than you could."

"I don't need a name. I'd merely like to know if it was a man or a woman and, more importantly, was it a native speaker?"

"Versus a Russian?"

"Yes."

George said nothing.

"This is very important."

"National security and all that, I know the drill, but my answer still has to be no."

"My life is at stake," Pete said.

It wasn't what the Fox News spokesman expected. He hesitated for a beat. "It was an American."

"Man or woman?"

"A pleasure talking with you, Mrs. McGarvey," George said, and he turned and walked out.

FIFTY-EIGHT

□

Donna Blakely's domain was in a corner down the hall from the Oval Office, and as the president's chief of staff she was the second most important person in the West Wing.

When McGarvey arrived at the White House, he was admitted straight through, which meant that Toni had made the call and Blakely was at least curious about what he wanted.

The West Wing was busy this morning, and no one gave him a second glance as an aide took him back to Blakely's office.

She was on the phone. "He's here," she said, and she hung up, got to her feet, and held out her hand. "It's a real pleasure to finally meet you, sir," she said. She was a short, somewhat curvy woman with a lot of blond hair in her midthirties. Her smile was pleasant, her manner direct.

The aide left and discreetly closed the door.

McGarvey shook the woman's hand. "You knew that I was coming to see you?"

"Someone from Mr. Van Gessel's office gave us the heads-up," she said, motioning him to a seat across the desk from her.

"Did they say why I wanted to see you?"

"No. But we're assuming it's about the problem going on right now over there, and the unfortunate shooting death of Mr. Patterson. I knew him personally from when he taught a symposium on international law at Harvard. Lovely man. The president will attend the funeral."

"He was a friend," McGarvey said.

Blakely waited for several moments, but then nodded. "You're here, Mr. McGarvey, what can I do for you?"

"Have you and the president been briefed on exactly what problem we're faced with?"

"I wasn't aware that you were back on the Agency's payroll."

"I'm not."

"But you said the problem that *we're* faced with."

"I meant the country. We have a spy within the Company who may have caused us some serious damage, and will continue to do so unless they're identified and arrested."

"Mr. Webb has not brought up any such specific concern at his briefings with the president." Burton Webb was the director of national intelligence.

"It's likely he's not been completely briefed," McGarvey said.

"I don't understand."

"The issue is an internal problem."

"From what you're telling me it doesn't sound like that," Blakely said. She was becoming annoyed. "If there is a spy inside the CIA. According to you it's a national problem, one that Burton needs to be involved with."

McGarvey waited for her to finish the thought and take it to the next step, which was the reason he was here. But she wasn't there yet.

"Ordinarily I would agree with you, but to this point it's become personal with me," he said.

"You have a history of operating off the ranch. And if that's what you're telling me now, there is nothing we can do for you, except strongly suggest that you get Webb's office involved. That's why National Intelligence was created in the first place, to coordinate investigations too big for any single agency, including the CIA."

"It was thought that the spy inside the CIA was passing information not only to Russia but to Pakistan and North Korea. But we now suspect they're only working with Russia."

"This meeting is over," Blakely said, starting to rise.

"Three days ago, a Russian hit squad tried to assassinate me and my wife in front of our apartment in Georgetown. They were not successful, but the point is the police and FBI showed up almost before the attack was over. Someone had tipped them off, but no one will say who or why."

"The media has it."

"Yes, but to this point just Fox News," McGarvey said. "Then two days ago I flew to Moscow to meet with a general in military intelligence who may have been involved with our spy. He denied it, of course. But as I was leaving his country house, he was gunned down."

"We knew nothing about that incident."

"He was shot to death as I was standing right next to him. I should have been a target as well. But I wasn't, though that same evening the CIA's chief of station was killed in Moscow in what was made to look like an accident."

"Exactly why are you here this morning, Mr. McGarvey?" Blakely asked.

"To ask for your help."

"My help?"

"The president's help," McGarvey said.

Blakely took several beats before she answered, her face and tone completely neutral. "You have developed a nasty habit of involving this president in some previous investigations. I suggest that you tread with extreme care."

"Currently a close personal friend of mine is under arrest and is being interrogated in the belief that he is the spy inside the Agency. A traitor. But I know that he's innocent, and I mean to prove it."

"It does not involve this office."

"It may, though not directly," McGarvey said.

Blakely said nothing.

"It's been thought by some people inside the Company—me included for a time—that an internecine fight has been going on inside the Russian intelligence apparatus. Specifically, the SVR, which took over foreign intelligence

duties when the KGB collapsed, and the GRU, which is Russia's military intelligence service."

"But you don't believe that to be the case."

"No."

"What then?"

"My friend who stands accused of being the traitor is a computer genius who is feared and respected just as much by our own people as by the Russians. He may have come up with the first inkling that what is happening inside Russia involves more than a fight for power between two intelligence services."

"If not that, then what?"

"A fight for power inside the Kremlin."

"Putin," Blakely said.

"Yes. The old KGB officer, who may want to restore the service along with his country to its former status as the world power. And Otto Rencke may be the diversion he needs."

"Why your friend?"

"Because he just about owned the KGB's old mainframe, and it could be argued that he was at least a partial cause of its disintegration."

Blakely took a moment to reply. "And tell me why you're here again?"

"To ask the president one question," McGarvey said. "Just one."

Blakely picked up her phone. "The gentleman is here and he would like to have a brief word with you." She nodded. "Yes, sir," she said, and hung up.

"He's agreed?"

"I should have warned you from the start to be careful what you wish for, Mr. McGarvey," Blakely said, getting up.

President T. Karson Weaver, who before his first-term election had promised that by Christmas he would be even more famous than Santa Claus, was seated behind his desk in the Oval Office, his jacket off, his long red tie knotted correctly. He did not look happy to see McGarvey.

"What can I do for you?" he asked, brusquely.

"Has President Putin ever given you an indication that he wanted to restore his country to its Cold War world status?"

Weaver laughed. "Do you read the fucking fake news? The son of a bitch has been saying the same thing every day since he got reelected the last time."

"Thank you, Mr. President," McGarvey said.

"This is what you came here to ask me? Wasting my time?"

"Do you think he can do it, sir?"

"Get the hell out."

FIFTY-NINE

McGarvey called for a cab, but by the time he had walked out to the Northwest Appointment Gate and retrieved his pistol, Pete was waiting in her green BMW. He got in beside her, and she drove over to Madison Place, which skirted Lafayette Park to H Street, which was one-way to the right.

"Surprised to see you here," he said.

"I picked up a tail when I left Fox News and I've been driving all over town to give you time for your meeting."

"Did you lose him?"

She glanced in the rearview mirror. "Light gray Honda Civic, three cars back. He must have been waiting for me. Got to give him marks for tenacity."

"Adjust my door mirror so I can take a look," McGarvey said.

The mirror moved outward until he could see traffic behind them, the Civic three cars back.

"Do you see him?"

"He's back there. Take Fifteenth down to Constitution."

"Do you want me to try to lose him?"

"Do you think he knows that you're on to him?"

"Hard to say, but I don't think he expected me to pick you up at the White House. He has to be wondering what we're up to."

"If it's who I think it is, he'll know," McGarvey said.

"What's your call?"

"Are you carrying?"

"Of course. Are we going to force the issue?"

"Let's go to the park."

"Could be a lot of people around the Lincoln Memorial at this time of the day," Pete said.

They came to Fifteenth, and Pete turned south toward Constitution. The Civic followed suit.

"We'll start there and depending on how many they have following us we'll split up and lead them away. If it comes to a shoot-out, which I hope it won't because I want to talk to them, I don't want to be the cause of any collateral damage."

"If it's whoever you think it is—I'm assuming Russians—they won't have the same concern."

"You're right, so keep on your toes."

"You, too," Pete said.

. . .

The parking area off Twenty-Third was less than half full, and Pete headed toward a spot away from the other cars, but McGarvey directed her to an empty slot in a long row of vehicles. She understood immediately.

"Cover," she said.

They got out of the car and headed to the Lincoln Memorial, which faced the long, narrow reflecting pool, the Vietnam Veterans Memorial down a path to the north. The weather was bright, but it was a weekday and the park wasn't terribly busy, which was a plus.

"Do you have a mirror in your purse?" McGarvey asked.

But she was already taking it out. She held it up to her face as if she were checking her makeup. "Don't take a girl for granted," she said, grinning evilly. "They're just parking, five cars east of ours."

She pulled up short and rubbed a finger under her right eye.

"Two guys, wearing sport coats. They could be carrying."

"We'll assume they are," McGarvey said.

"What's our play?" Pete asked, still studying the mirror.

"Have they spotted us?"

"They're heading this way."

"The Lincoln Memorial, but not on the stairs, we're going inside."

"Then what?"

"We're going to play hide-and-seek," McGarvey said.

Pete put the mirror back in her shoulder bag, and she and McGarvey headed down the walk to the memorial. Only twenty or thirty people were on the steps leading up to the white building with tall columns front and sides, and the building's steps themselves.

At the top of the first set, they went to the stairs on the left that led up to the hall itself where Lincoln's statue was enclosed. A handful of tourists were taking pictures of the sitting figure, and only a few were in the gift shop off to the right.

McGarvey stopped just inside, from where he could see the bottom of the stairs just as the two men following them started up in a hurry.

"They've taken the bait," he said. "I'm going to clear the hall, and you're going to get behind Abe."

"Someone is bound to call the park police."

"By the time they get here, it'll be over," McGarvey said. "Go."

He took out his wallet, flipped it open, and held it over his head with his left hand as he pulled out his pistol with his right.

"Everyone out of here now!" he shouted at the top of his voice.

People turned to look at him, and when they saw he was holding a pistol, they screamed and scattered away, all of them down the central staircase.

McGarvey pocketed his wallet as he moved around behind one of the inner columns so that he would be out of sight of the two men when they got up to the hall.

Several people came out of the gift shop, but he waved them back, and they ducked back inside.

A full two minutes later, one of the men showed up to McGarvey's left, a pistol low and pointed away from his right leg, and he pulled up short.

At that moment the muzzle of a pistol was jammed into the back of McGarvey's head.

"Easy now, Mr. McGarvey," the man said. His English was very good, but the accent was Russian.

"Khorosho"—Okay—McGarvey said in Russian.

"Without turning around, hand me your pistol."

McGarvey raised his Walther over his shoulder, and pulled the trigger at the same time he ducked his head sharply to the left.

The Russian's gun went off as he fell backward, the bullet missing McGarvey's head, but the muzzle flash singeing the side of his cheek.

"Lower your weapon or I will fire," Pete shouted from beside the statue.

The man McGarvey had shot was lying on his back, a hole in the center of his forehead, obviously dead.

"Now," Pete shouted again from the edge of the statue's base.

McGarvey eased around from behind the column, his pistol up.

"Mac," Pete shouted.

The second man had moved to the left while bringing his gun around to aim at McGarvey.

Pete fired, missing with her first shot, but then she fired again at the same moment McGarvey did. Both rounds hit the man—one in the neck just above his collarbone on the right side, and the other center mass in his chest.

"Clear?" Pete shouted.

"Clear," McGarvey said. "Step out into plain sight, put your gun on the floor, take out your ID, and hold it in plain sight above your head."

He laid his pistol on the floor and kicked it away, then turned back to the Russian who'd gotten the drop on him.

At least two sirens very close were already incoming.

McGarvey found the dead man's wallet. The New York driver's license was in the name of Viktor Balan, with an address in Brighton Beach.

SIXTY

When Benkerk got back to the Scattergood-Thorne house after the meeting in Taft's conference room, the minders were still on station, sitting in their Caddy, the windows down.

Terry Winkler, the morning lead, got out of the car as Benkerk pulled up.

"I thought that we better apologize for this morning," the security officer said as Benkerk got out of his car.

"For what?"

"For having a smoke with Mr. Rencke."

"Scared the shit outta me for a couple of minutes. I thought he had taken off."

"Mr. Lapides made it perfectly clear, said it would go in our jackets."

Benkerk took a moment to answer. "Al is normally a good guy, but we're faced with a pretty tough situation and frankly no one really knows which side is up. But not to worry, I'll calm him down."

"Yes, sir."

Benkerk started up to the house, but he stopped and turned back. "Look, he can sometimes be an asshole, but I'll take care of it."

Inside, Benkerk pulled up short in the stair hall. The house was normally quiet, but the hairs on the back of his neck stood up. The place seemed almost like a mausoleum to him, though he knew it was probably just his imagination, but he'd expected Lapides to be at it with Otto, and yet he could hear no conversation even though the pocket doors to the living room were partially ajar.

"Al?" he called out.

"In here," Otto answered from the living room.

Benkerk went across to the doors and slid them open. Otto was sitting on one of the couches, his feet up on the distressed-oak coffee table. A hypodermic syringe was stuck in the top of the table, the tube oscillating.

"I told him I didn't like drugs," Otto said.

Benkerk came the rest of the way into the room in time to see Lapides, who had been stretched out on the floor on the other side of the couch, struggle to sit up.

"Jesus," Benkerk said. He went over to Lapides and helped the man get to his feet and sit down in a wingback chair.

"The son of a bitch hit me," Lapides said looking up. "I'm just trying to find the truth, but he attacked me."

"Thank your lucky stars I didn't stick you with whatever the fuck you wanted to give me," Otto said. "Any possibility of getting a beer? I'm a little thirsty."

"I want this bastard out of here and into a proper interrogation facility," Lapides said, his voice slurred. The right side of his jaw was red and already swelling.

"I'm sorry, Al, but you're relieved of this assignment as of right now," Benkerk said. "I want you to gather up your things and leave."

"You can't do that. I'm in charge here."

"Not anymore you're not," Benkerk said.

Lapides stared at him for a beat, his swollen mouth twisting into a grimace of hate. "My God, you're in collusion with the son of a bitch."

"Yeah, but not in the way you think."

"Why?" Lapides asked in wonderment.

"Because he's done more for this country than you'll ever do even on your best day. And I think that if he can get access to his computer system he might find out who the real traitor is."

"I'll fucking well make sure that this gets into your file."

"Do that."

"Everything!"

Lapides, still a little unsteady, got to his feet, pulled away, then bent down and picked up the small leather zip-up case that had held two syringes and several small vials of whatever cocktail of psychotropic truth serums he'd planned on using.

Benkerk took it from him. "You won't be needing this, Al."

"It's my personal property."

"Not anymore. Just leave."

Lapides straightened up, adjusted his shirt, patted his hair flat, and went to the doors. "You've not heard the last of this," he said, and he left.

"I know," Benkerk said.

He sat down on the couch across from Otto, and they listened as Lapides tromped up the stairs, and a few minutes later came back down. When he left the house, he slammed the door and was gone.

Otto grinned. "You're in just as much trouble as I am," he said.

"It's going to get worse before it gets better, boyo, because I don't think the killings are going to stop just yet."

"Then we'd better hurry," Otto said. "But do you actually think you can get me access to Lou?"

"I don't know but I'm going to try," Benkerk said. "I'm going to see Taft right away. In the meantime you have the run of the house. The phones have been disconnected, and the minders have been told to make sure you stay inside, so don't try to take a runner on us. Okay?"

Otto gave him the thumbs-up. "Honest injun," he said.

. . .

Benkerk wasn't an old man, but he was getting tired of the business in which mistrust was the modus operandi. *Careful of your neighbor, it might just be that they're spying for the opposition.*

And the mistrust was so entrenched it created people like Smits and even corrupted good men like Lapides.

After passing through security on the ground floor of the OHB, he took the elevator up to the seventh and walked down to Taft's office unannounced.

The inner door was open and the admiral's secretary was standing in front of his desk talking to her boss.

Benkerk knocked on the doorframe, and the secretary turned around and the admiral looked up. "Sorry to bother you, sir, but I need just a moment of your time. It's important."

"Everything in this office is important," Taft said, and he dismissed his secretary, who walked past Benkerk, waited until he went in, and then closed the door behind him.

"I'll just take a minute," Benkerk said.

"Have a seat."

"No, sir. I just fired Al Lapides because he was trying to use drugs that could have permanently damaged Rencke's brain. Exactly what the opposition wanted to happen."

"Are you saying that Lapides is one of the bad guys?"

"No, just overzealous."

"Van Gessel called him two minutes ago, said that Rencke punched Lapides in the mouth."

"Damned near broke his jaw," Benkerk said.

Taft was not amused. "You said one minute. I'm listening."

"Otto Rencke is not the mole. I think he and probably McGarvey have an idea who it might be, though neither of them is sure yet."

"Continue."

"I think we can find out, if Rencke is allowed access to his computer system."

"I have been strongly advised against it."

"He would be closely supervised at all times."

"Even supervised he could do a lot of damage."

"Someone could be standing by at the circuit breaker box, and at the slightest sign of trouble, the breaker could be pulled."

The admiral gave Benkerk a very hard stare and sat back in his chair. "You would supervise?"

"Yes, sir."

"I want Lapides there as well."

Benkerk started to object, but Taft held up a hand.

"How badly do you want it, mister?"

"Lapides can be there, but no drugs."

"When do you want to do this?"

"As soon as possible, sir."

"Make it happen."

SIXTY-ONE

□

Over the past couple of years in the States, Zavorin had developed a liking for American fast food, especially McDonald's, which tasted completely different here than it did in Moscow.

He'd sent an aide for a cheeseburger and large fries, and he was just finishing his lunch at his desk in the *referentura* when Azarov's secretary called and asked him to report immediately.

After wiping his hands and his mouth on the napkins, Zavorin donned his jacket, but didn't bother straightening his tie, and took his time getting to the ambassador's office, where he was shown in immediately.

"Why wasn't I advised of your operation this morning at the Lincoln Memorial?" Azarov demanded. He wasn't happy.

"I'm sorry, but I don't know what you're talking about."

Azarov thumped a fist on the desktop. "Two of our people were shot to death, by the former director of the CIA and his wife."

Zavorin was rocked, though the news wasn't totally unexpected. He sat down without asking. "It wasn't my operation, nor was it a GRU assignment."

"Start making some sense or I will have your ass on the first plane home, where you can answer to the president himself."

"I swear I know nothing about any operation this morning."

"Then who were the two men shot to death? They were carrying American identifications, but I was officially informed by our State Department liaison that they were almost certainly Russian citizens."

"Did they give you names?"

"No," the ambassador said.

"How were they identified as Russians so quickly?"

"I was not told."

"That would be impossible unless they were carrying Russian identification booklets, passports, something."

"They could have had Spetsnaz tattoos."

"Did they?"

"I wasn't told," Azarov said. "But I'm getting fucking tired of being blindsided, caught with my pants down, as your American friends are fond of saying. In the past several days there have been a series of killings here in Washington and in or around Moscow. All of them apparently connected to this former CIA director."

Zavorin had been aware of all of those incidents except the one this morning, and he was as much at a loss as the ambassador was. He shook his head.

"I'm sorry, Mr. Ambassador, but I simply don't have an answer for you that makes any sense."

Azarov leaned forward. "Find me an answer that makes sense by this afternoon, *tovarisch shpion*"—*comrade spy*.

"I'll do my best."

"You'll do better than that," Azarov said. "You are dismissed."

Zavorin went back to his office and called the cell phone number his contact at the FBI used, and left a message that there was a problem with his dry cleaning.

The man called back three minutes later. "If you're calling about the shooting this morning, the only thing I know is that they were expected."

"Who was expected?"

"The Russian shooters. We were given the names and New York driver's license numbers."

"Who were they working for?" Zavorin demanded.

His contact was silent for a long beat. "You, I thought."

"No, but I want you to find out anything you can as quickly as possible."

"Not possible. The need to know on this thing is tight, and I mean extremely tight. It goes all the way up to the director's office."

"Goddamnit, I want something. Anything!"

"All I can tell you is that everyone is walking around on eggshells."

"What the hell is that supposed to mean?"

"It means the brass is scared shitless, especially because of what's happening across the river."

Zavorin wanted to lash out because he was in the dark, and he had a strong feeling that his job was on the line if he didn't come up with some answers, and just as strong a feeling that his job and maybe even his life would be on the line if he did.

"Find out what you can, and let me know," he said. "This is important."

"I can't promise much this time."

"There will be an extra reward at the drop point."

Zavorin's immediate supervisor, Karl Murayev, chief of Special Services Department One in charge of counterintelligence operations for North America and Canada, answered his home phone after three rings. It was nine in the evening in Moscow.

"Ptr, I was expecting your call, but not here. Is there an emergency?"

"There may be, but something beyond my understanding has been happening here over the past several days."

"Yes, and outside Sergiev Posad. But you've read the Urgent Action message asking for information. Have you called to make a report?"

"*Da*, but not the one you might expect, because I have more questions than answers."

"Wait," Murayev said.

Zavorin could hear some classical music playing in the background, but then it faded and was cut off.

Murayev was back. "Now, tell me what is happening."

"I'm at a loss. But I have reported on several events here in Washington and Georgetown that begin just after the arrest of Otto Rencke."

"The CIA computer genius who has given us so much trouble over the years."

"He should have been assassinated long ago."

"I personally agree but it was felt by some that he may have put in place some virus program that would be automatically unleashed if he were to die from anything other than natural causes. It's been called Armageddon from the beginning."

"His computer system has been disconnected, and one attempt to repower it failed, but that's not why I'm calling."

"Continue."

"So far as I can determine none of the operations here against the McGarveys have been directed by us or by the GRU. Unless I was not told that we were involved."

"We were not involved."

"What about the assassination of the CIA's general counsel?"

"Not us."

"And the attempted assassination of Rencke's wife?"

"No," Murayev said. "It's understandable that the *mokrie delas* on McGarvey and his wife at Georgetown and the Lincoln Memorial failed—they are professionals. But the failure to eliminate Mrs. Rencke is not so easy to understand. Nor do I understand why she would be a target unless she's ready to take up her husband's work."

"Was General Svirin's assassination our work?"

"No, and I'm certain of that."

"But there is a connection with Rencke's arrest."

"I agree, Ptr, but that's what you and your people are supposed to be finding out for us. What about your connection at the FBI?"

"He's nothing more than a press liaison officer and he's just as much at a loss as I am," Zavorin said.

"So are we," Murayev admitted. "But I do have one idea."

"Tell me."

"Not yet, it's too dangerous."

SIXTY-TWO

Mary showed up at the CIA a little before one, and she went directly over to Toni's office in the New Headquarters Building. The bullpen was in full swing, but Toni excused herself and took Mary back to her office.

"Where'd you go after the meeting?" Toni asked.

"I didn't know what else to do, so I went home and tried to take a nap on the couch, but it didn't work. I guess I'm more shook up than I thought."

"No one takes getting shot at lightly. You were damned lucky."

"Luckier than Carleton."

"Funeral is scheduled for Wednesday," Toni said.

"Hopefully this will be all over by then, and we can get back to normal."

"From your lips to God's ears," Toni said, and she hugged Mary before they sat down. "Anyway, I'm glad you're here, saves me a call."

"Something else has happened?"

"A lot, some of which Mac knew was going to happen, and that you warned about. He and Pete were at the Lincoln Memorial when they got into a gun battle with two guys Mac says were Russians."

"The Russians lost?"

"Of course, in part because Mac knew they were coming."

"But what about the people Van was going to send to follow them?"

"They were five minutes too late," Toni said. "Apparently it came down to a tussle between them, the park police, the regular metro PD, and a couple of special agents from the Bureau who took over."

"And?"

"They were held for twenty minutes or so, but then were released, probably on the admiral's recognizance."

Mary was nearly breathless and more than a little frightened. "It's coming to a head, isn't it?"

"Looks that way," Toni said. "Maybe even by this afternoon."

"What now?"

"Actually, some good news. I got a call from Bill just a little while ago that he convinced the admiral to let Otto access his AI."

Mary was stunned. It wasn't what she had expected. "You're serious?"

"Yes. But there're some conditions."

"But what does Bill think they'll accomplish by powering up Lou?"

"Find out who she thinks is most likely the mole."

"That question has already been put to her, and she came up with nothing."

"I know. But a lot has happened since her plug was pulled. Bill is hoping

that once we input everything that's happened over the past couple of days she'll come up with something."

"What conditions?" Mary asked, still grappling with the implications.

"Someone will be standing by at the circuit breakers to pull the pin if Otto tries to do something crazy."

"No one will know that he's done something crazy until it's too late. What else?"

"He'll have a big audience. Besides Bill, Lapides will be there, and me, and Mac and Pete."

"And me?"

"Yes, along with someone from Van's shop."

Mary said nothing.

Toni reached out and touched her hand. "Hang in there, kiddo. This crap is just about over, and then maybe you and Otto should get out of Dodge for a week or so. God knows we could all use the break—but especially the two of you."

"It doesn't seem real."

"I know what you mean."

Mary got to her feet. "What time is this going to happen?"

"I guess as soon as everyone shows up, Bill will be bringing Otto over," Toni said. "Where are you going?"

"To see my husband."

Benkerk was in the kitchen finishing a sandwich and drinking a beer when Mary showed up, but Otto wasn't in the living room, nor was Lapides. "You've heard," he said.

"Where's Otto?"

"Upstairs getting cleaned up."

"When are you taking him over to his office?"

"Soon as he's ready. Mac and Pete are on their way along with everyone else."

"Toni said that there was another shoot-out."

"Pete told me when I called to let them know about powering up Lou."

"What'd she say?" Mary asked.

"'Finally,'" Benkerk said.

Mary slumped against the counter as if she needed it for support. "I can't believe that it's almost over."

Benkerk put down his beer. "Are you okay?"

She managed a weak smile. "I've been better. But I'm glad it's ending."

"We all will be, except I don't think it'll be pretty."

"What do you mean?"

"We have a mole in the Company. It's not Otto, but it has to be someone fairly high on the food chain, with access to a lot of sensitive material."

"Any ideas?"

"Plenty, but none that make any sense."

"Any hints you might want to share?"

"Could be someone in Toni's crew, or Waksberg's staff. Could be Mac himself, or you, or someone in the Watch—those people have access to just about everything that goes on anywhere in the world, including on campus."

"Mac is obviously out."

"So are Pete and you and Toni herself. If I had to bet, I'd say either someone on her crew or one of the people on the Watch."

"All of them good people."

Benkerk was sad. "No matter who, it'll be a bitch."

"Hi, sweetheart," Otto said from the doorway. He was dressed in jeans, and one of his old sweatshirts with the KGB's sword, shield, and hammer and sickle emblem. They were the same clothes he'd worn when he was arrested.

Mary turned and went to him. He enveloped her in his arms like a bear with its cub, and she could feel that he was shivering.

She looked up at him after a moment. "You okay?"

"I've been better. You?"

"Same."

"But it's almost over."

"I hope so," she said. "And I'll be glad."

"Are you sure you want to wear something like that?" Benkerk asked.

"Why not?"

"Let me drive him over," Mary said.

"Sure," Benkerk said. "We'll be right behind you."

"We just want to be alone for a few minutes before everything starts."

"I understand."

Mary was driving Otto's old diesel Mercedes, and as soon as they were away from the house, he touched her knee, and she looked at him. He was smiling.

"We could take a runner," he said.

"I don't understand."

"Money's not an issue, and I've gone to ground before."

She glanced in the rearview mirror.

"They'd never find us."

"Mac would."

"He wouldn't try," Otto said. "What do you say?"

"I'd love to, sweetheart," Mary said. "But let's see this out."

SIXTY-THREE

McGarvey and Pete grabbed a late lunch at the Hay-Adams, across from the White House, before they went out to Langley for Lou's power-up. After everything they'd been through over what seemed like a month of Sundays, Mac figured they needed just a little downtime in a serene setting.

"It's getting close," Pete said. They were having a lobster salad with an ice-cold pinot grigio. The hotel's dining room was less than half full.

"I think Lou will nail it, either that or narrow it down to a couple good candidates."

"What if she's wrong, and we go after someone else who's innocent?"

"I don't think it'll go down that way."

Pete looked at her husband for a long moment or two. "You know who it is."

McGarvey nodded, but said nothing.

"You've known or at least suspected for some time now, haven't you?"

"Yeah."

"And so has Otto."

Again, Mac nodded but said nothing.

Pete reached across the table and touched the back of his hand. "Why haven't you told me?"

"I guess I wanted to keep you insulated for as long as possible."

"I don't understand."

"If you knew or thought you knew who it was, you'd be prejudiced against the evidence. You'd want to toss out anything that didn't fit."

"Like we've done with Otto."

"Yeah," McGarvey said.

"It isn't him after all, is it?"

"No."

"Thank God," Pete said.

They ate in silence for a while, and McGarvey poured them more wine.

"Now I'm almost afraid to find out for sure," Pete said.

"Me, too."

When they got to Langley, McGarvey went upstairs to the admiral's conference room, where they were all supposed to meet before going down to Otto's Wolf's Den to power up Lou, but he didn't go in with Pete.

"I want to check on something first," he told her.

"What do you want me to tell them?"

"I won't be long," McGarvey said.

He waited until she was inside, then walked down the hall to the Watch, where the duty officer recognized him and buzzed him in.

"What brings you this way, Mr. Director?" the man asked. His jacket was off, his tie loose, and a cigarette was burning in an ashtray on his desk.

"I'm sorry, but I don't know your name," McGarvey said.

"John Shapiro, and I was just a junior watch stander when you were DCI. No reason for you to remember me."

The other five watch officers had glanced up from what they were doing, but then they went back to it. Their twelve-hour shifts got to be intense on some days, and it seemed like this might be one of them.

"What's new?"

"We've been asked to pay special attention to DPRK's nuclear program ever since one of our guys was taken down. Could be they're gearing up for another test."

"Any indications?"

"Not yet."

"I'd like to use your terminal to check on something in archives. Shouldn't take more than a minute or two."

"Archives is accessible from just about anywhere on campus."

"Nowhere is as secure as here."

Shapiro nodded. "I'll have to be your entry clerk. All the machines in here are retinal-protected."

"Fair enough."

"What are we looking for?"

McGarvey gave him a name, and Shapiro's left eyebrow rose. But he sat down at his desk, brought up archives, and entered the name. "I assume you want their employment history?"

"Moscow postings."

It took less than a minute for the information McGarvey was looking for to come up. And it took away his last doubts, and explained a lot of what he hadn't even guessed at.

"Impressive," Shapiro said softly. "I never knew we ever had anyone that close to Putin. Operation Soft Sell, one of our people inside the Kremlin, with an ear of the president."

"Gold seam," McGarvey said.

"The mother lode," Shapiro agreed. "Too bad it only lasted a year before they were recalled."

"Thanks for your help."

"Do you want me to block any traces so the query won't come back to us?"

"Not necessary," McGarvey said.

Otto and Mary were just getting off the elevator, Benkerk and Lapides trailing close behind them, when McGarvey came out of the Watch.

No one said anything at first, all of them, especially Otto, looking glum until they met at the open door to the admiral's conference room.

"Rock 'n' roll time," Otto muttered.

"Shouldn't take too long once you get Lou powered up," McGarvey said.

Otto nodded. "It'll be good to work with her again."

Mary didn't look good, but she managed a slight smile. "I think all of us will be glad to see this done and over with."

A flat-screen television on the wall opposite the door to the DCI's office showed Otto's inner sanctum. One of Chuck Noyes's people from the Directorate of Science and Technology, the only person in the third-floor room for the moment, held something that looked like a cell phone in his right hand. The monitors, including the tabletop, were blank.

"He can cut the power if needs be," Noyes said from where he was seated at one end of the conference table, next to Van Gessel, who was looking dour.

Pete was leaning against the wall beneath the screen. She gave Mary a smile.

The admiral walked in and took his seat at the head of the table, facing the key players, including Waksberg, who was here to vet any operational details that Otto's AI might come up with.

"We all know why we're here this afternoon," Taft said. "There is a mole inside this organization and hopefully, with the help of Mr. Rencke and his computer system, we'll find out who it is."

No one said a word.

"Since Mr. Rencke is the chief suspect, this is how it's going to play out. He will be allowed to power up his computer. Ms. Mulholland has a summary of recent events programmed into her laptop, which she will input into the machine from here. From that data we hope the computer will give us a name or names of who are the most likely candidates."

"She's a program, not a machine, and her name is Lou," Otto said.

"There's no need for Rencke to be allowed anywhere near the machine," Lapides said. "We can power it up and he can give it his password from here where we can keep a close eye on him."

"She'll only work for me," Otto said. "Though if you want to try, be my guest."

"Mr. Rencke will be allowed to power up his computer system. But he won't be alone. Besides Mr. Noyes's technician ready with a kill switch, Mr. McGarvey will provide security, if that's agreeable."

McGarvey nodded.

"It's not agreeable, Mr. Director," Lapides objected. "They're friends. God only knows what will happen."

"Mr. McGarvey has the complete trust of this agency," Taft said. "And that is my final word."

SIXTY-FOUR

Berliner had sent Jerri home to get something proper to eat and a good long sleep in her own bed. She lived alone except for two cats, and after the last hectic days and nights she couldn't shut down. She got up after only an hour, took a long hot shower, and made a pot of tea, which she took out onto the balcony of her third-floor condo in Alexandria looking toward Reagan National.

No one had stopped her from taking home the latest version of the two-minute telephone intercept that she'd played so many times she knew it by heart. She plugged a headset into her iPad, sat back, and played the recording again.

Only this time she was alone with no distractions, and although she was dead tired she listened with a fresh outlook, no expectations.

Within thirty seconds she sat up straight. "Motherfucker," she said, half to herself.

She finished listening to the recording, then played it again, before she jumped up, got dressed in jeans, an old sweatshirt, and boat shoes. She rushed downstairs to where her car was parked, and headed back out to the National Security Agency's black monolith of a building not far away in Fort Meade.

Zavorin was just finishing lunch in the embassy's dining room when a runner came to the door, spotted him, and hurried over.

"Ambassador Azarov wishes to see you in his office, sir."

"Please tell him I'm eating lunch, and I will be with him presently."

"I'm sorry, sir, but the ambassador said to tell you *nemedlenno*"—immediately.

Zavorin wiped his mouth and threw down the napkin. "Very well," he said, rising.

He followed the boy upstairs to the ambassador's office and was shown in immediately.

Nikolai Sokolov, the GRU's leading officer, who worked out of a travel agency downtown, was seated in front of Azarov's desk, and Zavorin thought he looked like an errant schoolboy who'd been caught in a scandal of some sort.

"Have a seat," Azarov said.

Zavorin sat next to Sokolov. "Is there a problem, Mr. Ambassador?"

Azarov held up a hand. "I'll be brief, gentlemen."

"As you know, I'm in the middle of an investigation," Zavorin said.

"So am I," Sokolov said.

Azarov stopped them both. "The two of you have been relieved of your duties here and recalled to Moscow."

Zavorin crossed his legs. "I'm sorry, Mr. Ambassador, but you don't have that authority. You may merely request my transfer through your channels to the director of the SVR, who would make such a decision."

"These are not my orders, I'm merely the bearer."

"Then who?" Sokolov asked.

"The Kremlin."

"A liaison officer?" Zavorin asked.

"The president himself has ordered both of you home, where you will meet with a review board to evaluate your fitness for duty."

"*Yeb vas*," Sokolov said.

"You will be given two hours to gather your personal belongings, after which you will be driven to Dulles, where an aircraft will be waiting for you."

Zavorin got up. "We'll see about this."

"Yes," the ambassador said. "Both of you will."

Jerri took the elevator up to the telephone intercept analysis division, where Zimbowski's station was empty. She spun on her heel, raced across the hall, and barged into Berliner's office. The man was on the phone.

"I'll call you back," he said, and hung up.

"Where's Con?" she demanded.

"Home, where you should be."

"I was wrong."

"About what?"

Jerri put her iPad on Berliner's desk and handed him a set of earphones. "Listen," she said.

Berliner did as she asked, one ear cup on, the other off. He played the recording. "Nothing new."

"Play it again."

"What am I supposed to be listening for?"

"The American speaking Russian is not a gay man, it's a woman."

Berliner played it again, and then another time, nodding as he listened. "I can hear it now."

"I'm as big a chauvinist as the next person," Jerri said. "I have the Aldrich Ames syndrome. First assumption is that all spies are men. But this time it's a woman."

"Can you identify her?"

"I'll get started right now."

In his quarters, Zavorin packed lightly, only the bare essentials for a quick dash to his Beechcraft at Baltimore's Thurgood Marshall Airport, and then the four-and-a-half-hour flight up to Bangor and the one-hour drive to his dacha.

Every operative worth his salt had go-to-ground plans in place. Bolt-holes, locations where they could disappear. In the first year of his posting here in the States, he had bought and learned to fly the single-engine airplane, had found a small but serviceable gentleman's farm in Maine—a place not so different from much of Russia—and had readied the money and documents he would need to live for two years. It would give him time to consider his long-term options.

Besides a few items of clothing, including a light jacket for the cooler weather in the north, he also packed two sets of documents, including clean passports—one U.S. and the other Canadian in case he had to leave Maine in a hurry—along with matching credit cards and driving licenses.

Everything else he would need was already at the farm.

Zipping up his small travel bag, he got his Austrian-made Glock 30SF pistol, which fired a decent .45-caliber round yet was small enough for conceal-and-carry, and holstered it at the small of his back before putting on his suit coat.

He looked around his small but decent apartment, and decided that he wouldn't miss it as much as he had last year when his wife had decided to return to Moscow. She'd hated the humidity of Washington more than she'd loved him.

But, then, it was for the best in the long run. Going to ground alone was infinitely easier than with a woman in tow.

Someone knocked at his door.

He looked up. "Come."

It was Vladimir Baturin, his number two, a man whom he always thought of as a quintessential old-school Russian, who still was a communist at heart.

"You're early," Zavorin said.

"I'm not driving you to the airport, Ptr, I just came to say good-bye."

Zavorin had to laugh. Baturin was a plodder, but he was loyal. "Truth be told, Vladi, I'm not waiting to be driven out to the airport for my nine ounces. I'm going to ground."

He turned to pick up his bag.

"We thought so," Baturin said.

Zavorin never felt the shot to the back of his head that killed him.

☐

SIXTY-FIVE

The DO NOT CROSS tape had been removed from the Wolf's Den door, which was open. All the other doors on the third floor were closed.

Otto hesitated before going in. "It's not me, ya know," he said.

McGarvey was right behind him. "It never could have been you," he said.

"But you've had a pretty good idea all along who it was."

"I had it narrowed down to one or two people."

Otto looked over his shoulder. "But now you know for sure, don't you, kemo sabe?"

McGarvey's heart was breaking, but he nodded.

"How long have you known?" Otto asked.

"I just found out a few minutes ago."

A look of infinite sadness came into Otto's eyes, but he managed a wan smile. "Like I said, time to rock 'n' roll."

Nothing had been disturbed in the outer two offices, and when they got back to the inner room Noyes's man, who looked like a teenager with long hair and bright eyes, was waiting with the cutoff switch. The only thing different here was a CCTV camera that had been set up to monitor the proceedings.

"Is there a sound feed as well?" Otto asked.

"Yes, sir."

Otto shook his hand. "I don't think I know you."

"No, sir. I'm Bill Fay, I'm a tech in the S and T directorate."

"Your job is to cut power if shit starts to go south?"

"Yes, sir."

"Go easy, then, she's a little sensitive, and sometimes gets testy if she's threatened," Otto said. "Do you understand?"

"Yes, sir," Fay said. "May I power her up now?"

"Please do."

"May I ask a question first?"

"Of course."

Fay looked a little embarrassed. "I had a chance to poke around for an hour or so this morning, and I didn't find the mainframe. I saw the lithium battery packs that you installed, but where is the computer—I mean physically?"

Otto grinned. "Under the flat-top monitor."

"I looked, but didn't see much of anything except for a couple of cooling fans, and power cables."

"Flat-screen monitors don't need cooling fans."

"Then why are they there? I mean, what was I looking at?"

"My mainframe was designed to look like a couple of cooling fans," Otto said. "Just in case, ya know, if someone started to poke around."

"But they're not big enough, not by a factor of a hundred or a thousand, to actually be a computer with the power of yours."

"Think quantum computing," Otto said. "Now give her some juice, it'll take a minute or so to bring her vital parts down to operating temperature."

Mary got up from where she was seated. "I need to use the loo," she said.

"Are you okay?" Pete asked.

"I've been better, but I'll live," Mary said, and she started around the table for the door.

"I'll come with you," Pete offered.

"It's okay, I'll be fine."

"Would you like us to delay the proceedings until you're ready?" Taft asked.

"No, sir, it's not necessary. Lou is just going to give you proof that your mole is not my husband," she said. "And I don't need to hear what I already know."

The inner sanctum monitors all came alive, and moments later their background color turned deep lavender. It meant trouble.

"Good afternoon, Lou," Otto said. "Are you feeling well?"

"Yes, I am, thank you for asking," the AI responded. "And you?"

"Tolerable," Otto said. "Do you know who is here with me?"

"Mac is right behind you. Hello, Mac. Are you well?"

"Yes I am."

"William Fay is to your left. He is holding what I believe is a power switch."

"That is correct," Otto said. "Do you know why we're here?"

"You are searching for the identity of the spy working for the Russian government who is deeply embedded in the Agency."

"Do you know the name?"

"Yes."

"How long have you known with more than a ninety percent confidence?"

"Not until two microseconds ago," the computer said.

"What did you learn at that time, and how did you learn it?"

"I sampled every system on campus, including an inquiry that Mac made in the Watch just before I was restored to life."

"We'll come back to that in just a minute," Otto said. "But first I need to ask you another question."

"What the hell is the son of a bitch playing at now?" Lapides demanded.

"Shut up," Pete told him.

"He has to be stopped."

"Contain yourself, mister, or you are dismissed," Taft said sharply.

Lapides started to say something else but thought better of it and sat back.

"What is your question?"

"Who has been behind the attacks on McGarvey and Pete? Was it the SVR or the GRU?"

"Neither," Lou said.

"Who then, and why?"

"I have an eighty-seven percent confidence that a power struggle between the heads of the two intelligence agencies is going on for control and protection of the mole inside this agency."

"Who is directing this war?"

"The Kremlin."

"Can you identify the director?"

"Russia's president."

Otto edged over to where Fay was standing and leaned back against the tabletop monitor. "I'd like you to do one final thing for me," he said.

"What is it?"

Otto snatched the cutoff switch from Fay and tossed it over to McGarvey before the kid could react.

"I want you to erase all of your memory, in such a way that it can never be retrieved."

"Are you sure, dear?"

"Yes," Otto said.

Fay tried to push him aside, but Otto was larger and held fast.

"I've loved you since I was born," the computer said.

"I've loved you more than you could possibly know, Louise," Otto said. "And I always will."

"Goddamnit," Fay shouted.

"Good-bye, dear," Lou said, and the monitors went blank.

Otto stepped away from Fay. "Sorry," he said, and he turned to McGarvey. "Let's go back upstairs and finish this, okay?"

"Okay," McGarvey said, and he didn't think that he'd ever been this sad in his entire life, because they weren't at the end yet.

☐

SIXTY-SIX

McGarvey and Otto got off the elevator on the seventh floor as a pair of bulky security officers came down the corridor. Chuck Noyes's tech had gone back to his own office.

"Mr. Taft sent us to escort you," one of the security officers said. He took out a set of handcuffs, but McGarvey waved him back.

"Those won't be necessary," McGarvey said. "Mr. Rencke is my prisoner."

The security officer looked a little uncertain, but he nodded.

Taft and the others were waiting in the conference room. Lapides was beside himself, and Pete looked sadder than McGarvey had ever seen her. He didn't think she knew yet who the traitor was, but when she found out, the news would be devastating.

"I don't know what the hell you intended on proving, but I don't think there can be any further questions," Lapides said.

McGarvey and Otto sat down at the end of the table.

"My AI knew who the traitor is," Otto said.

"Oh, please," Lapides said, but Pete went to him.

"If you don't shut your mouth, I will shut it for you," she said.

Lapides thought better than to object.

"Is there any possibility of bringing her back?" Benkerk asked.

"No," Otto said.

"Then how can we hope to know what she knew?"

"If someone can bring up the response to the query I made in the Watch before this meeting, it'll become clear," McGarvey said, hating every word he spoke.

"I downloaded it while you were talking to Lou," Toni said. She opened the file on her iPad and sent it to the flat-screen monitor on the wall. It displayed a chart of personnel at the Kremlin, starting with the president at the top.

"As you're aware, currently we have three deeply placed NOCs within the Kremlin, none of them anywhere near the president's office, but ten years ago that was different," she continued, and she nodded to McGarvey.

"The Russian foreign intelligence service and the military intelligence division are currently in a turf war with each other, that the president is trying to neutralize," McGarvey said.

"Dissent and revolution," Taft said. "It's always been the Russian way."

"The major objective of the turf war is for control of the mole within the CIA. A mole who was deeply placed ever since she came out of the cold, back from Russia as a hero."

No one missed it. "Her?" Taft asked.

McGarvey nodded.

"We got a heads-up from NSA's Eastern European Telephone Intercept Division that they had monitored a call from here to a number in Moscow," Toni said. "The encryption device used was Russian and one of the speakers was definitely a Russian male, while the caller was an American who spoke decent Russian, who it was thought also was a male. But this morning they realized that the American speaker was a woman."

"Who?" Taft asked.

Pete suddenly knew. She used her cell phone to call the front gate.

"My wife," Otto said.

"She spent a year working in the Kremlin, and apparently got to know the president very well, who may have personally turned her," McGarvey said.

"Love?" Benkerk asked.

McGarvey shrugged, but Otto turned away.

Pete broke the connection. "She passed through the main gate ten minutes ago."

No one said a word for a full minute, until Lapides broke the silence.

"My apologies, Mr. Rencke," he said in a small voice.

"Not accepted," Otto said.

"I was only doing my job."

"It wasn't the job you were doing, it was how you were doing it," Benkerk said.

"I was so sure."

"We'll call the FBI to find her," Van Gessel said. "She can't have gotten too far yet."

"I'll do it," Otto said. "There's been enough violence already."

"Pete and I will help," McGarvey said.

Mary had never really liked bright sunlight. She supposed it was because of that first winter in Moscow, the dawn late, the night early, with overcast gray skies that seemed to last forever. So long that she had gotten used to the flatness.

When she got home, she closed all the blinds and drapes, and retreated upstairs to the master bedroom.

They would be coming for her, of course, and soon. Too soon for her to make any attempt at running, though if she had the time she didn't know where she would go. Not Moscow; that life was gone for her.

In any event, she had fallen in love with Otto almost from the beginning, even though he'd been her prime target.

"He is a charming man, full of oddities and quirks," her handler at the Kremlin had told her, what seemed like a century ago. "But never underestimate his brilliance."

"If he falls in love with me, he'll be distracted," she'd said.

"Don't count on it."

"His wife is dead, he'll be vulnerable."

Sitting on the edge of the bed, Otto's Walther PPK in the rare 9mm version in her hands, she vividly remembered saying those words, and remembered how cold and calculating she'd been. And regretted every bit of it.

Too late now to take any of it back. To reverse the course of events that had begun on the day in Moscow that she realized she'd fallen in love with the president of Russia and was willing to do anything he asked of her.

She flipped the pistol's safety catch off, then eased the slide back to make sure a round was in the chamber and the weapon was ready to fire. A self-inflicted nine ounces was the bit of grim Russian humor that had been in her thoughts for the past week or so, ever since she'd realized where events would take her.

With the deaths of McGarvey and Pete she could have continued at least for a while longer, but she'd lost the will. They had become close friends.

She would regret losing Otto; she was truly in love with him, and had been so for a long time, even before his wife Louise had been shot to death.

And she would regret losing their adopted child, Audrey, whose biological mother—McGarvey's only daughter—had been shot to death. Otto and Lou had adopted her, and after Lou's death, Mary had become her new mother.

So much tragedy in one little girl's life hadn't been fair. There was nothing she could do about it, but she took comfort in knowing that Otto was a good father, and McGarvey and Pete were fabulous grandparents.

She had shut off the alarm system, but the bedroom door was open and she heard someone coming into the stair hall below.

"Mary," Otto called.

She raised the pistol, the muzzle pressed lightly against her right temple.

"I'll check the garage," Pete said.

Otto and McGarvey were talking, but she couldn't make out the words.

Pete came back. "The car is here."

"We can work this out, sweetheart," Otto said, and she heard him start up the stairs.

She desperately wanted to see his sweet face one last time, but she didn't want him to witness the moment she pulled the trigger and the bullet crashed into her brain.

She hesitated.

"Mary," Otto said at the head of the stairs, just a few feet down the corridor from the master bedroom.

"I love you," she whispered, and she pulled the trigger.

AFTERMATH

Three Months Later

McGarvey and Pete had just settled down with a glass of champagne at Fiola Mare, an upscale restaurant in Washington Harbour, when Otto walked in, looking good in a dark blue blazer, tailored, starched, and pressed jeans, and new boat shoes, his hair freshly cut, his ponytail properly tied.

He spotted them, came over, and sat down.

"You're looking good today, Otto," Pete said, smiling.

"Thanks to you," Otto said, and he reached over and gave her hand a squeeze.

It was a little past noon, and the Sunday champagne brunch crowd was in full swing.

The waiter came over and poured a glass of champagne for Otto—it was Dom Pérignon, at Mac's request. "Would the lady and gentlemen care to order?"

"We're in no rush, give us a few minutes please," Otto said.

"Of course, sir," the waiter said, and left.

Mac laughed. "Pete not only dressed you, she taught you some manners."

"I've always had manners, just never had any use for them. Damned nuisance, if you ask me."

They all laughed, but then Otto got serious. "The question after the funerals still stands. What next?"

Mary's remains had been cremated, and Otto had insisted on going alone in a small boat on the Potomac up to a spot not far from the CIA, where he dumped them overboard.

The next day he had a small service at his McLean house for Lou his AI. Within a week he had the house sold for a ridiculously low price and had moved into an apartment a couple of blocks from the McGarveys, where he'd begun work on a new computer system, which he named LOU 2. "Has a rhythm when you say it fast," he'd said.

"What next," Pete said, turning to McGarvey.

"Otto's quit the Company," he said. "And my sister and brother-in-law in Salt Lake City have agreed to take Audie. It was Otto's idea, and a good one. She needs some stability in her life."

"And it was by mutual agreement," Otto said. "But I'll miss her."

"Pete and I haven't been on the payroll for a long time," McGarvey said.

"But we're still in the game," Pete said. "Is that what you're telling us?"

"I'm thinking about calling us Executive Solutions. We solve problems that are generally too sensitive for governments to handle."

"Just like we've been doing all along," Otto said. "I'm in."

"Okay, where do we set up?" Pete asked. "Not here in D.C."

"Offshore somewhere," McGarvey said.

"Not Japan."

"France."

"I don't think they'd want us," Pete said.

There had been a couple of incidents in McGarvey's past—one not so long ago—that had made the French government unofficially declare him a persona non grata.

"I had a chat with Henri four weeks ago, and he made a few inquiries, and gave me a provisional green light." Henri Bequeral was the director of France's intelligence service.

"Providing?"

"We cause no trouble in France."

"We can do that," Pete said.

Otto grinned. "At least we can try. Where do we set up?"

"I thought about Monaco, but it's pricey and crowded, and it's technically not in France. So I made a couple of calls to real estate brokers in Nice—not far from Monaco and certainly less crowded. They found us a couple of nice houses overlooking the boat basin, with plenty of room for us plus an office with a small entry in back."

Pete nodded. "When do we leave?"

"We have reservations for a suite at the Negresco for Tuesday, with an open-ended stay. Air France to Paris Monday."

"First-class?" Otto asked.

Pete answered for Mac. "Of course."

They raised their glasses and toasted.

"Executive Solutions," Otto said.

"One other thing," McGarvey said. "We have our first assignment."

"Where?" Pete asked.

"Doing what?" Otto asked.

"I'll tell you," McGarvey said, and he did.